DEAD

LIKE

LAZARUS

By Tim Mahoney

First Edition
Copyright © 2015 Tim Mahoney
Cover design by Zoe Shtorm
Proofreader: Kathleen Lewinski

ISBN: 978-0-9908974-2-2

Other books by this author:
Dead A Long Time
If the Dead Could Speak
Secret Partners
Jack's Boy
We're Not Here
Halloran's World War

Dedicated to the memory
of George Grapman, a good horseplayer
and an even better person.

This novel is based on real crimes of the Gangster Era. The Barker-Karpis gang committed its most notorious crimes from its base in Saint Paul, Minnesota. The gang had a secret partnership with certain politicians and policemen in that city.

The two most powerful figures in that underworld were Jack Peifer and Harry Sawyer, as depicted in this novel. Their sidekicks Sam Tanaka and Pat Reilly are also historical characters.

The accounts of Ma Barker, Alvin Karpis, Fred Barker and others associated with the gang are based on historical research.

CHAPTER ONE

It was a lonely Saint Patrick's Day.

It was a snow-bound Saint Patrick's Day.

It was the richest Saint Patrick's Day of my life.

In honor of the man who chased the snakes out of Ireland, I stayed home and sober on his day. Home was Aunt Doris's cabin in the forest outside Eagle River, Wisconsin. As for sober, well, I had no friends in Eagle River, and there wasn't an Irish tavern within a hundred miles.

I had boiled up a corned beef and cabbage dinner for myself and the dogs. After enjoying that, I thought I'd honor my Irish ancestors by having a cup of tea. I'm a coffee man, usually. So for the whole winter, I'd never brought Aunt Doris's tea pot down from its ledge above the old wood-fired stove.

That's when I discovered the cash. Last fall, Aunt Doris had hinted that she'd hidden money as her final gift to the Powers family. My sister Mona had more or less torn the cabin apart looking for it. And here it was, rolled up and rubber banded in four bundles inside that black enamel tea pot.

I counted it four times: $3312.

I'd have to split it with my sisters, but my share of $1104 was equivalent to a year's pay.

I celebrated with a cup of Irish tea and a home-made scone. I was becoming quite the baker in my isolation.

With a small fortune in hand, I began to admit how much I missed Saint Paul. There was nothing Irish about Eagle River, nothing to celebrate on Saint Pat's, except being one day closer to a mushy spring. Eagle River might have worked if I'd been a deer-hunting, muskie-fishing guy. The men up here — Finns, Germans, Norwegians, French-Indians— they were decent enough, but silent and solitary. There wasn't a horse parlor in town, and you couldn't buy a Racing Form anywhere in Vilas county.

Worse, the thermometer, and the population of available women, lingered near zero. Sitting at the drum-stove with my dogs, staring at a red barn surrounded by snow, I realized how much I missed city life. I forgot all the dangers and began to think fondly of that lively, corrupt little city, where I seemed to recognize half the people on the street. I knew how to get things done in that town. In running away from Saint Paul, I had sentenced myself to solitary confinement in a snowdrift. I discovered that a man alone is not a man at all.

So as the sun descended over the pine trees for another long night, I worked through the long distance operator to phone Sam Tanaka.

"A voice from the past," I said.

"Maybe it should stay in the past," he said.

"Don't hang up," I said.

"Why not?"

"First Saturday in May," I said. "At odds, I think. Looks promising."

"Speak."

"A pair at five-to-one at least."

He didn't say anything.

"Sam? Anybody talking about me there?"

"Perhaps."

"Swede and Rico?"

After a hesitation he said, "They're laying low."

"I'm thinking of making an appearance," I said.

"Up to you."

"Come on, Sam, melt the ice, will you?"

"Wait."

He left me holding the phone, long distance charges racking up, for about five minutes. I was using an old-fashioned candlestick phone, so I rested the ear-piece on the desk and petted Snowflake left handed and Hula Girl right handed. They watched intent as a white-tail buck, heavy with antlers, devoured a sapling in the snow-covered garden.

When Sam came back to the phone I let the dogs go, and they scrabbled at the windows, barking at the deer. I shouted into the phone for Sam to wait as I let the dogs out. They chased the buck into the woods, and he bounded away, no contest.

"What the hell is going on?" Sam asked.

"Deer versus dogs," I said. "The deer ran away."

"I know the type," said Sam. "Look, maybe Jack is interested. More interested than I imagined. He thinks you learned something with Harry. He's intrigued. He's got the upstairs guest room, you can have it for a few days."

"Really?"

"I'm surprised too."

"I could leave tomorrow," I said.

After a pause I reconsidered.

"I really need to be sure about Swede and Rico."

"They're out of favor with Jack."

"Oh? May I ask why?"

"Why ask a question that can't be answered?"

"How's the snow cover? Should I bring my golf clubs?"

"Are you kidding?"

So the next morning I packed a suitcase, put the dogs in the back seat of my Essex Terraplane and slalomed down the snow-packed driveway. Both dogs got panting-excited about any road trip, but for me it was six dull hours of icy driving.

I was exhilarated by my first sighting of the Saintly City, its outer ring guarded by the brick fortresses of Minnesota Mining and Hamm's Brewing. Construction crews were doubling the size of the Hamm plant. The shrewd brewers who had survived Prohibition were going to bubble up a fortune now. I was returning to a changed world: President Roosevelt had closed the banks and opened the beer halls. I didn't vote for him, but had to admit he'd made people happy.

I avoided downtown and its Loop and the tangle of autos, trucks and streetcars. I crossed the Mississippi on the easy side and drove along the river to the Hollyhocks casino.

I let the dogs out to relieve themselves on Jack's big brown lawn. The winter's snow clung only in the shadows, but the ground was frozen as hard as pavement. Sam was right, we were weeks away from golfing weather.

Sam was on an errand, so Violet greeted me on the big porch. The Hollyhocks dining room didn't open until five, but behind her bustled waiters and cooks and porters, all male and either Colored or Japanese. The walls wore the cardboard remnants of a Saint Paddy's party: shamrocks, shillelaghs and leprechauns.

Violet was gangland's loveliest woman, a thin, icy, Scandinavian blonde, a former underwear model and tennis ace with blue eyes and a perky ski-jump nose. She wore a black gown that hid her figure but not her movie-star looks.

"Jack has your room made up," she said as the dogs and I

followed her up the wide, carpeted staircase. The casino was dark, one woman with a broom in there, sweeping amid felt tables. In Jack's office, Suzy the Doberman stood to guard her territory but let my dogs pass with only a snort. When we reached the turret room, Violet pushed open the door without stepping in. She fended off a thousand passes a year, but need not have worried about me. I was not such a fool as to rattle her husband's cage.

"Call the desk," she said, "if you need anything."

"The Master?" I asked.

She pursed her lips. Her husband, feared boss in the underworld, was amusing to her.

"The Master is out being masterful," she said. "Saph will send up a drink if you like."

"Maybe a little meat for the dogs?"

"Saph," she said, "will provide," and then closed the door, glad, I felt, to be rid of me.

So the dogs dined on steak and potatoes and I, road weary, took a nap in the bed. It was dark when I awoke. I crept downstairs to see the office door cracked open. I knocked, pushed, and there sat Jack, in tuxedo, at his desk.

Suzy the Doberman, that dispirited creature, barely rattled her chain as I stepped over her. I thought of suggesting that Jack let her roam free once in a while. But I didn't want to renew our relationship with a lecture.

Jack extended his hand over the desk, and said, "Good."

He had the oiliest hair of any man I'd ever known. Despite his fearsome reputation, a rogue's twinkle lit his blue eyes. They gave the sense that a soul was trapped in there somewhere, if shrunken to the size of a walnut.

"Sit sit sit sit sit," he said.

He crossed his arms over his shiny tux jacket.

"So."

"I'm back," I said. "Took the winter off."

"Florida?"

"Not exactly."

He waved me off. "No matter. How's Harry?"

I wobbled my hand.

"What does that mean?" asked Jack.

"We haven't talked in a while," I said.

"Oh." He kicked back in his chair. From a desk drawer he pulled a quart of Canadian Club. He poured us both a heavy drink in water glasses.

"He's a good guy, for a Jew."

"Harry? Sure, I like him."

"But ... " Jack said.

I waited.

"But ...? "

"Well," Jack said, "everybody's blaming everybody for that bloody mess in Minneapolis. I can't blame you for taking a powder."

I shrugged.

"Okay, well see..." Jack reached over to finger his venetian blinds, his view a bare oak tree.

"See," he said, "I can't find the boys. And I need to."

"I've been out of touch, Jack."

"But you can *get* in touch," he said, and turned, pointing a finger at me. "You can slip into Harry's world. I can't. Sam can't."

"So who do you need?"

"Shorty or Ray. Actually, Ray is the brains of the outfit so make it Ray. But Shorty would do. Either one. And soon. Urgent!"

"Are they back in town?"

"If they were in town, would I need you?"

"Jack, I've got to ask. Swede and Rico."

He shook his head. "They won't be a problem."

"Both of them have it in for me, personal."

"And why is that?"

"I gave Rico the brass knuckle treatment," I said. "And Swede, he probably blames me for his fingers."

Jack looked sideways. On the long wall he had posted photos of prize fighters, baseball players and race horses. I knew he wasn't looking at them, but thinking of an answer.

"Saph will speak with them," he said.

"They don't forgive, Jack."

"Saph is the soul," he said, "of forgiveness."

Actually, Saph was the soul of back alley beatings. But Jack's assurances made me feel better. It was common for men to "wear a halo" bestowed by Harry or Jack. Always that halo cost something, but in my case the price would be cheap: I would connect Jack to Fred Barker or Alvin Karpis. It didn't seem so much to ask.

That night I ate a steak and baked potato dinner in my turret room, saved the Caesar salad for desert, and fed the dogs meat scraps. No matter Jack's assurances, I would avoid Rico and Swede. That wouldn't be easy, since I'd have to mix with low characters if I was going to find the Barker-Karpis gang.

Last I'd heard, in January, Barker and Karpis were headed for Reno. But they never stayed anywhere for long. One guy from the Barker-Karpis gang, Larry DuVol, had taken the rap for three murders the gang committed last December, during the Third Northwestern bank robbery. DuVol was the only member of the gang who was caught, and wasn't naming names. Other guys, who'd had nothing to do with that crime or with the Barker Gang, were facing trial in Minneapolis. The local cops, it seemed, had a special talent for arresting the wrong guys.

So where were Fred Barker and Alvin Karpis? It would take delicate probing to find out.

My last call for the evening was at my former apartment, top floor of an elegant brick building. It stood on the hillside between the sleazy Seven Corners and the holy Cathedral of Saint Paul. I would have phoned, but last I'd heard Janie didn't have a telephone, so I tapped on the door. I heard her shuffling feet and the rattle of a safety chain.

"It's Powers," I called out.

She opened the door, puzzled look on her face.

"You're alive!"

"There were rumors to the contrary?"

"Certainly. Come in."

She stepped back. She was a delightful woman in her early twenties, a little chubby, with sparkling blue eyes and red hair. She wore a light blue bathrobe that may have been her father's. Or it may have been a lover's. I hadn't talked to her all winter.

She didn't look pregnant, but unless something awful had happened, she was.

"You've done wonders," I said, looking around my old place. She had mixed her furniture with mine. She'd been sending $40 a month to my sister, and had the sublease until January.

"How are Snowflake and Hula Girl?" she asked.

"They miss you."

"Oh, I doubt that. Coffee?"

"French pressed?" I asked.

"Of course."

I had converted her to the True Coffee Religion last summer. As she put the kettle on the stove, I stood at the window staring down at the autos and streetcars crisscrossing Seven Corners. With beer declared legal, half the storefronts had hung out signs that said SCHMIDTS or HAMMS or ALTWASSER. Seven Corners had always been a raucous district of bordellos, pool halls, dice dens and speaks, but for more than a decade, the taverns had pretended they weren't selling beer.

Janie walked to the window. "Take your coat off and stay awhile," she said.

I handed her the rumpled topcoat. A quizzical look crossed her face.

"So what's new in the news biz?" I asked.

"Oh," she said, and hung the coat in the closet. "I'm getting the cops."

"Where?"

"The Daily News of course."

"You're back? I thought you got the heave-ho?"

"Major Hoople found me a spot. He says the ads are picking up Goggles is getting promoted, a byline and everything. I'm his legman now. Goggles takes the weekend off, but crime knows no holiday."

"You've had the whole winter without a job?"

She bit her lower lip. "My parents helped. I think, to be honest Powers, I think the editor has romantic feelings for me."

"Oh," I said.

"It's a little embarrassing.," she said.

"In love with your boss."

"Come on, Powers, he's too old for me."

Last summer, Harry Sawyer, the baddest bad guy in town, had ordered me to silence Janie. After my warning, Janie had quit snooping into the case Harry was worried about: the case of the Burned Ladies. I was sorry, though, that Janie had come to gangland's attention at all.

But now that Janie was pregnant, she had higher priorities than writing gangland exposes. If she was going to work under long-time police reporter Goggles Thornton, well, he knew where the foul lines were in this game.

"You know how to play it, right?" I said. "You write what the cops tell you and only what the cops tell you. Every sentence you write should end with the phrase: *police said.*"

"Oh now you're a writing teacher? That's quite a resume you've got there, Powers. Bootlegger, gangster fugitive, writing consultant."

"Since you're on cops, keep your ears open," I said. "Fred Barker and Alvin Karpis."

She frowned. "Everybody's looking for them."

"I need to get one of them on the phone, that's all."

"Powers, are you mixed up again? I thought you were out. Isn't that why you skipped town?"

"You sit in an igloo for three months and see how you like it."

"He's written me."

"Larry?"

"I burned the letters."

"What did he say?"

"Never mind."

"Did he mention Fred or Karpis?"

"No. Never. Not when we were dating, not in a letter. He never admitted anything to me."

The kettle whistled but she did not answer its call.

"He's lost his mind in prison. He thinks he's got magical powers that will spring him free."

She shook coffee grounds into a chrome-and-glass French press.

"When he gets out," she said over her shoulder, "he'll come for me."

She poured steaming water into the press. "I'm afraid Powers, I admit it. Our prisons are leaky. Guys have bribed their way out."

"He's got no money to pay bribes. I have sources, I'll check to make sure."

"Would you?"

"And you keep an ear out. Shorty, that's Fred's gangster name. Ray, that's the code name for Karpis. You're running cops for the Daily News? Jeez, that paper lives on cop news. You'll be hearing all kinds of stuff you can't print."

"I hope I don't hear anything about you, Powers."

"What do you mean?"

She depressed the plunger.

"Your coat weighs twenty pounds."

I shrugged. "It's a dangerous town."

"So that's why you came back. You missed the danger."

She poured coffee into cups that were leftovers from my married days, fancy with gold trim, painted with roses. I rarely let myself wonder about the woman who had left me. It was like a big, black hole in the ground, and I didn't want to walk anywhere near it. Peggy was, as far as I knew, living near Pearl Harbor. But these coffee cups, and this apartment, brought it back to me, the days when I was a happily married, high-living rum runner.

I sipped. The coffee tasted bitter.

Janie said: "I thought you wanted out of the gangster life."

"One guy, one favor, that's it."

"A favor that requires you to carry a gun?"

"Guns plural," I said. "There are people who don't care for me. Look, beer's coming back and the breweries are hiring. Maybe I can catch on at Altwasser or Hamm's. You understand, Janie. You grew up on a farm. I hated being cooped up all winter."

"So you came back to go straight."

"Kind of," I said.

"Hmm," she said with a sly smile.

CHAPTER TWO

I didn't dare enter the Green Lantern. Its creepy patrons would rat me out to Swede and Rico as fast as they could drink a nickel beer. Instead I drove toward the Capitol. In the shadow of that great white edifice lived Pat Reilly, the Green Lantern's bartender and gangland's idiot savant. He had been kicked out by his wife and was now a guest of his long-suffering mother. Mama Reilly was part-owner of a laundry. She worked twelve hour days as Pat lolled around like a bachelor bum, drinking beer.

He answered, holding a can of Altwasser.

"Canned beer?" I said.

"It's modern."

"Can I come in?"

He belched. "Why not?"

He backed into a living room that was tidy, except for the beer cans. They were scattered like buoys marking danger spots in a river channel. Pat's teeth were growing fouler, stained by his Lucky habit. He extinguished a cigarette, opened the blinds to let in a sliver of sunlight.

"I thought you was in Florida?" he said.

"Not even close."

"Well, it's been a rough winter."

"How's Harry?"

"Shitty. He's giving up. What the hell is he going to do now? The breweries are crushing him, ruining all the old bootleggers. All of a sudden, booze is legal and Harry is a big fat nobody."

He swigged beer and said: "He's giving me the Lantern."

"Giving?"

"He's drinking more than ever. Want a beer?"

"Gout," I said.

"Still?"

"Never goes away," I said.

"You poor bastard."

"Looking for somebody," I said.

"You got a Derby horse?"

"Too early to tell. Looking for somebody who used to know Harry."

"I can't see a horse."

"The Derby? It's too early Patrick. You've got to wait for the odds to settle, and let the rubes pick a favorite. When I work my figures, I'll let you know, but in the meantime, I need to see somebody."

"Who?"

"Shorty."

"Huh."

"Or Ray. Either one."

"Good luck."

Pat swilled.

"Pat, you know everything, come on."

"I don't know nothing that nobody else don't know," he said, "only I don't know it sooner."

"What?"

"I'm in the twilight of my career as, you know, a messenger boy. In one ear and out the other. Nothing sticks to me. I don't listen to what I'm hearing. I don't see nothing that don't see me first."

"Okay. Look, I know these fellas got their pictures in the Post Office. I'm not J. Edgar Hoover. I don't want to electrocute them. All I want is a phone call from Shorty or Ray."

"What's your number?"

"I'm not settled. Call Myrtle. Leave a number. I'll call back."

Pat shook his head. "That don't work. Those boys don't leave their number."

"Call Myrtle at five o'clock any night, then. I'll make it my business to be there."

"How's Myrtle?"

I shrugged. "I'm going there next."

"Who wants these guys?"

"Me."

"They owe you?"

"Nope."

"Harry's cooled down."

"Yeah."

"Now that they nabbed those Minneapolis guys," he said and shook his head. "Poor saps. Rotting in jail for something they didn't do. I thought our cops were bad."

"They're all bad. Hey, there's twenty in it for you, Patrick."

"Great, I can retire."

"Plus the Derby tip."

"What about running a horse wire at the Lantern? You want to go in?"

"Don't do it. All that telegraph equipment. And when the cops bust you, you go broke. Running a crooked game in this town, all you do is enrich the cops and lawyers. Jesus, Pat just run an honest tavern. People will be drinking until the Second Coming."

"And possibly after," said Pat.

CHAPTER THREE

Myrtle was as good a gangland source as Pat, or so I told myself when I knocked on her door. She stepped aside, let me into a dark apartment that smelled of loco weed. The marijuana smoke had somehow not killed her parakeets, Charles and Amelia. They occupied one sunny corner, chirping happy in their cage, like they were on a treetop in the Amazon.

Maybe it was the dope making them happy.

"Well, buster," said Myrtle. "I heard you were dead."

"Dead like Lazarus," I said.

"Among the goddamn living," she said with a goofy smile. "Well, come in."

"I am in."

"All the way in."

I shed my overcoat, wrapped her in my arms and kissed her a long time.

"I'm not clean," she said.

"But still adorable."

"Oh, Mick. It's been a bad winter."

She sat on her elegant mohair couch, swathed in a purple robe. She leaned forward, arms on thighs, studying me, as if she couldn't believe I had returned.

"Get some daylight in here," I said.

"Don't. Hurts the eyes."

I pulled the curtains anyway.

"Tell me, kiddo," I said.

"Shit," she said.

I sat in the chair across from her.

"Andrew left me."

I was glad to hear it. "Sorry," I said.

"What a prick," she said and lit a joint. "Don't start smoking this crap. It makes you sad."

"I'm smoking it as I breathe. Did you love him?"

"Nah," she said. "But he treated me right. Look around. Did you ever see such furniture? Persian rugs! From goddamn Persia! Look at that vase. It's like Papa Alt's mansion in here. Except no servants."

She waved smoke away.

"You know, Myrtle, I'm still a little sweet on you."

"Ah Mick."

"We're perfect. Two ruined statues in a weedy garden."

"Cut the poetry." She blew smoke. "Where you staying?"

"Dump downtown," I lied.

"How long you in town for?"

"Until the first Saturday in May."

She looked over her shoulder at the sunlit window.

"I'm finished, Mick. Thirty five. Look for my obit in the Dispatch."

"What are you talking about?"

"I can't pass a store in this town but they call the cops. Chicago too, every fur shop seems to know I'm coming. So I take the train to New York last month," she blew smoke, "and they got my picture in the Macy's. I'm there ten minutes trying on furs, and these two mugs rush me out. Shove me down on the sidewalk. They'll give me a beating if they see me again. Stepped on my hand, see? Broke my pinky finger. It's crooked now."

She lay back and sputtered those heavy red lips.

"Professionally," she said, "I've had it. A thousand miles away,

Mick, and they got my picture in a book."

"I made you an offer once."

"I ain't living on no farm."

I shrugged.

"Is that where you were all winter?"

"No, I was in Florida," I lied.

"Oh yeah?" She rolled over. "You don't look tan. They had a cloudy winter down there?"

"I need something."

"I told you it's my time of the month right now."

"Freddy Barker and Alvin Karpis."

"What do you want with those assholes?"

"Just a phone call."

"If I see those hillbillies I'm running the other way."

"I've put out word that they should call here."

"Here?"

"Five o'clock, any day."

"Are you nuts giving out my phone number?"

"Myrtle, everybody knows your phone number."

She hugged herself.

I didn't want Myrtle to know I was staying at the Hollyhocks, so I fumbled. "I can't have 'em calling my hotel. Are you kidding? The switchboard operators? They eavesdrop. Hey, I'll make you dinner."

"I don't want dinner. What'd you give out my number for, Mick?"

"You must've heard something about the hillbillies."

"Yeah, well."

"Come on."

"One of the punks came on like Romeo Never mind who. Not Fred or Ray. One of their errand boys. Sent me a card from California."

"Where?"

"Lost Angeles."

"When?"

"Last month."

"Where is it?"

"Lost Angeles? It's in California."

"The postcard."

"I threw it in the trash where it belongs."

I rose to walk toward the kitchen.

"It's gone, Mick."

The kitchen was gleaming clean, because Myrtle never cooked. I stepped open the trash can, saw a dead flower bouquet but no card. I backed into the living room.

"I had a dream, Mick."

"While you were doped up?"

"While you were gone. I dreamed the Professor got out of Waupun, but he didn't know me no more. Went off with a whore to Sarasota. How do you like that?"

"But it's only a dream."

I kneeled at her side, rested my hand on her knee.

"Myrtle, the Professor's never getting out of Waupun."

Her eyes began to flood.

"I know."

"I'm here, I'm sweet on you, what's wrong with me?"

She looked up at me, teary.

"I don't know. I can't shed him, Mick, I can't, he needs me. He'd hang himself if I wasn't out here waiting for him."

I touched her cheek. "Mrs. Eaton," I said. "Can Myrtle come out to play?"

The phone rang.

"I don't want to subscribe to no magazines," she complained on the way to answer it. She raised the phone to her ear and then turned with a look of fright.

"It's for you."

CHAPTER FOUR

"Shaky Powers?" said a harsh voice.

"If you want Mick Powers," I said, "ask for Mick Powers."

"I was told to ask for Shaky."

This was followed by a fit of coughing.

I waited it out, phone away from my ear.

Recovered, the voice wheezed: "We're outside."

I turned to the window.

"Who is we?"

"We'll see you out here."

He hung up. Down on the street, double parked, was an idling yellow taxicab. A tall angular figure wearing a gray suit and hat burst from the drugstore, crossed the streetcar tracks, and entered the cab.

I had never seen this guy before. I grabbed my overcoat. In one pocket was a cheap chrome revolver with a pearl handle, in another an Army Colt .45. Even carrying my arsenal, I resolved not to get into the cab.

The parakeets chirped as I kissed Myrtle and rushed the door.

Downstairs, the taxi had pulled in front of a fireplug that was surrounded by melting snow.

"Get in," said a fellow from inside.

"We'll talk out here," I said.

I stood my ground on the curb. One fellow leaned forward to

pay the cabbie. Then they both got out. The tall fellow hacked coughing. The shorter fellow, dressed expensive, stuck out a hand like he was a greeter for the chamber of commerce.

"I'm George," he said. "Excuse Monty, he's got a cold."

George was a handsome man of average build and blond hair. He wore a cashmere topcoat, creased fedora, shoes shined to a mirror finish.

"You were expecting us, I take it?" asked George.

"Not exactly," I said.

A puzzled look crossed his face. "Jack didn't set us up?"

"Jack?" I said.

"Yes, Casino Jack."

I looked toward Monty. It was obvious that George would do all the talking, and Monty would do all the coughing.

"Casino Jack?" I said.

"Yes," said George. "The nightclub man with the Japanese servants. Oh, don't play dumb, fellow."

"Maybe I know Jack but I wasn't expecting anybody."

George looked toward Monty, who shrugged.

"How do you like that?" said George. "And here we are in the age of communication."

Monty laughed. He was maybe six-three and a hundred fifty pounds of bones. He had the hawkish expression and pale face of a man who'd been sick a long time.

"May I suggest," George said, "that you telephone Jack?"

"He doesn't take calls," I said.

George scuffed his soles on the sidewalk.

"Oh, he doesn't take calls," he said. "May I suggest a visit? Are you in possession of an automobile?"

I looked from one man to the other. "Look, I don't know anything about this."

"You are known as Shaky Powers, correct?"

"Mick," I said. "Mick Powers."

"Jack volunteered your services as a tour guide."

"Tour guide?" I said.

George nodded. Monty nodded.

"What are we touring?"

"Lake properties, I was told."

I said: "Why don't you gentlemen have a cup of coffee across the street and let me make a phone call?"

The two crossed the streetcar tracks while I climbed the back stairs to Myrtle's apartment. The door was cracked open. Myrtle stood naked, except for sky blue panties, at her bay windows.

"There wouldn't be so many peeping toms," I grumbled, "if you didn't tease them."

She stood mesmerized.

"Who are those guys?" I asked.

"Never seen them."

I picked up her phone.

"They stink like Chicago to me," she said.

"You can smell 'em way up here, eh?"

"Oh, there's a train every hour."

"Very perceptive."

She crossed her arms over her breasts. "I should know those guys."

I dialed the Hollyhocks. Saph answered and shouted for Sam and a minute later Sam said: "What's up?"

"Two mugs from out of town," I said.

"So?"

"Jack sent them. But I don't know anything about it."

After a pause, Sam said in a low voice, "The Master is not quite himself lately. Let me see."

He left me holding the phone. In the drugstore across the street, George and Monty were sitting at a window booth, hats on the table.

Sam fumbled the phone and said, "They're looking for a

summer place. East of town. Near the lakes. Good fishing."

"And so?"

"Help them," Sam said. "Jack owes them. They're friends of the Italians."

"The Italians," I said.

"Find them a cottage for the summer," Sam said. "They're looking to escape the city heat."

"Okay," I said. "But remind Jack we're living in the age of communication."

Myrtle, goose-bumped arms crossed over her breasts, held a cigarette lighter in one hand and flicked it. No flame.

"Friends of the Italians," I said. "I wonder what that means?"

"I'll tell you exactly what that means," she said.

"Spill," I said.

"Starts with a C- and ends with P-O-N-E. We don't have enough troublemakers? We bring them from out of town?"

"Capone's in prison, in case you haven't heard."

"Prison don't stop those guys."

I patted her butt.

"Let me go earn some money," I said.

I pulled my Essex in front of the drugstore and tapped the horn. George sat in the front seat, threw his cashmere coat between us. Monty sat in back, drinking dark fluid from a medicine bottle.

"You're straight now?" asked George.

"All squared away."

"Not too close to town, no too far in the boonies," said George.

"I know just the place," I said.

"Now we're communicating," George said.

I drove them through the swell part of downtown. The bankers and insurance clerks were leaving, the night creatures beginning their prowl of Saint Peter Street. Would boozing be half as much fun when it became legal?

As we passed the Civic Center, George asked: "Do they have much of an opera in this town?"

I said I wouldn't know.

"Well," he settled into his seat, "we'll be here all summer. Won't we Monty?"

"Won't we what?" said Monty.

"Be here all summer?"

"Federal Building," I said, when we passed it.

"Right across from the opera house," said George. "Seems fitting. I imagine J. Edgar is an opera fan."

"Horse racing fan," I said, "or so I hear."

"Dreadful sport," said George. "I don't suppose you wager on it."

"Occasionally," I said.

"Really," said George, "opera would be a much more enriching use of your time. He should start with something simple, shouldn't he, Monty?"

Monty coughed.

"I would recommend," George said, "the Barber of Seville. It's a simple *opera buffa* that anyone can enjoy. It's in Italian but you don't need to speak the language to enjoy it. I've taken Monty to see several performances, isn't that right Monty?"

"Very nice," said Monty. "Good singing."

"Good singing," George muttered in disgust. He tapped me on the shoulder. "The Barber of Seville, remember that now. The Barber of Seville, and you'll be an opera lover for life."

That was a silencer for maybe ten minutes until we approached the Hamm Brewery.

"Ah," said George. "Legal beer. The nation has come to its senses. Did you hear that, Monty? I said the nation has come to its senses."

"I heard you," coughed Monty.

"Don't drink it myself," said George, and patted his flat belly.

"I'm a cocktail man." He looked at me as if seeing me for the first time.

"How do you fit in, Powers?"

"Me?" I said.

"Your name's Powers, isn't it?"

"I do a favor here and there," I said. "I know everybody in town, pretty much."

"He knows everybody in town," George said to Monty. "Now that could be helpful, couldn't it, Monty?"

"I guess so," said Monty.

As we turned onto Highway 61, we blew past a shallow ring of suburbs and entered the countryside. It was that awful time of year, neither winter nor spring, the black loam either hidden by snow or turned to muck amid last year's corn stalks. Here and there stood a forlorn farmhouse, cows that had barely survived the winter, rusty trucks and muddy tractors.

However curious I was about these guys, I knew better than to ask questions.

George, turning his hat in his lap, said: "We're looking for quite a big place."

"Oh?"

"Monty's got a substantial family, and I expect we'll have visitors from Chicago."

"How many people are we talking about?"

"Six to eight, depending," George said.

We turned off at the resort town of White Bear. Its modest downtown included drugstores and cafes, a pool hall, a sweets shop, and a big market: Bloom's Cash and Carry Grocers. "Everything you need," I said. "Right here in town."

When we rolled up to the shore, the lake was icy at the edges, but calm.

"Two popular lakes here," I said. "You're looking at White Bear. Bald Eagle's up the road."

Monty, chewing gum, said: "Fish?"

"Plenty," I said. "Walleye, muskie."

I drove them along the lakeshore and they gawked at cottages. A boardwalk featured kiddy rides, hot dog stands and taverns, all closed for the season.

"I imagine it livens up in summer," George said.

"Streetcar comes out here," I said. "Brings pretty ladies."

"Well, Monty's married. So am I. Monty's got children."

"They'll enjoy the lake," I said.

"So," George said, "you can rent us one of these cottages, correct?"

"Sure you could…"

"I'm in need of an arm's length transaction, if you catch my meaning."

"I catch your meaning."

"As close to the lake as possible, as many rooms as possible."

He turned to Monty.

"What's your assessment?"

Monty coughed.

A half hour's quiet drive later, I dropped them off at the Hotel Saint Paul, the most expensive joint in town. From there I drove alone to the Hollyhocks and parked behind the garage. Sam and I began to lay out the Derby, each with our own tasks.

"So Sam."

"So Powers."

"Who's calling me Shaky?"

"I never heard of this."

He was lying. Sam has heard of everything.

"I'll bet the Swede's spreading that around," I said. "I don't like it."

We were sitting in his retreat, at the back end of the Hollyhocks garage. A mechanic's light hung from a workbench as our only illumination. Sam wrote on scrap paper, I used pencil and a Catholic school notebook.

"So two guys come to town," I said. "One's an opera buff, the other is a TB skeleton. They're from Chicago. They want to spend the summer at the lake."

"So?"

"I was under the impression Chicago had a lake of its own."

Sam looked up from his scrap paper, which he had stapled together into a book.

"I have something for you, Powers."

He lifted one haunch, drew his wallet out of his hip pocket and produced a fifty dollar bill.

"For you." He handed it over. "Clench your teeth and take it."

"Payday," I said. "So when were you going to tell me?"

"Tell you what?"

"About this money."

Sam sighed. "Mick, when will you learn to trust? The Master always comes through. The Master is far seeing. Think about it. It took him years to put together this nightclub. The cash, the slot machines and roulette wheels, the real estate, top class liquor connections, the furniture, hiring discreet help, fixing everything with the cops and politicians downtown. Do not underestimate the Master. He sees many, many moves ahead."

"Jack, sure, I get Jack. But these Chicago guys are spooky."

"Powers, work your figures, please?"

I turned to a fresh page in my notebook. I subscribed to Watch Clocker, a mail order service. Every week I got sheets of numbers, private clockings from wise guys at the race tracks. From these I extracted my own speed figures, equalized for various track conditions. There's no two racetracks run the same, that's the point. A horse can run like Man O' War over the Jamaica track, and plod like a mule at Havre De Grace.

Sam worked the class angle. A horse's first race counted for nothing with Sam. In the horse's second race, only his ability to leave the gate quickly counted. From then on, Sam kept book on who-beat-who in any race at a mile or longer. Put together, we had speed and class angles that, with luck, could extract a pile of cash from the Kentucky Derby win pool.

We agreed that the likely favorite, Ladysman, had run weak times and had beaten nobody special.

"They want their money up front," I said.

"Who are we talking about?"

"The landlords. At White Bear. We're talking maybe three hundred for the summer, at least"

"It will be provided then."

"How about providing it now?"

"Your financial demands tend to annoy me, Powers."

"I'm not a banker, Sam, I need folding money."

He sighed and walked into the sunset and toward the nightclub. The Hollyhocks patrons were well into their steak dinners and Sam was free of them now, having risen above head waiter to become Jack's Man Friday. But he was no happier for the promotion.

Having a wife and children in Japan hung around Sam's neck like a stone. I wondered what kind of deal he had worked with Jack for his eventual emancipation. Sam was once a waiter on the Empire Builder. Someday soon, maybe if we hit it big in the Derby, Sam would take that train to Seattle in the first leg of his journey home.

I leaned on the polished fender of Jack's olive-green Packard. The circular driveway was jammed with expensive cars. The Hollyhocks drew its share of bankers, moguls and tycoons, but was a particular favorite of the legal crowd. There were more lawyers in the Hollyhocks than in any courthouse in Minnesota. The infamous criminal defender DeNoblis, known for his whiskey habit and his indiscretions, let the valet take his car. He escorted a fur-wrapped lovely, certainly not his wife, up the wide stairway. A moment later, a yellow cab disgorged my new Chicago acquaintances.

Violet rushed the door to greet them.

George was accompanied by a toxic blonde and Monty was followed out of the cab by Myrtle.

Violet kissed George on the cheek. That told me he was somebody. Violet was not a kisser.

Myrtle and Monty climbed the stairs to the velvet carpet. The toxic blonde turned to gaze at the Mississippi sunset. George was arm-in-arm with Violet. They entered the gilded doorway, followed by the blonde. Myrtle, wrapped in silver fox fur, was having some kind of problem with her high heels. She kicked and fussed and Monty dropped to one knee to help her.

Powers, why the jealousy? I asked myself. Myrtle is loyal to no one except the Professor.

Still it made me feel rotten, and left out. When they all disappeared into the dining room I returned my attention to my horse notebook. But soon it was full dark, and Sam's lamp wasn't bright enough to work by. What was keeping him?

I crossed the lawn and climbed the front porch. An older woman dressed in a shimmering wrap was laughing with a man young enough, and hefty enough, to be a college football player. I stood away from them and looked into the big windows.

There at a candle-lit, white-clothed table sat the four of them, the blonde hanging on to George's arm, Monty reading the menu, Myrtle smoking a cigarette, its end heavy with lipstick.

Sam trotted up and discreetly handed me a wad of money.

"Every priest has his altar boy," I said.

"Speak English, please, Powers."

"George is the golfer, Monty is the caddy."

"Now I understand."

"George escorts the high-priced blonde, wears the cashmere, does all the talking. Monty's just tagging along. I've got a feeling about this George. Who is he, Sam?"

Sam shrugged.

"And if he really is a big shot Chicago gangster, what's he doing in the Saintly City?"

CHAPTER FIVE

Swede Fanlund owned a 1932 blue Pontiac. It was a long, four-door sedan with whitewall tires and spoke wheels. It had a chrome radiator and headlights, and the spare tire was set into the fender, just off the driver's door. Its pumpkin-orange Minnesota license plate was B 301 522.

I remembered all these details because I'd been studying that Pontiac through my racetrack binoculars. I'd been parking my Essex on the sunny side of the Cathedral, walking into the shadows of the Chancery, and spying on the Swede.

Swede in his Pontiac was parked downhill and across the street at Herb's Garage. From the corner of Herb's parking lot, Swede had clear view of my apartment. He was always alone and he too was using binoculars.

I had seen him parked there three days in a row.

What this meant I could darkly imagine. Over the past two years, Swede and his partner Rico had become the first-call assassins of Saint Paul's underworld. They worked for everybody and nobody. They had been responsible for three murders that I knew of, and probably plenty more. Saint Paul's gangster masterminds were far too clever to commit their own murders. They hired Swede and Rico, who enjoyed killing, never talked to the cops, and worked cheap.

Both of them had it in for me. I had left Swede to freeze in an alley last January, and he had lost pieces of three fingers to frostbite. Rico I had sucker-punched with brass knuckles. If it weren't for the fact that I was useful to Harry Sawyer and Jack Peifer, I'd have been murdered by Swede and Rico long ago.

And so now, on Cathedral Hill, with Swede in the double sites of my binoculars, I wondered. Had Swede heard I was back in town? Did he figure I'd show up at my old apartment?

Or worse, was he spying on Janie?

It was possible that Janie was his target. The more I thought about it, the more likely it seemed. Janie's snooping into the case of the Burned Ladies had alarmed Harry. He'd asked me to shut her up. I had warned her, and she had lain low all winter. But now she was back in the game, reporting for the Daily News.

Maybe word of that had reached Harry, and he'd reasoned that I'd had my chance to bully Janie out of town, and had failed. If I was right about that, Swede was stalking her now, and one day soon would show up with Rico in the car. That would be the last anyone would ever see of Janie Vetter.

I still had friends in this town, so I dropped in on one of them, Sergeant Billy McAmbly. He was the lone identification specialist for the Saint Paul Police. He worked in the Bertillion Room on the second floor. His main weapon in Saint Paul's laughable fight against crime was a camera.

We had played ball in high school, me a first baseman and Billy the catcher. We had been friends for 25 years now, and last fall, I had made a sneaky donation to help out when his daughter had been operated on at Mayo. I'd made that donation through a priest, but Billy found out. I'd never come out and say, *Billy, you owe me,* but he *did* owe me.

Billy grunted.

I said, "How's Maureen?"

"Back to being a pain in my ass," he said. "Thank God. I owe you Powers."

Well, the Irish. Sometimes they're mind readers. And for all their faults, they do have a sense of obligation.

"I won't forget it," Billy said. "You and Doc Sherman. He performed a miracle, and then cut his fee to what I had in the bank. I won't ask where you got the money."

"Well, I do need a favor, Billy."

"Shoot."

"Swede Fanlund has been watching my apartment for three days now."

"Well, you don't live there anymore," Billy said. "Or did you move back in?"

"I leased it to the kid reporter, the red head."

"The one you're in love with."

"Billy, a wrecked middle-aged gangster and a pretty college girl? What would she get out of that? Your old friend Mick's a sap, but he ain't a fool. I like the kid. I admire her. She's the daughter I'd hoped to have. When she's around, I feel like the human race might have a future after all."

"What's Swede want with her?"

"I can't tell whether he's after her, or figures I'll show up there. I think he blames me for his fingers."

"Too bad it wasn't his trigger fingers. What about the girl? What's he got against the girl?"

"Remember last year, the Burned Ladies? I don't know why, I don't know how, but that's a crime neither Jack nor Harry wants solved. And this college girl, well, she's got her faults. She's been on that case. She's stubborn and she's nosy."

I looked around. The pebbled glass door was closed, no shadows in the corridor. I couldn't be sure if anyone was behind the black curtain back in Billy's file room so I said: "We're alone?"

"Essentially," Billy said.

"What does that mean?"

"Well, somebody seen you walk in right? So somewhere in this nest of vipers, somebody's tongue is wagging."

"I need a little help."

"How little?"

I lowered my voice to a whisper, leaned across the counter, my lips two inches from Billy's hairy ear.

"I need a search warrant executed by a cop in the know."

McAmbly whistled. "Where do you come up with a search warrant? That's the hard part. Executing it, that's easy. You're playing golf with judges now?"

"I can get the paper," I said. "I need boys in blue who can play along."

McAmbly lit a Chesterfield and it bobbed in his lips. He raised his thick dark eyebrows and said: "The den of iniquity?"

"Not those guys, Billy."

"Crumley and Bulldog are the right guys," he insisted. "Best cops money can buy."

"You could do it."

"We're known to be friends. I haven't been a street cop for fifteen years. All of a sudden I'm knocking on gangster doors at midnight?"

"But you can find a street badge who needs a little extra cash.

"I'll think about it." He shrugged. "Best I can do. What's Swede got coming to him?"

"Couple of decades in Stillwater, I hope."

CHAPTER SIX

Myrtle's phone rang at exactly five o'clock.

"Say your piece," said a voice.

It was Karpis. Fred had a girlish Ozarks twang. Karpis sounded nasty, like the streets of Chicago.

I said: "Remember the guy who shot a piece of his pecker off?"

"Yeah."

"He wants to see you. In person. Big deal. Don't call. As soon as you can."

"It'll take me a couple of days," said Karpis, and then hung up.

I put down Myrtle's phone. It was one of those modern ones, earpiece and mouthpiece all one. I looked out the window. A fat old peeping tom was staring across at us. I drew the curtains.

"My work is finished," I said. "Now, you're out of it, Myrtle, you don't have to worry."

"So cancel all those dinners you were going to make me."

"I learned how to bake bread. I can bake all the bread you can eat."

"I don't care for bread, it's fattening."

"How about a pork chop dinner?

"With sauerkraut?"

"Yup."

"And pickled beets."

"Let me get a pencil if it's going to be a big order."

"And chocolate cake. I feel German tonight."

"I can buy a cake," I said.

"What's stopping you then?"

"Nothing. Hey, I've got nice wheels now, Essex Terraplane, six cylinders, plush seats."

"We'll go for a drink after dinner. Celebrate the return of booze."

I went grocery shopping at Essenmeyers but detoured to the Hollyhocks. I parked around back, walked Snowflake and Hula Girl, and asked the cook to feed them. Sam was in the pantry scolding a busboy when I beckoned him out.

"This is a bad time," he said. "Jack's not here."

"No, it's a good time," I said. "Walk with me."

We slipped out the kitchen door, where it smelled of moldy kitchen waste. We walked over the frozen earth to Sam's sanctuary corner of the big garage. The main doors were closed. Sam led me to the side door.

"Tell Jack I arranged his rendezvous," I said. "It will be a couple of days."

"Okay."

"Make sense for me, Sam."

"If it is possible."

"These Barker boys are bank robbers. That's not Jack's game."

Sam shrugged. "I don't tell the Master what to do."

He walked into the garage and shut the door on me.

I brought Snowflake and Hula Girl up to my turret room and played roughhouse with them for a few minutes. When I descended the back stairs I saw, at the big doors of the garage, Sam talking with Serious Bobby.

The garage doors were flung open. Both men stood admiring Jack's olive green Packard. Serious Bobby was dressed for summer weather, in a Palm Beach suit and straw hat. He held that hat in one hand, revealing a bald head. He wore thin gold spectacles and his reddened face hinted at a diet of steak and beer. Sam was dressed for work, in rough shirt and baggy pants. Together they looked like a garage mechanic talking to a banker.

I slipped back behind the kitchen.

As they say when a horse race goes wrong, all bets were off. The end of Prohibition was shaking gangland to its foundations. Serious Bobby had been a collector and negotiator for Police Chief Big Joe Ryan all during Prohibition. The Hollyhocks, and every other speakeasy in town, filtered their bribes through Serious Bobby. But Big Ryan wasn't chief anymore, and dispensing booze was no longer illegal. So what was Bobby here to negotiate?

And if Jack wasn't home, why was his Packard in the garage?

I'd had many brief dealings with Serious Bobby and one personal close call. Last fall, he'd proposed to my sister Mona, who's fifteen years younger than he is. I believe they were both blind drunk at the time of said proposal. I also believe they decided to get married after only one date. The day after that date, Mona borrowed and wrecked Bobby's beautiful red-and-white Auburn speedster.

End of engagement.

There's one last part of the mystery: I'm pretty sure Serious Bobby is a homosexual. The only sense I can make of his proposal to Mona is that he wanted to squelch the rumors about his inclinations. He needed a flashy woman to go around with. Mona was that. She was flashy.

I walked around to the shady side of the building and sneaked a look from there. Serious Bobby, in black-and-white shoes, was climbing the wide porch of the Hollyhocks. Saph McKenna, Jack's sad-eyed bouncer, let him in, and shut the gilded glass doors.

I crossed the wide lawn and entered the garage, passing gleaming Packard and headed to Sam's sanctuary. There a lawn chair was pushed in at a rough table. Nailed to the wall above that table was a wood crucifix. Underneath it sat a jade statue of a meditating Buddha. The bench was scattered with wrenches and pliers, two lanterns, a gas can, pencils in a holder, a notebook, and stack of Racing Forms.

The side door was open. I found Sam. He was raking leaves off the bare tundra that would evolve into his garden.

He looked up at me, rake poised.

I said: "So Jack is in, I take it, but not to me."

Sam wiped his hands on dirty trousers.

"Michael, why ask questions that cannot be answered?"

"I don't know, Sam, I don't like it when my friends lie to me."

"Jack is not in."

"Then what's Serious Bobby doing here?"

"Jack is not in as far as you are concerned. He has other appointments."

"I see."

Sam shook the rake at me.

"Powers, can't you understand that we are all here to play our parts? You have played your part. You will be rewarded."

"All right."

"Tomorrow at noon you must find other accommodations."

"I see."

"But your work is appreciated and further patience will be well rewarded."

"Look, Sam, I myself cut the deal for the protection money that kept this casino running. I was the go-between for Jack and Serious Bobby. I negotiated for Jack, at a table in the goddamn Town Talk diner. Bobby and Jack couldn't be in the same room, and that wasn't even a year ago. What's changed? Bobby's not here for the roast beef. Something new is in the oven. The Ozarks boys are invited back to town. Chicago gangsters are circling White Bear Lake. And Serious Bobby is up talking to Jack right now. I'm just curious."

"You are not the only one who's curious."

I nodded.

Sam pointed up at the heavens. "Only He is omniscient."

"Maybe He doesn't know what's going on either," I said.

CHAPTER SEVEN

Myrtle's friend Loretta had stringy hair, a pock-marked face, a hefty build, huge breasts, and was just shy of 30 years old. She wore pleated red trousers and a shiny blue blouse, and walked into the room on spiky high heels.

"It's twice the dough," Loretta joked, "for a threesome."

Myrtle grinned.

The room service waiter had set us up with a drinks cart, rum, and juices. I played bartender. Loretta plopped onto the couch.

"Mind if I smoke?" she asked.

She removed a golden case from her purse and sprang it open. In it were tiny home-rolled cigarettes wrapped with an amateur twist.

"Myrtle indulges, how about you?" Loretta said.

"Go right ahead," I said. "But that stuff makes me dizzy."

Myrtle, shoes off and set at the edge of the rug, walked over and lit the cigarette in Loretta's pink lips.

"Havana screwdriver?" I asked.

"Why not?" said Loretta, "I'm always getting screwed."

I delivered the drinks, one to her, one to Myrtle, one for myself. I stood looking out the windows, across Rice Park, to where the Division of Justice lived, behind the stone castle walls of the Federal Building.

The women smoked. I drank. I wanted everybody relaxed.

When I turned back to look at them, Loretta was horizontal on the couch, her stocking feet in Myrtle's lap. Myrtle gave her a foot rub through the stockings.

"I need a quiet favor," I said.

"Oh boy," said Loretta.

"Myrtle says you know how to shut up," I said.

"Do I?"

"One hundred dollars," I said.

Loretta shrugged. "A girl's got rent to pay."

I crossed the room, picked up a manila envelope from the secretary desk, and dropped it in her lap.

"You've been with Swede Fanlund?" I said.

"I never talk about my customers. I never talk *to* them, if I can help it."

"All right," I said. "The envelope contains bonds…"

I left out how I had acquired them. The bonds had been the property of the Third Northwestern Bank, until the Barker Gang robbed it, just before Christmas. Their boy Larry DuVol had delivered my share of the loot, including a few bonds, in return for services rendered. Looking back, I wish I had not rendered those services, but swimming in the Sea of Regret wasn't going to help me now.

"These bonds are no good to you," I told Loretta, "or anybody. They're hot. They're non-negotiable. What I need you to do is get into Swede's apartment. When he's asleep, put these bonds somewhere, anywhere he won't come across them for a few days. In a closet, or behind the dresser, or buried in a bottom drawer. That's all you need to do."

Loretta looked at Myrtle. "What'd you stop rubbing my feet for?"

Myrtle swished her drink.

"Them spikes is going to ruin your feet," Myrtle said. "And you got such pretty feet."

"Do you think this is something you can do?" I asked Loretta.

She yawned.

"Hide and seek," she said, "yeah I can do that. But how about deucing me up? You're a man with plenty of dough, I can smell it through your pockets."

"Okay, two beans, but you can never spill."

She pursed her lips. "I'm not a talker."

"Which is why Myrtle recommended you."

"I thought she was hot for my body."

"Maybe she is but right now…"

"Are you hot for me, Myrt?"

"Sure," Myrtle said.

Loretta led Myrtle's hand up her pants leg.

"Dopey feeling," Loretta said, and giggled. "I like it."

She fixed me with a stare. "For you to climb aboard, it's ten dollars extra."

I dragged over the desk chair. I sat at Loretta's side, and grabbed her bejeweled hand.

"This is important to me," I said. "This is going to save my life. Myrtle says you don't care for the Swede, he's treated you rough."

"I don't care for your sex in general," said Loretta.

"Then you won't care if Swede goes away for a while, because that is the plan."

The marijuana cigarette had gone out between her fingers. She handed it to Myrtle and said, "Light me up, honey."

"Listen, Loretta," I said, "two hundred dollars is a lot of money and this job's got to be done right and you can never talk about it. Swede has all kinds of sporting girls up there, I understand, he'll have no reason to think it was you who planted him."

"As a bonus," said Myrtle, "he will be in prison quite a while."

Loretta sucked on that cigarette, kept the smoke in, then laughed.

"Fine with me," she said. "Disgusting. He feels you up with that chopped-up hand. Surgeons done that? Or the butcher?"

Loretta slurped the orange remnants of her drink. "You think you could leave us alone, sport?" she said. "Me and your friend."

"Sure," I said.

She unbuttoned her blouse to reveal a ratty white bra and a chubby belly that hadn't seen sunshine all winter.

"A backrub is what I need," she said, and removed the blouse and rolled over on her belly. Myrtle lurched into the bathroom for a tube of the hotel's body oil. Then she leaned over Loretta, unhooked her bra, and began a slow massage of her back.

"Oh, God help me," sighed Loretta. "A girl needs her rest."

Gangsters and prostitutes gave each other, far too often, a certain social disease. I'd never had it, and wished to avoid it. My inner animal wanted a three-way with Myrtle and Loretta, but he was overruled by that cautious fellow known as Shaky Powers. Shaky knew many gangsters who had leaky pipes. Doctors had a tough time curing it.

So I soothed my inner animal with coffee and cake in the Garden Cafe downstairs. I sipped and looked over the forlorn, gray Rice Park. Streetcars clanged by, and across the way, people ran up and down the stairs of the Post Office. I thought I spied, at the second floor window, that skinny, cheroot-smoking Agent Heater, J. Edgar Hoover's man in Saint Paul.

I ordered chocolate cake for Myrtle as she sidled up.

"She's asleep," Myrtle said. "The poor kid."

"Can we count on her?" I asked.

"Oh, she needs the money, and she really doesn't like these gangsters, so we're safe with her. I think. But life is a gamble, Mick."

With a gleaming heavy silver fork, she cut into her chocolate cake.

"I could live here," she said. "Lap of luxury."

"Twelve bucks a day," I said. "Plus room service and bar tab.

That's all it would take. Live like a Hollywood star."

"I known her since high school," Myrtle said.

"You told me."

"The boys always treated her rough. You know, bad skin, chubby with that ratty hair. Of course, she dropped out like the rest of us. Jeez, it's a rough world, Mickey Powers, no wonder we want our fancy hotels and chandeliers and champagne and chocolate cake."

She ate with a satisfied moan.

"Oh God, I could live here." She looked at me. "Did I say that already? You finished your cake? Give me that fork, will you?"

She admired both silver forks, twisting them so they gleamed in the reflected sunlight. She licked them clean. She slipped them into her purse.

I sent Myrtle home on the streetcar, returned to the Hotel Saint Paul lobby, and asked the elevator girl to take me up to three. This floor was occupied by dentists, accountants, lawyers, a union office, and finally, farthest from the elevator, the Saint Paul Protective Association.

On the pebbled glass door were stenciled those words, and the image of a policeman's badge.

I rattled the door.

Serious Bobby answered.

His Palm Beach suit had been stripped off to trousers, white shirt, red suspenders. He stuck out his hand and we shook like bankers about to make a deal. An enormous oak desk in one corner was immaculate, and bare, except for a green felt blotter. We stepped to the windows overlooking Rice Park. Bobby's bald head gleamed in the sunlight.

"I need a warrant sworn out," I said.

Bobby's blue eyes twinkled behind his eyeglasses.

"How much is that?" I asked.

"A warrant for whom?"

"A gangster."

Bobby bit his lips. "Probably a thousand. Depends on which gangster."

"Did you pull that number out of your hat?"

"Powers, be serious, will you? Judicial services," he said with a faint smile, "get expensive."

"A search warrant for Swede Fanlund's residence."

Bobby shrugged. "I don't know … What's he done?"

"I just need the warrant. Probable cause. Simple. It's boiler plate, Bobby, they do it every day, you just need a judge's signature."

"You're working with Jack again, aren't you? You've been seen."

"I'm friends with Sam Tanaka. Sure."

"Would this warrant have Jack's approval?"

"I have no idea. Bobby, look. I know all about Irish Kinkead and his shenanigans in the County Building. The man can do anything, you know it and I know it. Jack pays to run his casino, and we know exactly how much, don't we? Kinkead could set this town on fire if he wanted to."

"Excellent, excellent reasoning," said Bobby. "The price just went down to twelve hundred dollars."

"Down?"

"While you were babbling, it had risen to fifteen hundred."

I sat on the desk. Bobby stood at the sunny window. I noticed sweat stains under the arms of his shirt.

I said: "We live in a city where any number of people will end a fellow's life for five hundred bucks. Even cheaper in some cases."

"Well." Bobby shrugged.

"So that's why I'm offering five hundred."

He laughed. "Make me a serious offer, Powers."

A light rap came to the door, a shadow on the other side. Bobby held up one finger and strode to the door, opened it, and there stood Big Joe Ryan.

He looked me over. He was a giant at six-six and 275 pounds, in a fine suit with gold-rimmed eyeglasses and the sagging chin of a man who enjoyed his meat and drink. He had brown dull eyes and thick lustrous lips, almost like he used lipstick.

He lifted his chin toward me, as if Bobby should explain my presence. Then they walked out into the hallway and left me alone.

Big Joe Ryan, tossed out as chief, remained on the force and was still feared in the station house and on the streets. He and his new partner, Lieutenant Charles Tierney, had lobbied to form a Kidnap Prevention Squad, just the two of them. This was meant to comfort the mansion-dwellers up on Summit Hill. A cynic might say it was a taxpayer-provided bodyguard for a wealthy few.

It was Big Ryan who stomped back in alone, and slammed the door behind him. He unbuttoned his jacket, revealing the strap of a shoulder holster. He threw his hat on the desk.

"What's this about a warrant?" he said.

I sat in the big oak chair, pretending a comfort I didn't feel.

"Poking around," I said. "For possibilities."

He nodded, slowly, like a judge who had heard your defense but whose soul held no mercy.

"We can't do those kinds of things anymore," Big Ryan said. "Bootlegging's over. Haven't you heard? We walk the straight and narrow from now on."

"I see," I said.

"Heard from any old friends lately?"

"Me? I haven't really got many friends. Just got back to town, you know. Florida for the winter."

"Bullshit," said Big Ryan.

I spread my hands, helpless.

He said: "You were over in Minneapolis last Christmas, weren't you?"

"Me?"

"Don't fucking lie to me Powers."

"I don't like that town," I said. "Never go there. Too many Swedes."

"Stand up."

I did and he shouldered me like he was a linebacker, knocked me to the wooden floor. I was dizzy, but it felt oddly pleasant, lying there on my back, looking up at the white tin ceiling. It felt pleasant right up to the moment the big cop kicked me hard in the ribs.

He opened the door.

"Bobby," he shouted down the corridor.

As I lay writhing in pain, Serious Bobby peered in. Big Ryan patted him on the back and walked out the door.

Bobby helped me to my feet.

My suit jacket was ripped at the underarm, and Bobby helped me get it off. I removed my shirt and sleeveless T-shirt to see an ugly purple swelling at my left ribs. Bobby searched the desk drawers, and came up with a bottle of aspirin and a pint of gin.

He looked at me with pity.

He phoned the desk for ice. Then he walked toward a tiny bathroom, soaked my undershirt in gin, and came back and applied it to my ribs. He told me to hold it there while he retrieved a glass of water, and handed me three aspirin.

"I think I need to drink the gin," I said.

He shook his head. "That's old bootleg stuff."

I moaned in pain.

"God I hope he didn't break anything," Bobby said. "You know he's been like that, Powers, since they knocked him out as chief. He took it real, real personally. He hasn't been the same guy. Seriously. He's, I don't know, he's got something to prove."

I swallowed the aspirin.

"Yes," Bobby said, "he's got something to prove and he's on a mission to prove it."

He patted me on the shoulder and handed me my shirt and suit jacket.

"Five hundred, Powers. I can get your document. Seriously. Five hundred down, no further payments, just give me a few days."

He cocked his head. "Say hello to your sister. She's a fun gal. Tell her no hard feelings."

I threw my gin-soaked undershirt into their little sink, buttoned my dress shirt, and threw jacket and tie over my shoulder. My ribs throbbing with pain, I put my hand on the doorknob.

"Nice doing business with you, Powers. Come again anytime. Seriously."

CHAPTER EIGHT

On the first moment of April 7, just when the clock passed midnight, the City of Saints went crazy with beer. Men, women, even children and dogs, roamed the dark cold streets, lurching from tavern to tavern. Many of those former speakeasies poured free suds for all. Streetcars and auto traffic merged into an unmovable jam at the Seven Corners. Down on the levee, teenage boys shot fireworks over the Mississippi. A nightclub down there had flung open its doors and brassy rhythms floated over the drunken celebration.

Swede Fanlund missed it all.

On the afternoon of April 5, two lowly uniformed policemen had climbed the back stairs of Fanlund's Saint Peter Street apartment, knocked and were let in. The next morning, a small inside item appeared in the newspapers, noting that Douglas "Swede" Fanlund, aka "The Mechanic," had been arrested in connection with the deadly robbery of the Third Northwestern Bank in Minneapolis. Bail was set at $10,000. Witnesses called to an overnight show-up had sworn that Swede was one of the inside gunmen during the bank robbery.

That last part was a pleasant surprise to me. But Swede looked like a thousand other guys in the Twin Cities, and there were many witnesses, and witnesses were often wrong.

So with Swede in a Minneapolis jail, and Rico in Florida, I could feel easy, at least for a while. I concentrated on the Kentucky Derby and on finding Jack's Chicago friends a place for the summer.

After cruising the shores of both White Bear and Bald Eagle lakes, I settled on the biggest cottage I could find. It had a for-rent sign pasted on the big screen porch. It was across from the lake and a fishing dock. The locals may have called it a cottage, but it had four bedrooms, gleaming hardwood floors, a private water tank in back, one bathroom inside and an outdoor shower in the rear. The owner's wife had died a few weeks ago. He didn't want to stay the summer without his wife. We made a handshake deal: the whole summer in return for $400 cash.

Back in town at the Hotel Saint Paul, I left a sealed note for George and Monty. Then I drove to Myrtle's apartment. She had never worked a day since I'd known her, and when she was gone in the daytime, it was usually lunch with Loretta and her Free Love Group. I walked Snowflake and Hula Girl around the neighborhood, ruminating on where I would move after the Derby. I couldn't poach on Myrtle forever.

Upstairs in her apartment again, I had cleared a sunny corner near the birdcage for my notebooks and racing forms. It looked like the fat cat owner W.R. Coe was going to enter two horses: Ladysman and Pomponious. By the rules of Churchill Downs, this would cause the horses to be coupled: a bet on either was a bet on both. Thus, bettors would believe they were getting a two-for-one bargain. They could make one bet, and if either Ladysman or Pomponious won, they would cash the ticket.

The rubes can never resist a bad bet.

This was just the scenario I'd been hoping for. The casual bettors would overload Ladysman and Pomponious, driving the odds down to insane levels. This would fatten the odds of the other horses. Using Sam's class notes and my speed figures, I focused on three long shots: Head Play, Brokers Tip, and Charley O. There are no guarantees in horse playing or in life, but I was pretty sure I had worked out three good bets.

I packed my pipe with Havana Gold and lit it, opening the window. Out there was a brick alley and from it swirled the lovely breezes of spring. I blew smoke out the window so as not to poison the birds and dogs. Across the alley was the drawn shade of peeping tom, not interested in gawking at a pipe-smoking horseplayer.

I was scraping the dottle out of the bowl of my pipe when I heard footsteps in the hallway. The dogs, having become accustomed to people in the halls, set up a late alarm, barking, howling, hair standing stiff. I opened the door just as a man was about to knock.

He was short, red hair underneath a flat cap, wearing a black shirt and rumpled trousers.

I had the door open only a crack, keeping the furious Snowflake and the growling Hula Girl away with my foot.

"Looking for Myrtle," the man said. "Myrtle."

"She's not here," I said. "What's your business?"

This guy fixed me with a punk glare. He was maybe thirty. He hadn't bothered to shave. His forearm was tattooed with a crude blue Christian cross.

"I'll come in and wait," he said.

"No you won't," I said. I closed the door, snapped the lock.

The dogs were in full homicidal rage. I picked up Hula Girl and carried her squirming black furry mass into the spare bedroom. Snowflake bayed at the door. A ferocious knocking began.

I took my .45 off the dresser, put it in my pocket, closed Hula Girl into the bedroom and stepped up to the door.

"Take it easy, fella," I said through the door, but the knocking had already ceased. I went from window to window and finally from the kitchen I saw this little man cross the side-street. He got into a long, luxurious Hudson, a rich man's car driven by a roughneck. That big car made him seem even smaller. I noticed he wore cowboy boots just as he shut the door and fired the car's engine.

He drove away slow. The car had Oklahoma plates. And I had a bad feeling. I copied the plate number into my racing notebook.

Back at horse racing, I studied my times and did my sums for my three choices. Handicapping can be totally absorbing, and I don't know how much time passed before the phone rang.

I picked it up and said: "Yes."

"My bellman informs me," said a cultured voice, "that you wished to communicate."

Somehow, George's velvet tones managed to switch me into high-falutin' mode.

"I have arranged for lakeside accommodations," I said. "I anticipate they will prove satisfactory."

"We'll rendezvous," he said, "in the lobby. In perhaps ten minutes?"

When I pulled up to the Hotel Saint Paul, George was waiting in the flower garden. Accompanying him was not Monty, but a big rough-looking older man with a big nose, white hair and and a sparse mustache. George got in beside me, the older man plopped into the back seat.

George had oiled his blond hair and smelled of aftershave.

"So," he said, "I'd nearly despaired of hearing from you."

I grunted. I thought I'd done a pretty quick job.

"The distinguished gentlemen in the rear seat is known to all as Dad."

I shook Dad's strong hand over the seat.

As I weaved out of the city and onto Highway 61, George sat silent and Dad hummed a tune I couldn't identify. The cracked-open windows let in air that was both moldy and sweet. Nobody said a thing until we pulled up in front of the cottage I'd rented.

George and Dad got out of the car. George stretched while Dad ambled over to the nearest tree and peed.

I said: "The owner will let us have it a few days early, since we paid up front."

"Spectacular work, old fellow," George said, and clapped me on the back.

I winced.

"What's the matter?" asked George.

"Sore ribs," I said. "You know, pissing on a tree might not be the best way to introduce yourselves to the neighbors."

He waved that off. "The poor old fellow can't hold his beer anymore."

George wore a starched shirt straight from the cleaners, a knit burgundy tie, gold pin underneath to keep the collars in line. An alligator belt held up golfing trousers that ended at the knees, where dark blue socks took over.

He walked up the stone path to the screen porch. He ran his hand over a home-made wood sign that declared the cottage's name: IDLEWILD.

"Idle," George said. "I like anything with idle in its name, don't you Dad?"

The old man stumbled over the grass. His tie was loose, shirt unbuttoned at the neck, belly bulging.

"Power of suggestion," said George. "A very dynamic thing." He gave me a friendly backhanded tap. "And your name, Powers, very suggestive as well. Do you have the keys?"

I handed them over, a tiny chain connecting two slugs of brass.

"Only two?"

"You can get more made."

"I'm very well aware of that. Dad will want his own key and so will our guests. We'll make do, I suppose."

Dad and I followed as George entered the screen porch, glanced at the net hammock and the striped chairs, and then unlocked the front door. The owner had cracked the windows but the cottage smelled of stale winter air and mice. The living room was painted a sunny yellow. I opened the windows as George went room to room. The owner had set in home-made screens, but it was sloppy work, and I envisioned a buggy summer for these guys. They might complain, but I planned to be gone by then.

"Ice box," George called from the kitchen. "How very primitive."

"It is a vacation cottage," I said.

"Indeed," said George.

Dad belched. He leaned into the front windows. There was hardly any wall. Those windows occupied nearly all the space on the lake-view side of the room.

"Boat?" he asked.

"I think you'll have to rent your own."

George appeared in the living room, hands jammed in his trouser pockets. His face beamed with satisfaction.

"'Did you see the back yard, old man?"

Dad grunted.

"Fenced, private, and perfect for parties," George said. "It promises to be quite the summer for parties."

On the way back to town, I drove them through White Bear Lake, pointing out the taverns that had sprung up and the new ice-house and beer store. This was an enormous converted boathouse, covered in peeling white paint. Just about any rube could get into the beer trade now, and there was hardly a business they wouldn't convert.

My passengers said almost nothing on the way back. Dad hummed an anti-melody that suggested he was either tone deaf or hard of hearing. George smoked Camels and blew the smoke into the slipstream. There was no question that Dad was a gangster. Just the fact that his real name was a secret told me that. But what was he doing with these fellows half his age?

As we approached the industrial ring of the city, George tapped the dashboard and said: "They sell radios for this model Terraplane, don't they?"

I nodded.

"Well get with modern times, won't you? Live. Enjoy life. Why, in Chicago, they broadcast operas on the radio. Get a radio put in, will you? Enjoy it while you've got it, I say."

"Right," I said to shut him up. I figured he was just irritated by Dad's awful humming.

As we passed the Hamm Brewery, Dad said: "They're going to make a fortune."

"Hamm's," I said, "Oh yeah. Millions."

He whistled in appreciation of all that beer and money.

I dropped them off at the Hotel Saint Paul, where a dignified doorman in heavy uniform opened the doors to let them out of my car.

Standing beside the lobby doors, smoking a cigarette, was the red-haired tattooed punk who'd pounded on Myrtle's door.

George walked into the lobby, but not before tapping the red-headed punk on his shoulder. The punk followed George and Dad in, and the big glass doors closed on them all.

CHAPTER NINE

"Whoever he is, he knows your name."

Myrtle shook her head. "You know me, Powers, I don't go for shrimps or wimps. So cross him off, will ya? I can't help it if some runt comes knocking. Maybe he read my name on a bathroom wall."

She blew smoke.

"Thirty five or so," I said, "prison tattoo of a Cross?"

"Cut it out."

"Mean looking son of a bitch with a nasty glare."

"That describes half the men in this town."

"Drives a deep blue Hudson."

"Stolen, no doubt."

"Oklahoma plates."

"Well now we're getting somewhere, Powers. Let's see, who do I know from Oklahoma? Well, there's Will Rodgers. Maybe it was Will Rodgers, looking me up for advice on his rope tricks."

I said, "I'll be finding my own apartment after the Derby."

Her face looked noble and sad in the filtered sunlight of her living room.

"I don't mind you so much, Powers. You're someone to talk to."

Staring into her full-length mirror, I knotted my black tie. I wore my best dark blue suit, fresh from the cleaners. My shoes were scuffed but I could get a shoeshine downtown. I picked up my gray fedora, set it jaunty on my head, walked over and put one arm around her plump shoulders.

"Don't take it personal, Powers, but it's your dogs I'm growing fond of."

"Noble creatures, aren't they?

"We should be more like them. Loyal, territorial, always hungry. See there's no such thing as stealing in a dog's world. They're like me. If they see something they like, they just snatch it up."

I left Myrtle in charge of Snowflake and Hula Girl. I drove downtown to the Bankers Building, paid the garage man for two hours' parking, and got myself a businessman's shoeshine and a haircut.

I walked three blocks, careful to stay out of the mud, through the tangle of Saint Paul's dark, narrow streets. Streetcars ground around the loop, shoppers rushed among the stores, a few men, clinging to another century, sold coal or ice from horse-drawn wagons. Cars zig-zagged impatiently, horns honking, and the April wind blew down from Cathedral Hill. I passed a newsstand without even glancing at the headlines, busy rehearsing my speech.

At the bronze doors of the Hamm Building, I hesitated just a moment, trying to settle the jitters. Just go, I told myself. I walked down the corridor past a busy, smoky pool hall. Where the carpet ended, a hand-drawn sign said:

HAMM'S BREWERY HIRING HERE.

A lady in a polka-dot dress, with frizzy white hair, who looked liked she'd been eating quite well, handed me a pencil and a clipboard. I sat in a chair in the hallway, among other rubes, most of them men, scribbling to fill in the form. I checked OFFICE WORK. I checked HIGH SCHOOL GRADUATE.

I practiced my speech in which I touted my facility at math. I would neglect to mention it had been acquired at the race track. But in fact at Sacred Heart I had breezed through Algebra Two. There was no question that I could handle the simple tasks of say, an apprentice bookkeeper. At almost forty-two years old, I didn't want to start rolling barrels around the brewery floor.

Once I finished my application, I handed it back to the frizzy-haired lady. I stood like a Catholic schoolboy, hands behind my back, waiting for a grade from my teacher.

"You can go on in then," she said. She handed back my application, separated from clipboard and pencil. "You are a Number Two. Please stand in the appropriate line for your number. Two."

Well, of course lady, I didn't say. I'm not going to stand in the inappropriate line, am I?

I wandered into a room full of murmuring applicants, bumping and milling and generally looking unsure of themselves. Only two tables at the far wall were Number Twos, accepting applications for the office, and I shuffled over there and almost applied for a job.

What stopped me was a familiar face near the back door.

Serious Bobby stood near a red door. His hands were behind him as he leaned back into it. He was speaking to a very tall, thin, elegantly dressed man with oily dark hair, parted in the middle. I recognized the tall man from photos in the newspaper. He was William Hamm, occupation millionaire brewer, resident of Saint Paul, Minnesota and Palm Beach, Florida.

Hamm had taken over the brewery not two years ago from his father, who had died after guiding it through the treacherous shoals of Prohibition. The son was now maybe 35 years old, a prince of the city, handsome, divorced, and the most eligible man in town.

Mister Hamm turned his back to me. He and Serious Bobby were not exactly arguing, but there was some point of contention. I backed out of the hallway. The frizzy haired lady was taking a cigarette break. I sidled up to her and said: "Ma'm, could you tell me who that fellow is along the back wall. The one wearing eyeglasses talking to Mr. Hamm?"

She peered in.

"Oh that's Mr. Robert Pearson. He's our hiring agent."

"Could you tell me how long he's been with the firm?"

She looked in, as if she could read the answer somehow from his face.

"Oh, I don't know," she blew smoke, "I believe he's a consultant to Mister Hamm."

"And do you know where he worked before becoming employed here?"

"I haven't the vaguest idea," she said.

"Thank you ma'am," I said and walked toward the lobby.

"You haven't turned in your application, mister."

"Oh, oh," I said, flustered. "Changed my mind, sorry, and thanks so much for your courtesy."

I bought Janie lunch at Swensens' Ice Cream Parlor in the basement of the Emporium Department Store. Janie had convinced me, over the last couple of weeks, that she had tamed her inner tiger, and had quit her crusade to reform Saint Paul. Instead, she was working on a book, to be put out, she hoped, by some famous New York publisher.

"This is America, Powers," she said. "You can't get away with murder."

I didn't argue. Writing this book would keep her mostly home, and by the time she got around to the dangerous questions ... well, I'd deal with that when, and if, it happened.

It was a late lunch. Janie looked flushed and tired. I ordered the grilled cheese and she the hamburger-deluxe. We finished with vanilla malts and only after we'd slurped them up did I come out with it.

"You want a piece of the puzzle?"

She leaned across at me. "Sure, why not?"

She wore a black blouse with pearl buttons that hid her swelling pregnancy pretty well.

"Okay, let's talk about the puzzle," she said.

I was going to be her main source for this gangster book. But the agreement was, both Harry and Jack would have to be dead or in prison before it could be published.

"All right," I said. "Serious Bobby Pearson."

"Yeah."

"You've heard of him."

She said a hesitant yes.

"He's a bagman-negotiator-diplomat. He shuttles among the factions. The sheriff. The County Attorney. The State Police. The Saint Paul cops. The City Council. The Minneapolis cops. The State House. He delivers money and messages designed to keep everybody happy and well-fed."

Janie, lips around a straw, slurped.

"He's been at it for probably ten years. He started in real estate. He was your man if you wanted to disguise your ownership of speakeasies, horse wires, bordellos, pool halls, slots palaces, dice rooms. Let's say you were on the city council and didn't want the world to know you were dispensing booze or running a card game. Serious Bobby was your man."

"Okay."

"How does such a fellow turn up as hiring consultant for a rapidly expanding Hamm's Brewery?"

Janie shrugged.

"He's a high school dropout. He's got no experience in brewing, accounting or general business. I'm more qualified to be a brewery consultant than he is. So what does that tell you?"

"I don't know, Powers, stop toying with me, I'm exhausted."

"Serious Bobby is a gangland insider. He knows where the bodies are buried, literally, and his flapping lips could generate a thousand indictments. My conclusion is, William Hamm hired such a man under pressure from the gangsters."

"I see."

"You're aware that during Prohibition, the Hamm Brewery sent out the occasional barrel of real beer, right? And this was an illegal act, right? For which they had to pay off somebody, right? And that means that the Hamm family had, however reluctantly, engaged underworld figures in protecting their business."

She shrugged.

"So, Janie, you've been asking yourself, what's going to happen to all these bootlegger-gangsters now that booze is legal? The answer is, they're going to muscle the legit businesses. And what better way than to get your hands around the hiring process, and fill the brewery work floor with your gangster buddies?"

I slapped the table.

"So there's a chapter in your book. The intermingling, that's the word, right, of business and the underworld."

She pushed away the malt. "I didn't need that," she said.

"The information or the malt?"

"The calories. I don't know how I can ever make something of this, unless somebody's arrested and tried."

"Nobody's going to be arrested unless and until the G-men step in. Are you kidding me? In this town? This shakedown could go on for decades."

"Well, I see how it works," she said.

"Oh do you?"

" I appreciate it," she said. She pulled out a skinny reporter's notebook and a pencil. "On background," she said. She began writing. "Let me take a few notes."

"For your book, not for the damn newspaper," I said. I'd already calculated the odds. She was knocking out three or four pages a day. Just writing a draft of what she already knew would take six months. Sometime in there she would have a new baby to deal with, so I figured that would add another six months. We agreed that when she finished the first draft I would read it, there'd be corrections, a second draft, and only then would she begin asking questions. This would buy me, and her, two years. Anything could happen in two years. Maybe I'd be in Cuba, maybe she'd be married or working in Chicago. Procrastination can be a strategy. Anything worth doing is worth putting off.

She stopped scribbling when she saw me staring at her ring. She slapped her hand on the green Formica table and said: "For God's sake, here, look at it."

I held her hand. It was a thin ring on the marriage finger of her left hand, gold, filigree if you looked close enough.

"It was my grandmother's, okay?"

"Hmm. There's no guy?"

"I'm tired of everybody glancing at my belly and then looking for a wedding ring. Okay?"

"Are you going back to Wisconsin to have this baby?"

She closed her eyes and growled: "I don't know. All right? There's a lot of things I don't know. Powers, mind your own business, you're not my father."

CHAPTER TEN

The Derby was setting up well for Sam and me. There was not just one coupled entry, but two. Catawba Stables put in a hopeless pair that would appear to be a bargain to the casual bettor. That left the three best horses, Broker's Tip, Charley O and Head Play, to drift all over the board as longshots.

After all the payoffs I'd made to have Swede Fanlund framed for bank robbery, I had about $350 left from my find at Aunt Doris's. In the week before the Derby, Sam and I started making our bets. We let the downtown bookies know we'd consider any of those three horses at 10-1. We put down five dollars here, ten dollars there, whenever the odds rose. The odds were generous enough that we could bet all three horses and still win money.

We worked our angles on Monday morning and again on Tuesday, and when we broke for lunch, Sam returned to the garage with two ham sandwiches, two iced ginger ales, and instructions.

"Jack wants you to check in on the boys."

"What boys?"

"Out at White Bear."

"I thought *you* were his errand boy."

Sam shrugged.

We ate sandwiches, we drank ginger ale. We worked our speed figures and class angles in the April sunlight, just off the garden Sam had spaded.

"Well," I said, "Mr. Khayyam won the Chesapeake at Havre de

Grace. Set a track record it says here."

"And beat nobody," said Sam. "And will be coupled with Ladysman at even money. He's a toss."

"Anything special out at White Bear?" I said, rising out of the lawn chair.

"Just see if they're okay. Courtesy call. Ask if they need anything."

As I walked to my car, that request made sense to me, in a way. Jack was paranoid about phone taps. He didn't want to call his friends at White Bear Lake. But why not send Sam? I shrugged it off and drove north toward the lakes.

When I arrived, I first thought there was trouble. The Idlewild cottage was surrounded by cars. There were three cars jammed into the sandy lot astride the house, four lining the street in front, and two parked on the grass facing the lake. These were late model Buicks, Packards, DeSotos and one I recognized: A dark blue Hudson. This was parked under a budding tree in the shadows of the cottage. Its Oklahoma plates confirmed that this car belonged to the rude runt who'd come knocking at Myrtle's door.

A party was going on around back, in the fenced yard. It was a high, raw-wood fence, and I could hear the party but not see it. I knocked on the gate.

A tiny, smashed-face woman answered. I felt as if somebody had smacked me in the gut with a shovel. This was the dangerous drunk Paula Harmon. Her fingers were all diamond rings. She wore a one-piece black bathing suit that clung to her, tight and sexy. She held a highball in one hand, and a cigarette in the other.

"Oh, hello," she said, "I know you, don't I?"

I steadied my impulse to take off running.

She tilted her head and blew smoke high into the air.

"Well come in," she said, and stepped back. "Don't just stand there like a dummy."

I stepped into a grassy yard. A phonograph balanced in a

windowsill played fiddle-guitar western music. Men stood around a steel barrel that had been turned into a barbecue. The lid was flung open to reveal a small pig on a spit, its skin roasted crisp.

Three women sat in the shade of an umbrella table, two more on the steps. Down those steps walked Ma Barker, carrying a tray of buns.

I heard the gate slam behind me. I looked back to see the old man they called Dad had slammed the gate. He was wobbly drunk already, dressed in trousers and undershirt. I willed myself to approach the men around the barbecue. George was smoking a cigarette, playing chess at a picnic table with Monty. Alvin Karpis was using a long fork to poke at the roasted pig. Fred Barker, solicitous, took the tray of buns from his mother.

The rude runt who had come knocking for Myrtle sat on a milk carton, playing tug-of-war with a miniature bulldog, a stick in contention. The partiers either didn't notice my entrance or dismissed me with a glance.

Fred slid the tray of buns onto the picnic table and offered me a handshake.

"You set this place up?" he asked.

I nodded.

"Nice place," he said.

I began to see the fundamental difference between Fred and Karpis. Fred wanted people to like him. Karpis didn't give a damn.

Fred inclined his head toward the barrel smoker. "We're about to cut the pig," he said.

He turned to Karpis. "Ray is doing the honors." He handed Karpis a huge rusty knife.

"Juicy," said Karpis. He stabbed the pig, and using that knife as a server, began plating huge portions of roast pork onto white porcelain plates.

"Jack sent me ..." I started to say but Karpis' finger went to his lips. He took a plate of roasted pork, flooded it with barbecue sauce and topped it with a roll.

"Get some and follow me," he commanded.

In consideration of gout, I took a modest portion of meat and two buns, and climbed the steps into the kitchen.

"Oh mister …" Ma Barker called.

"Hello, Mother," I said, and escaped her.

In a galvanized tub set on the kitchen table, a mountain had been built of chipped ice and bottles of Hamm's beer. Karpis opened a bottle for me and one for him and beckoned me into the sunny porch.

It was quiet, except for the hillbilly music. We had a view of the calm lake, nobody swimming this early in the season.

Karpis and I sat at a rough table on the screen porch. Flies pestered us, and Karpis waved at them.

"What do you hear from our friend the nightclub man?" Karpis said.

"He wants to know if you need anything."

Karpis seemed to consider that seriously. He cut a piece of bread-and meat, fed himself, swigged beer.

"I'll tell you what you can do for me," said Karpis.

But I had to wait a moment as he chewed. "You know the fellow with the cars, don't you?"

He meant Tom Filben.

"I do."

"We need a rich man's car. It has to look convincing, it has to be disposable."

"I could tell him that," I said.

"Also a chauffeur's uniform and cap."

"Okay."

"That should do it," he said. "Aren't you going to eat?"

"Sure," I said. The pork was beautifully roasted, succulent and full of smoky flavor, without need for sauce.

"The fellow playing with the bulldog," I said. "I don't know him."

"What did you need to know?" Karpis said.

"I've been seeing him around town," I said. "That's all."

"He's Fred's brother Doc. Anything else?"

"I guess not," I said. "How are the neighbors?"

"We sent them a case of beer. They're our friends now."

"Good, good," I said. "Jack was hoping for good relations."

Karpis pushed away his half-eaten plate, leaned back, worked a Chesterfield out of the pocket of his white linen shirt. He lit it with a silver lighter, stared at me through the smoke. The look of his eyes changed. They were like hard winter coal.

"I'm not going to like seeing you around," he said.

"What do you mean? Jack sent me."

He tapped ash to the gray-painted wood floor. I followed that ash as it drifted over his polished brogans.

"We've got enough friends, okay?"

"Sure," I said.

"So beat it."

I stood up. He was a greasy-haired skinny punk, and I could have kicked his ass in a schoolyard fight, but somehow I was afraid. His eyes were spooky, riveting, cold, without a hint of humor or pity. He gave commands with a natural, unthinking authority.

"I'll see the car guy," I said.

Karpis turned his back on me, smoked his cigarette, and stared at the lake.

I stopped at the White Bear Hotel and rented a room. In the bar I was the only patron, me and the bartendress staring at the lake, a lone tiny white boat plowing across. The bartendress was probably 80 years old and had a yappy curly-furred dog. In the corner was a woodstove, fired up as if it were midwinter. The picture window looked through budding trees. I ordered a double Crab Apple whiskey with a Hamm's beer to wash it down.

She delivered and sat knitting near the stove.

I stared at the lake and drank.

So as it turned out, doing Jack's bidding, I had rented a summer home for the Barker-Karpis gang. But it was a bigger gang now, joined by Doc Barker, and three Chicago gangsters. Certainly, they were here under Big Ryan's protection while they planned some monster job. What bothered me was my memory of a guy I had never met, named Oscar Erickson. He was a laid-off dining car waiter on the Empire Builder. He'd been selling Christmas wreaths door to door and had the bad luck to drive through Como Park on December 16. He was a sincere, helpful young man, people said, and just married. The mistake of his life was offering Fred Barker help in changing a tire.

Wham! Two shots in the head. Dead in the morning.

The killing of two Minneapolis cops didn't sit right, but the murder of that poor unemployed sap, that was getting between me and sleep. I'd had a role in that, although minor and unintended. The Barker-Karpis gang, I had discovered too late, was far more vicious and trigger happy than they needed to be. Maybe they had to shoot it out with those Minneapolis cops, but a wreath salesman?

"Mae, is it?" I called to the bartendress. "Do it again."

I drank and stared at the lake. Time seemed to drift all over the place. As fresh and lovely as it smelled outside, in here it was the stench of alcohol. Mae knitted, the dog snoozed, I stared and drank.

With the last half-sober thought, I realized I was stuck running this errand for the Barker gang. I had to see Filben on their behalf, or risk taking a dead swim in the Mississippi. But after that I was through. Play the Derby, get the hell out of town. Summer in Eagle River. I could stand it in summer. And then … and then? Well, someday my sisters and I could sell Aunt Doris's farm, split the money and then maybe I would try my luck in Havana.

A good town for gamblers, I'd heard.

I ordered again, I drank again. "I'm staying upstairs," I said. "Not driving in this condition."

She returned not a twitch, not a blink. She went back to her knitting.

I drank.

I stared at the lake.

After a while, I saw nothing.

I woke up at 4 a.m. with gout pain. My big toe was throbbing so bad I could barely stand the air to touch it. I took a bath, but the soaking didn't help. It would be hours before the drugstore opened.

Near 8 a.m. I eased my socks and shoes on, limped to the car, and drove to the Walgreen's up the street for a big bottle of aspirin.

It only helped a little. I limped into William Paul's Cafe for a breakfast of weak coffee, brutally-cooked eggs and stale toast.

I mulled my choices. I didn't know any Minneapolis cops I could trust. The flaming demise of Sadie and Rose last year had shown what happens to people who trusted the Saint Paul cops. The sheriff was under the thumb of the County Attorney, Irish Kinkead. The chief of the State Police was Harry Sawyer's drinking buddy. That left me only one choice: The Division of Justice, and its special agent in charge, Roland Heater.

A throbbing hangover accompanied my limping self as I met Heater in a place no gangster had ever been seen: The Saint Paul Public Library. A massive stone building, it was across Rice Park directly from the Federal Building. Up its marble stairs, three floors, in a sunny space behind stacks of history books, I met the head G-man.

His teeth were stained from his cheroot habit. Otherwise he was well groomed, but with a wool suit too heavy for spring. We sat across from each other at a study desk.

"Hurt your foot?"

"It'll be all right." I whispered: "The Third Northwestern robbery."

"Uhmm-hmm."

"Two cops and a civilian dead."

"Right."

"I know who done it and I know where they are."

"Well, that's mildly interesting."

"I want immunity."

"I can't give you anything like that," Heater said, and spread his arms. "First of all, there's no federal crime."

"What do you guys do over there?"

"Bring me a kidnapping, bring me white slavery, bring me interstate auto theft. Otherwise..." he kicked back in his chair.

"Come on."

"Powers, there are political factions in this land of ours who absolutely loathe the concept of a national police force. They have allies in Congress. Our Director is constantly fighting rear guard actions against them. We can't start swooping down on civilians and kicking in doors. That would play right into the hands of our political enemies."

"So bank robbery, murder, that's not..."

He lifted a tiny notebook out of an inside pocket, and a golf pencil. He licked the tip of that pencil.

"Who you got?"

"Fred Barker," I whispered. "Alvin Karpis. They're also wanted for the murder of the sheriff of West Plains, Missouri."

"I'm aware," said Heater.

"They're living with Fred's mother at the Idelwild cottage on Bald Eagle Lake. Apparently Fred's got a brother named Doc, another vicious punk, here from Oklahoma. He's got a cross tattooed on his arm, and if he didn't get that done in prison, I'll buy you a hot dog."

Heater wrote.

"Joining them somehow is this mob from Chicago. Three guys. One named Monty, another named George, and an old guy everybody calls Dad."

"Chicago," muttered Heater.

"They didn't come here to have a pig roast," I said.

Heater scribbled.

"They're there right now," I said.

Heater pushed himself back against the window. His hands worked over his face, as if trying to pump up tired muscle.

"Mother, did you say?" Heater asked. "Who's the mother? They go around with their mother?"

"A plump little old country lady," I said. "Does the name Arthur Dunlop ring a bell? Because he was her boyfriend until last May, when the Barker Gang had him bumped off."

"Okay."

"She has a little bulldog. One of those miniatures. Dotes on the dog. A whole gaggle of pretty young ladies goes around with the gang too."

"Cars?"

"What is it with you guys and cars? Why do you obsess on cars? Okay, Doc drives a Hudson with Oklahoma plates. The others, I don't know. Lots of flashy cars."

He closed his notebook and sighed.

"I'm not going to involve the local police," he said. "The Director won't have it. He's livid against the Saint Paul cops and the Ramsey sheriff too. Let me see what I can accomplish at the state level. Leave it with me, Powers. I do have your phone number, don't I?"

"Look, Heater, here's what I want in return. There's a young reporter, name of Vetter, Janie Vetter. She's chasing cop cars for the Daily News, but she hopes to be a book writer. If you ever get any of these characters into handcuffs, I want you to cut her in, as a favor to me, okay?"

"Uh," said Heater.

"Is that a yes or a no?"

"That's an uh," said Heater.

CHAPTER ELEVEN

Sam and I reserved a side table at the Royal for the Kentucky Derby and placed our final bet through Pat Reilly. We backed three horses: Brokers Tip at 8-1, Head Play at 5-1 and Charley O at 6-1. All spring we had been laying "winter book" bets on those horses at high odds. Our combined bets totaled $200 on each horse.

We listened over the Royal's radio speakers as the Derby went off. Ninety seconds later, the horses were in the stretch, with Brokers Tip and Head Play dueling, leaving all the others far back. Even before they crossed the finish line, Sam and I danced in a fog of cigar smoke, over a scattering of ripped tickets. Apparently the finish was so close that the jockeys got into a fight after, and maybe even during, the race. The placing judges had to be consulted to determine the winner. Either way, we couldn't lose. The judges ruled for Brokers' Tip, who officially paid $19.86 for $2. We did better than that, placing clever bets in future books all over town. In the end, Sam and I split nearly $3,000.

Even after subtracting the cost of the bets, our profit was equivalent to a year's wages for, let's say, a traffic cop, or a meat cutter at the Union Stockyards. Sam was $1200 closer to Nagasaki. I had cash for a year's living.

Myrtle and I celebrated with a modest dinner at the Lowry Terrace Cafe, but delayed the main celebration a week. We planned to attend the re-opening of the fabulous Plantation Nightclub. I owed her a big night out in return for her hospitality.

So on the Saturday following the Derby, we were dressing in her bedroom, the dogs eyeing us, suspicious, from the bed. They could always sense when they would be left behind.

"You can stay if you can pay half the rent," Myrtle said, her back to me, her face angled in at the dresser mirror. "Now that you're a rich gambler."

She applied bright pink lipstick.

I said: "I guess Myrtle's run out of sugar daddies."

She compressed her lips, examined the result, and said: "We've got each other figured, haven't we?"

Over her shoulders she buttoned a silver sequined blouse. She shrugged and stepped back from the mirror, her eyes never leaving its reflection.

"What is it about us, Mick? Why can't we do what's good for us?"

"We're going out to have a good time, aren't we?"

She rubbed my hair like she was a teacher and I a schoolboy.

"That's what I like about you, you don't use no Brillcream."

"That's what you like about me?"

"Among other things."

Out in the living room, her parakeets set up squawking.

"But you're not my type, Mick. I like a ruthless man. A ruthless man understands the nature of this world, and he takes it on with both fists. A woman can work with a ruthless man, but she can't have a fellow who won't stand up for her."

I lay back on the bed and petted Snowflake and Hula Girl.

I said, "I thought we'd have children, and so did she."

"Oh," said Myrtle, and grabbed her sequined purse, "your runaway wife. She was no good for you Mick, that's why you moon over her. See, that's what we want, everything that's bad for us."

"How am I mooning? I've barely said a word about her."

Her lips pursed, skeptical.

"A wild horse gets broken once," she said. "After that, she don't have no spirit."

I was still living out of a suitcase and I rustled in there to choose a weapon. The .45 was a heavy cannon compared to the silvery pocket revolver Jack Peifer had given me. I left the .45, slipped the shiny revolver into my coat pocket.

Myrtle placed a purple turban over her curls.

"It's going to be a big night out there," she said.

The Plantation Nightclub was an amusement park for adults, perched over the far shore of White Bear Lake. It had been run as a wide-open speakeasy for years by the gangster Benny Harris. But in 1931, people were flush out of booze-and-dancing money, and some were even out of gas money. The Plantation was twenty miles from Saint Paul, in a resort town that had tourists only ten weeks a year. When times got tough, the Plantation had no chance, no matter how swank it was.

Apparently, Repeal revived Benny Harris's hopes. He spent a fortune on repairs and added an ice-based cooling system. The Plantation was now open legal, complete with air conditioning.

To judge by the number and quality of cars in its circular driveway, Benny was going to collect his bet. Myrtle got out of the Essex when the schoolboy valet opened the door. She was shimmering in silver, set off by an ermine fur stole.

A lanky, elderly Colored man, in a blue coat with brass buttons, opened the Plantation's big red door for us. Benny Harris was one of the few crooks I didn't know, so I couldn't lobby for a better table. I tipped the doorman but it didn't help. A gawky schoolgirl hostess led us to a table too near the orchestra. I tipped her but that didn't help either.

I said: "We get rube seating, I guess."

"Sir," the hostess said, "we are absolutely jammed to the walls tonight."

"That's all right little girl," said Myrtle.

The orchestra's instruments were laid carelessly at the bandstand. Our table was set with tulips in cut glass and a tall white candle over spotless linen and gleaming place settings. If the cooling system was working, it wasn't doing much for the smoky air. Myrtle refused a boy's offer to take her coat.

"I always keep my animals nearby," she informed him. "This place is full of thieves."

She put a cigarette in her lips and I, gentleman, lit it. We ordered martinis, which made my gout foot twinge. I sat facing the orchestra and Myrtle kept looking over my shoulder, trying to spot friends in the crowd.

"Trouble," she said.

I turned.

"Don't gawk," she said, and then hid her face with her hand. "Oh god."

A punk approached us, sending a ripple down my spine to my scrotum. Here, dressed up like a kid for church, was Doc Barker. He swayed with drink, steadied himself with a grab at the back of an empty chair.

Whoever dressed him had trouble getting him into that suit. The sleeves too long, the tie sloppy.

"Myrtle," he slurred. "You should of come with us."

Myrtle cast her eyes down as if there were something interesting on her empty plate.

"You too, champ," Doc said and brushed my shoulder.

Our martinis were delivered, the waitress making deft moves around Doc.

"Now Kentucky, that's a party town," said Doc. He stepped back, waved one hand. "You missed it," he said, and stumbled off.

I turned my chair so I could watch him.

"Louisville," muttered Myrtle. "He wanted me to go with him to Louisville. Why would he imagine I want to hang around a race track with fifty thousand screaming drunks?"

She ate the martini olive off the toothpick.

"Who would go to Louisville with that mob of hillbillies?" she said. "The Barker Gang," she sputtered. "Look at them."

Doc made his way through the crowd to tables in the center of the room, at the premier spot, separated from the dance floor by a row of potted palms. There he joined the gang: Alvin Karpis with a dark-haired teenager dressed in white. Freddy, with Paula sitting in his lap. George and Monty, each beside women who looked like showgirls. Dad, standing cocktail in hand, telling a joke or story. Doc arrived, lunging at the table, grabbing a drink.

"I wonder what they did with their poor mother," Myrtle said.

"I've met her," I said, "she's a fabulous cook."

"Oh yeah?"

"Southern fried chicken," I said.

"That's not all she's cooking up. She wouldn't stop harping at the boys until they got Doc out of jail. I don't understand it. Doc's the meanest of them, and somehow the mother dotes on him." She sipped at her martini. "They bribed him out, you know. Rumor is, he learned something in the joint. They say he learned a taste . . . for men. Those man fuckers are the worst kind, the very meanest. They're better off in prison."

The cigarette girl bowed before our table and I, feeling Derby generous, bought Myrtle a pack of Pall Malls and tipped too much.

Joe Sanders and his Night Hawks returned from their break, picked up their instruments and dropped into a low-crawling tune. Myrtle closed her eyes and swayed to the music. I sipped the martini, which went down like battery acid. Beer may have been legal, but booze not yet, and the Plantation was pouring bathtub gin.

I am not a dancer, so Myrtle spied somebody she knew and flew off to swing with him. I was feeling a bit used, her escort to a good time, and a relatively sober drive home. I made up my mind, sitting there alone, that I would find my own digs now, and search for a woman who could tolerate the future I had in mind.

Myrtle stayed out on the dance floor and after a few minutes I wandered toward the restroom, down a dark hallway, behind a black curtain, where a bank of pay phones lined the wall of a noisy steamy kitchen. Between each phone was a small open window, giving a view into the sweaty busy folks preparing the meals. In the men's room I stood at the urinal peeing onto ice when the door opened and then pissing next to me was Ralph Tallerico.

"What do you know, Shaky," he said, "I thought that was you."

I tucked in my manhood and zipped up.

He took a casual piss, his back turned to me, as if I were nobody to fear. I edged to the sink, began washing my hands, looked in the mirror to see my frightened, reddened face. I tried to catch my breath.

Tallerico zipped up.

"I see you came with that Summit Hill slut," he said.

I simply stared at him.

"You bring your brass knuckles?" he asked.

He grinned at me, one missing tooth in front, the one I'd knocked out. Hands on his hips, he spread his jacket so I could see his vest and shoulder holster.

"Dental work," he said. "Going to be expensive."

I did my best to glare right through him.

"Powers, you're nothing but a Catholic schoolboy," he said. "Swede wants a piece of you, or I'd take your right here."

Trying to be casual, I pulled a paper towel out of the dispenser and wiped my hands. I could feel the weight of that revolver in my pocket, it was like gravity sucking at my hand.

"I've got friends," I said. "You should know that."

Tallerico laughed. "Friends? In this town? You belong to the Elks or something?"

I leaned against the wall. I realized that if he was going to shoot me he wouldn't be talking. I put my hands in my pockets. The left, my shooting hand, wrapped the revolver.

"I'll see you squirm," Tallerico said. "I'll see you shit your pants and beg. Swede will beat his rap. And then the three of us will get together, and we'll have a payday."

He bumped past me, grabbed the door handle, and bulled into the dark hallway.

It was time for a second martini and then a third. The second one I drank listening to the orchestra alone while Myrtle danced. The third I sipped with George at the bar during the band's intermission. He was drinking a cocktail called The Cosmopolitan. I'd never heard of it.

He was dressed for spring in a salmon shirt, dark blue tie, off-white jacket and trousers, brown-and-white shoes.

"The women in this town," he said. He whistled. "Low quality."

I shrugged. "Depends on where you find them."

"I suppose that's true," he said. "So, how long have you been Jack Peifer's man?"

"Oh, we go back," I said.

I kicked the barstool over to make room, rested my elbows on the bar.

"What's the rundown on his wife?"

"The lovely Violet," I said.

"Stunning creature," said George, and sipped. "Rumor has it that Peifer shot his cock off. So I was wondering how he could possibly keep that gorgeous creature satisfied."

"Tip of his pecker. Just the tip."

"Have you seen it?"

"His pecker?"

"The damage."

"I'm not on intimate terms with his male equipment," I said. "It's just, you know, stories go around."

"Rumors," said George. "They're just another form of communication."

I looked around. None of the drinkers or bartenders seemed to be paying attention to us so I drew from out of my left trouser pocket the shiny revolver. I could hide most of it in my hand, it was that small. It had a no-snag hammer, and a thin profile, held only four rounds of ammo, if you wanted the hammer to rest on an empty chamber.

"This is the gun that did it," I said. "Jack gave it to me. Didn't want it around anymore."

George looked at the gun and smiled.

If I hadn't been at the end of my third martini, I might not have committed such a foolish indiscretion. Feeling a bit like a sheepish amateur, I palmed the gun back into my pocket.

"Tip of his pecker," said George. "Then it's a bad-luck gun."

"It wasn't all luck," I said. "He was drunk out of his mind."

"You know what they say about a gun that has drawn blood."

"I don't think I do."

He never did give an answer. He raised his eyebrows. Dealing with a rube like me was testing his patience.

"In a few short months in office," he said, "Franklin Roosevelt has managed to ruin this country. Can you imagine another president confiscating gold? He's a dictator like Stalin or this man Hitler in Germany. Shutting the banks and confiscating gold. It will be a sad Fourth of July with the entire country on its knees. Street riots wouldn't surprise me, not at all."

I reduced my martini to a frosty mist.

"What we need in the White House is a communicator, not a dictator."

"Don't let me drink another," I said, "I'm wobbly already."

"So are you a Cubs or a White Sox man?"

"Neither," I said. "In this town, it's Saints versus Millers."

George sputtered. "I thought a fellow like yourself would follow the major leagues."

Across the vast, smoky expanse of the nightclub floor, I saw Rico, arm around Myrtle's waist, escorting her to the big red door. My blood ran with a drunken heat that overcame all caution. Heart pounding, light headed, I pushed over the stool next to me, said "Excuse me," and left George drinking his Cosmopolitan.

I crossed the floor like a missile tracking its target. It seemed like I was aware of nothing and everything: the cigar smoke, the chatter, the beautiful women, the potted palms, the half-drunken men in their best suits, the waitresses in flame red, the gleaming floors, the plush red carpet.

I pushed out the double doors and stood breathing the crisp air, struggling for it, but strangely calm and focused. There across the muddy lot, at a dark green Studebaker, Rico slapped Myrtle and pushed her into the passenger seat of his car.

I marched across the mud. Rico was leaning into the open door, his hands around Myrtle's throat. I could hear her gasping as I rounded the hood.

I think I shouted.

Something flashed brilliant and beautiful. Bells and whistles sounded in my ears. Rico turned toward me. His mouth opened and his face took on a look of exquisite surprise. I felt like I had been lifted off the earth into a dizzy, noisy heaven. I was shocked when Rico fell back against the Studebaker. He twisted. He collapsed. They say he was hit by all four bullets, but I don't remember anything after Myrtle's choking scream.

CHAPTER TWELVE

If Harry wanted me dead, he wouldn't have sent Pat Reilly.

If Harry wanted me dead, he wouldn't have sent Pat Reilly.

If Harry wanted me dead, he wouldn't have sent Pat Reilly.

That thought whirled through my brain as I watched Reilly mount the rickety back stairs of my new home in the slums.

"Pat!" I cried. A lump clogged my throat when I opened the door. "Good to see an Irish face."

"Don't give me that Irish bullshit," Reilly said.

"Beer?"

"Now you're talking."

I opened two bottles of Altwasser and handed him one.

"Warm beer?" he said.

"Waiting for the ice man," I said.

We stood in a dark, sparse kitchen in a tenement owned by the Archdiocese. A tiny table and two cheap chairs were the only furniture besides icebox, stove, and stained, half-sized leaky bathtub. That bathtub doubled as kitchen sink. On the table was a pile of newspapers and detective magazines, and a bag of groceries delivered by the Essenmeyers boy. I hadn't been out of the apartment in almost a week.

"So what's the latest?" I asked.

"The latest?"

Pat said this over his shoulder as he did a walk-through. There were only two other rooms, a combined bedroom-water-closet off to the side, and a parlor overlooking Marshall Street. I was up on the third floor, below me two destitute noisy families living on Catholic Charity.

I caught up to Pat at the parlor windows. He had his shirtsleeves rolled up and banded. Even from behind he smelled of bad breath.

I had been keeping the windows closed, since they had no screens, but Pat opened one and stuck his head out, looking up and down the street.

"Come on, Pat, what's up?"

Satisfied that no one had tailed him, he sat sideways in a lumpy chair and lit a Lucky.

"The word is Commodore."

"Commodore," I said.

"Commodore," Pat said. "Ten to them, same to Harry, so twenty the night, and we'll let you know when it's safe to leave."

"That clever Harry," I said, "knows how to profit from any situation."

"That's how you show your gratitude?" said Pat, blowing smoke.

"No, no, no, tell Harry I'm squirming with gratitude."

"He figured you would be."

"Squirming, yeah. They allow dogs at the Commodore?"

"Do I look like a desk clerk?"

Actually, he did.

"We'll be around for a favor," Pat said. "You know that."

"Of course."

"And I need a tip on the Belmont."

"I'll place the bet for you personally."

"And stay the hell out of the Green Lantern."

"I can do that."

"And nobody knows nothing about nothing at all."

"Goes without saying."

"That's why I never said it, because it don't need saying. All right," he dropped that Lucky butt into the beer bottle, where it hissed. I escorted him to the back door, shook his limp, sweaty hand.

"Tell Harry thanks," I said, "and I owe him a big one."

"Tell me something I don't know," Pat said.

I watched the little guy trot down the stairs, sick fear and blessed relief battling for what remained of my soul. I could hardly remember Saturday night at the Plantation: all darkness, mud and fog as I stumbled along the lakefront. I do remember flinging the pistol with all my strength across the lake, and the splash it made unseen, a gulp in the dark as the lake sucked it down. All that chilly night I straggled like a hunted animal through the woods along the lakeshore. In the morning, from a drugstore phone booth, I called Billy McAmbly at home. He said if the cops were looking for me, he hadn't heard about it. He drove me to see Father McCarthy O'Sullivan.

Since then I'd been hiding in this charity apartment. The shooting of Rico did not make the Sunday papers, and on Monday the news was short and played on inside pages. The headline might as well have said: Just another gangster shooting. Myrtle Eaton, the only witness, told police and reporters that two Italian men who "appeared to be from Chicago" had ambushed Rico in the parking lot. One Italian did all the shooting, the other drove the getaway car, Myrtle said.

Rico died without saying a thing. The White Bear cops had turned over the case to the Saint Paul Police Gangster Squad.

Police noticed bruises around Mrs. Eaton's throat, which she declined to explain.

After a single day's mention in the papers, the case disappeared from the news.

I had not dared to visit Myrtle, and only by the grace of Billy McAmbly was my Essex sneaked back to Herb's Garage. I entertained dark thoughts of creeping over to Herb's at midnight, and turning my tailpipe on this city forever.

But that was before Pat's visit. Encouraged, I left the groceries for the next tenant, dropped my best suit at the cleaners, and took a cab six blocks to the Commodore.

It was in the mansion district, the only hotel on Summit Hill. The Commodore was six stories tall, solid brick, with a generous lawn, and a single, humble sign which spelled out its name vertically. The lobby was beautiful blond wood, lit by a humungous glass chandelier. The smartly attired guests in the lobby glared as I passed them. I wore tweed trousers and a white short-sleeve shirt, under-dressed for this swank crowd.

"A room was arranged by a Mister Reilly," I whispered to the clerk.

"Yes," he said, flipping through cards attached to a metal tray. With a straight face he said: "Your baggage, sir?"

"It," I said, "it got lost, the railroads lost it, it will be expressed up from the Union Depot this evening."

"Sign here, sir," he said.

And then I was in the elevator. The raven-haired operator was high-school cute in her brassy uniform. I said, "Nice evening, although I suppose you don't see much of it, trapped in an elevator."

She half smiled, as if to fend off a lunatic.

"Do they allow dogs, do you know?"

"Dogs?" she said. "Here? At the Commodore?"

"I guess not," I said, and she let me off at the fifth floor.

I unlocked the door, closed it behind me, and for the first time in a week, felt safe and calm. I opened the window and let in the spring breeze. The trees were just leafing out, the perfume of lilacs wafted over from rich peoples' yards.

The Commodore. This was where Harry stashed a guy to keep him safe from gangsters and cops. As long as you kept stuffing money into Harry's pocket, you were safe at the Commodore. It cost you double, but being a gangster was expensive.

This was one of the hotel's smaller rooms, but it seemed spacious because the bed folded up into the wall. I pulled down that Murphy bed, lay on its fresh sheets and took a long, sweet nap.

I fell asleep innocent and woke up a murderer. A dark soulless chill came upon me as I awoke to fading sunlight. I tried to force this feeling back to the depths of Hell where it had come from. I couldn't shake it. Michael Powers, guilty as sin.

He'd had his hands around Myrtle's throat, hadn't he? I recalled that justification again and again. He'd pushed her into the car, intent on kidnapping, or maybe murder? Either way, Myrtle was going to get it, just for being my girl. I was working a job for Jack, and couldn't be touched, but Myrtle ...

The thoughts just kept churning. At sunset I walked past mansions, lush lawns and the Cathedral to visit Janie. It was a risk, but only a ten minute risk, a five block walk between the Commodore and my former apartment. I badly needed company.

Janie and I climbed up to the rooftop. A wooden deck, surrounded by picket fence, occupied one corner. We sat in lawn chairs, turned our backs to the wind and the Cathedral, and looked over the city as it lit up. A long narrow grain barge floated placid down the Mississippi. The taverns at Seven Corners began to glow.

Janie had always had a rough ride at the Daily News. They started her on the wedding pages. They promoted her to the county beat, but then laid her off. I had something to do with that layoff, but my intentions were honorable. When she came back from furlough they'd given her the junior spot on the cops beat, but now that she was obviously pregnant, and unmarried, they'd put her back to weekends, when there was nobody else in the newsroom.

"So Janie, what do you hear about the Ralph Tallerico thing?"

"Not much," she said, and smoothed her scotch-plaid skirt over her goose-bumped legs.

We had carried coffee up, the French Press and two cups. I rattled my cup and saucer, a bit wind-chilled myself.

"Who did it Powers? Who did the world a favor?"

"No idea," I said.

"Yes you do or you wouldn't have brought it up."

"Chicago Outfit hit," I said. "Don't you read the papers?"

"Powers, you liar, you do know something. It was your friend Myrtle who witnessed."

"You first."

The wind blew her red hair into her face.

"Chapter and verse," I said.

"Well, they're letting me have a couple of shifts, like I'm a charity case, the shifts nobody wants, Saturday and Sunday nights. Nobody's in the newsroom, see, so there's no embarrassment. So I'm sitting around the copy desk doing crossword puzzles when I get the call."

"Okay, Saturday night."

"I'm listening to the police radio. We got a new one. It tunes to the cop stations directly. White Bear Lake constable calling for assistance. Wants the homicide squad from Saint Paul, and an ambulance."

"Okay."

"So I drive a photographers car out there."

"To the Plantation."

"Yes, late Saturday night. It's after deadline, so no urgency, but I want to get out of the newsroom, so …"

She sipped coffee.

"The ambulance was gone by the time I got there. The stiff is being loaded into the M.E.'s van. The M.E. is a part-timer from

Ramsey County, I don't know him, he won't say much, but tells me the stiff is named Ralph Tallerico."

"So…"

"So after I picked myself up from the ground I said, Ralph Tallerico, the Saint Paul torpedo? The M.E. shrugs. He doesn't know Tallerico from Herbert Hoover. It's Saturday night, and he wants to be out drinking."

"So who did they send? Saint Paul, I mean."

"Inspector Crumley."

"Oh boy."

"So I go talk to him, and after he grabs my ass and looks down my blouse he says: Come see me later, little girlie, I'll show you what we've got on this turd."

She sputtered.

"Well I know that's a trap, so I go talk to your friend Myrtle. She's all wrapped up in her furs, sitting on the nightclub's porch, looking shell-shocked. She's got the furs wrapped around her neck but I can see she's all purple and swollen. The band's playing inside. A crowd of gawkers was gathered around this Studebaker and the police cars. There was a lake of blood near the left front tire."

"And Myrtle says…"

"She has bruises on her face too. I ask if she needs a doctor and she says: What are you talking about? She tells me how a long dark car pulls up with Illinois plates. Two dagos get out, that's her word, dagos. One pins her to the hood, that must have been where she got the bruises. The other guy plugs Tallerico, one shot after the other, as he falls back against the car. Then the one guy lets Myrtle go with a shove and off the killers roar off toward Chicago. She's pissed, you know why?"

"Why?"

"Blood spatters on her fur coat."

"I see. And Inspector Crumley says…"

"White Bear Lake has a well-known gang problem, he says."

"Oh, White Bear Lake does."

"The criminal element from Chicago loves to vacation at White Bear, he says."

"Right."

"I've been around long enough to know this: Whenever Saint Paul cops want to cover up a crime, they blame Italians from Chicago."

"Janie, I remember when you were a naïve college girl."

"So who are the cops covering for, Powers?"

I lit my pipe. Wind blew the smoke away.

I said, "Ralph Tallerico put a bullet into Rose and Sadie, and then poured acid on their faces. And he did it just for the spending money."

"You're not answering my question."

"Do you think you could dog-sit Snowflake and Hula Girl for a few weeks?"

She lay back in the chair, taking in the sight of the rising full moon.

"Just a couple of weeks," I said.

"Where are you going?"

"I'll be around, but I'm kind of unsettled right now. The dogs are with my friend Billy, but they can't stay there, that house is too crowded as it is. And the dogs are on the lease here."

"I don't know … "

"I'll come over. Twice a day. I'll feed 'em, I'll walk 'em."

"Maybe," she said. "But Powers…"

A streetcar clanged out of the Selby Tunnel.

Janie leaned over the fence. Looking at the city, she said: "I don't trust you, Powers. You're playing me for a fool."

"I am?"

I stood at the fence next to her, both of us ruffled by the wind.

I kissed her on the lips. A warmth flooded through me, and

then she pushed me, gentle, away.

"Don't do that," she said. "I don't love you, Powers."

"Of course not," I said.

"And you don't love me, either. You're just lonesome, that's all."

"Okay."

"I'm looking for love," she said, "real love, not what you gangsters call love. I'm looking for a man, a good man to marry and have a family, a big family with him. So I guess I'm still naïve. I believe there's a good man out there who will marry me despite, you know… "

I stammered. If I were an honest young man with bright prospects, I'd marry her in a heartbeat. Pregnant or not. Her pregnancy had brought out my urge to protect and shelter someone.

"Oh," I said. "Marriage, yeah. I see Janie. I see what you want now."

CHAPTER THIRTEEN

"How many Catholics," Myrtle asked, "does it take to fill the Fair Grounds?"

"How many drunken Catholics," I corrected her. "About a fifty thousand, I'd say."

"It makes a German Baptist feel out of place," she said, and blew Pall Mall smoke into the breeze.

We were sitting at a picnic table that was sticky with tree sap. The air was heavy with an approaching thunder storm. Myrtle drank beer and I ginger ale. All around us swarmed thousands of Catholics from all over the Twin Cities. They were attending a beer picnic disguised as the Holy Name Parade. Mass and sermon had been held inside the race track and now, released from liturgical suffering, the crowd clogged the beer and bratwurst tents.

A cute family begged our pardon and sat with us, mom, dad and two tiny blonde girls. Myrtle's face went tight with feigned politeness.

"Nice to meet you," she told the family, and beckoned me into the sunshine.

"People like that give me the creeps," she said.

"People like what?"

"Wholesome," she said, "why did you drag me out here with all these holy rollers?"

"To thank you."

"This is your way of thanking me?"

"It's a festival, can't you tell? I don't like to be alone these days."

She put an arm around my waist, lay her head on my shoulders. She looked girly, a yellow dress with a big blue bow at the throat.

"That doesn't explain why you're a Holy Name guy all of a sudden."

"Bratwurst?" I asked.

"Plenty of kraut," she said.

At a sausage stand I flagged down a boy in a white paper hat. "Two with kraut!"

Myrtle and I ate bratwurst under the shade of an oak tree, to which a wooden bench had been nailed. All around us, the shuffling feet of the Catholic horde raised dust. Across from us, children lined up for the carousel.

"Mick," Myrtle said, licking mustard off her chubby fingers, "why don't we start fresh, you and me?"

"How's that?"

"Get a place together," she said.

"An apartment, you mean?"

"Some people say you're slow on the uptake, but I say that's baloney. Yes, you dumb Irishman, an apartment, split the rent, you and me?"

"Move in together, permanent?"

"How dim are you? Living in sin, ain't that how you Catholics say it?"

"This is a serious proposal?"

"Proposition," Myrtle said. "We split the rent."

"You're springing a surprise on me."

"What do you want, an engraved invitation?"

"I'd like a little time to think."

"Don't think too long, cowboy, your horse is getting restless. Look here, I always kind of liked your place on the hill. Why don't you throw out that college dingbat so we can cohabit in style?"

"She's on the lease," I said, "until January."

"Does she frighten easy?"

"Let's not mess with the kid."

"Of course not. The cute ones get away with everything."

"She's okay. She can't help being young. Look, she agreed to take the dogs for a couple of weeks, and I was hoping you could walk them once in a while. I don't want to be seen on the streets around there too much."

I fumbled for the zippered leather pouch that held my tobacco.

"Myrtle, I just don't know from day to day what's going to happen to me. See, I can't leave the Commodore right now. Harry's trying to work something out for me."

In shaky hands, I began to fill my best pipe, a Dubliner, with Havana Gold tobacco.

"Yeah," she said, "I was afraid to bring it up, you and me living in sin. I knew you'd back out."

"I'm not backing out. I'm waiting for the fog to clear."

Myrtle sat glum, arms resting on her thighs.

"Only one man I ever met could stick by a woman," she said, "and wouldn't you know, the state of Wisconsin locked him up for life."

We were watching a clown juggle bowling pins in the Tent of Smiles when I saw Father McCarthy O'Sullivan in the gaggle of passersby. At six-foot-six, he was hard to miss. I patted Myrtle on the leg, promised her a quick return, and stalked the priest. He stood at a pile of hay bales, surrounded by parishioners who had bought him a cardboard tankard of beer. I flagged him with a wave of the hand. He followed me around the back of the beer tent, and into the shade under a canvas flap.

"I'm out of that apartment, Father," I said, "and thank you."

I handed him a white sealed envelope.

"Twenty dollars for Patrick's Pence," I said.

He nodded. His bad eye fluttered as he folded the envelope into the front pocket of his black trousers. He'd had a couple of beers, his neck flush at the Roman Collar, his good eye watery.

We ambled along a fence that separated us from the mob of pedestrians and mess of stalled traffic along Snelling Avenue.

"So Father, if you've got a minute, I know this guy, good friend of mine, but he had the misfortune to be born Protestant."

Father Mack sipped beer.

"And so," I said, "he was wondering about the Sacraments, in particular, you know Confession."

"It's a morbid curiosity Protestants often have."

"So if this Protestant man came to you with a big sin, I mean, a Mortal, Mortal sin, could you, you know, offer forgiveness?"

He looked surprised. "Absolution? To a Non-Catholic?"

"Forgiveness, maybe," I said. "Because this Protestant, he caused bodily harm to another."

"Intentional bodily harm?"

"Sort of," I said. "He stabbed a guy."

"Grievous harm?"

"The guy he stabbed died, Father."

Father Mack looked down at me.

"After an altercation," I said, "that the other guy started. See the guy who died, he'd been causing bodily harm to the Protestant's wife."

Father Mack upended the tankard, spilled the last drops of beer near his shiny black shoes.

"Tell the man he's better off a Protestant," he said. "You see, Michael, the problem with us Catholics is we think we can commit any sin, and then wash it away in the Confessional."

"But we Catholics have to pay for our sins in Purgatory, right Father?"

"Michael, there are certain aspects of our Faith that are simplified, the better to teach them to schoolchildren."

"So there's no Purgatory, then? Is that what you're saying? There's no place of suffering between Heaven and Hell?"

"There is such a place, Michael. Look around you. You've been there all your life."

CHAPTER FOURTEEN

Harry Sawyer was the Chief Justice of the Gangland Supreme Court, and for six nights at the Commodore I awaited his decision. It was like being in a luxury jail while an unseen judge decided your fate. Whatever it was, there would be no appeal. I rarely went out that week, and absolutely avoided the dives downtown. It was a slow Tuesday night, June 14th, when I ordered a bowl of chicken dumpling soup at the hotel bar. I was reading the funnies in the Evening Dispatch when two women walked in. One of them was Ma Barker.

The other woman I knew only by her first name, Sylvia. The last time I hid out at the Commodore, last winter, she'd fallen asleep half-naked in my bed. Whiskey, and my backrub, had sent her into dreamland.

Sylvia was very tall and lanky, maybe thirty years old, with long bleach blonde hair that ended in a flip. She wore a blue jumper and slippers, which made her obviously a current guest of the hotel. Ma Barker wore an ill-fitting white dress that came down only to the knees, where it met the rolled tops of her support stockings. She limped toward a table as Sylvia said: "Will this be all right, Mother?"

Ma Barker sat, and across the empty bar room, nodded at me.

I could not help but walk over.

"Mister Powell," Ma said.

I shook her sweaty little hand.

"This is Sylvia."

Ma may have forgotten our meeting last Christmastime, but I didn't. By the gleam in her eyes, neither did Sylvia. We shook hands as if we'd just signed an insurance deal.

Ma looked around. "Do they have table service?"

"Of course, Mother," said Sylvia. "Will you join us Mister Powell?"

"Oh..."

"Please?" said Sylvia.

"I'll order desert," I said, and pulled back a chair.

Ma Barker almost disappeared behind the menu. Sylvia's knee brushed mine underneath the table.

"We've just checked in," Sylvia told me, "and mother is famished. Have you been here long, Mister Powell?"

"A while," I said. "I'm between apartments."

"So you're a native."

"Kind of," I said.

Sylvia was playing dumb, and so was I, on the theory that the less Ma Barker knew, the better.

"Well we..." Sylvia indicated Ma and herself, "are from Missouri. Both of us. What's good here?"

"Well, I'd recommend the fried chicken, except that it could never approach Mother's recipe."

The compliment went unnoticed. Ma dropped the menu to the beige tablecloth. "Don't they have a ladies room?" she asked.

"Right past that curtain," I said.

I watched her waddle off. She had gained weight since I'd first met her on Robert Street last year. She had a tummy bulge now. Life up north had been good to her.

Sylvia sighed.

"It's Mick, remember?" I said. "Mrs. Barker might know me as Patrick, but my friends call me Mick."

"I remember you, slugger," said Sylvia. She stuck a cigarette into her lips and I fumbled in my jacket pocket for a match. "You're Mister Magic Fingers. I never forget a good massage."

Sylvia wore, as far as I could tell, not a hint of makeup, despite her rough complexion. No lipstick on those pale lips, either. It was like she had given up trying to look glamorous. She inhaled smoke, let it out, careful to blow it away from me.

"I forget," she said. "How do you know the old bat, anyway?"

"Oh, she cooked me dinner. Last fall. I met her walking the dog."

"The dog," Sylvia said, "my God, that woman and her yappy bulldog."

"She's driving you a little crazy, I take it?"

"We've already seen every movie that's out," said Sylvia. "I'm the entertainment committee, see?"

"I thought I'd seen Mother at a party at a lake house, maybe. Recently. So I guess the whole family's back in town."

"Well, her sons don't want her around. Whenever they're up to something sneaky, they send her away, see. Besides, all she does is start arguments."

She picked up the menu. "What's good? The roast beef?"

"Don't each much beef," I said. "Never ordered it here."

"You're not one of those vegetarians, are you?"

"No," I said.

"I never met one of those. I'd be curious. How do you live on string beans?"

She let the menu fall. "I'll have roast beef. Don't they have table service here?"

"She'll come around," I said. "So it's you and Mother?"

"And some people wonder why I drink."

"What can I get you?"

"Whiskey sour."

"How about Mother?"

"She's against drink and for the Bible."

"She used to take the occasional drink."

"Now her stomach's acting up, so she …"

I snapped my fingers for the attention of the lazy bartender.

"… says drink is the Devil's pitchfork."

Mother walked out of the restroom. I stepped up to the bar, ordered Cokes for me and Ma, a whiskey sour for Sylvia, and carried three drinks back to the table.

Ma Barker sat and put one hand to her breast.

"Thank Jesus they have an elevator," she said.

"Is Jesus an elevator boy now?" asked Sylvia.

"My ticker," said Ma, "is functuatin'."

"It's what? You eat too much fried food, dear," said Sylvia.

"You can't get decent corn bread up here," said Ma, reading the menu.

Sylvia took down half her whiskey sour in one gulp.

"My Herman," said Ma. "Herman loved my cornbread."

"Don't start, Mother."

"That's when my heart trouble started. With poor Herman."

"I know, Mother. Let's eat in peace now."

Ma wiped a tear.

"I can't bear to think of that good boy in his grave."

A young waitress pushed through the curtain and into the dining room. She stood hands on hips, as if trying to decide which table to serve, although we were the only diners. Finally she approached us.

"I'll have the chocolate cake," I said.

"Roast beef dinner," said Sylvia, "extra gravy."

"I'm too tore up to eat," said Ma.

"She'll have the fried chicken," said Sylvia.

"But no cornbread," said Ma. "I can't stand northern corn bread. It makes me sick to my innards."

The waitress grimaced and backed away.

"They mistook him for a burglar," said Ma.

"Who for a burglar?" I asked.

Sylvia pursed her lips, subtly shook her head.

"My Herman," said Ma and burst out crying. "The police shot him like a dog in the street."

She picked up her beige napkin and dabbed at her tears.

"He's lost, my boy is lost to me. My Freddy and Doc is all that's left."

"They love you, Mother," said Sylvia and patted Ma's hand.

"Jesus has sent me tests and trials," declared Ma.

"Yes he has, Mother," said Sylvia. "And you have borne up strong beneath them."

Sylvia rolled her eyes at me.

When I finished my desert, I took the elevator up to my room and tipped the raven-haired girl a dollar.

"The blonde eating in the bar," I said, "might care to know my room number."

So I wasn't surprised when two hours later, just as I was drifting off to sleep in the easy chair, a discreet tap came at the door.

I opened it to see Sylvia.

"Thank God," she said. "The monster sleeps. What do you have for booze?"

"I can send down."

She grabbed the phone. "Rye and setups," she ordered. "And quickly, please."

She put the phone down and stood by the writing desk, which was thick with Racing Forms.

"You know what they say," she said. "Horseplayers die broke."

"Everybody dies broke," I said. "It's the nature of death."

"Touché Mister... remind me."

"Powers, Michael Patrick Powers, that's the real name my sainted mother gave me."

"You're fast with the tongue, aren't you Michael Powers?"

And with that she gave me a long wet kiss. She pressed herself against me and then pushed me away.

"I'd been wanting to do that," she said, and then lifted a silver cigarette case from her purse. "I'm naturally impulsive. "Smoke?"

"Pipe," I said.

"Einstein smokes a pipe, I heard."

"I can do a equation," I said. "If it involves six horses and a crooked jockey."

"Then help me figure out how to kill this old woman without her sons finding out."

I laughed.

"Because they're vicious bastards," she said. "Don't cross them, Mick, in fact, you're better off walking a wide circle around them."

"I've met them."

"Then you know." She blew smoke. She walked to the door and opened it a crack.

"Where the hell is the bar boy?"

She closed the door.

"They don't want Ma around, you know why? Because she constantly fights with the gang's girlfriends. She's obsessed. Her sons should put no other female before her. Imagine that, the vain old bat. She finds fault with all the girls. She snipes, she picks, she criticizes. She carries tales from one to the other and gets the girls fighting among themselves. So I, me, I'm her jailer."

"How did you draw the lucky assignment?"

"My husband," she said, and drew her finger across her throat, "dead."

"Oh," I said, "sorry."

"I'm unattached, see? A spare tire on the gangsters' limousine."

A tap came to the door. The raven-haired elevator girl rolled in a steel cart, draped with linens, and topped with glasses, a pint of rye, water in a pitcher, a bottle of Altwasser ginger ale, and a silvery pitcher of ice.

"Put it on the room tab," I said, and handed her a quarter.

Sylvia mixed the drinks. I said: "Light for me," and she said, "to hell with that."

We clinked glasses. We drank. She sat in the easy chair and I lay back in the recliner.

"I'm getting out of this life," said Sylvia. "I've never seen anything like it. These boys don't give a damn for the human soul. My husband, he was one of them back in Tulsa. Well, he wasn't really my right-married husband if you want the truth, but then, see, one of their jobs went wrong and bang-bang, they left poor Earl lying in the dirt. And oh they were all best friends, see, blood oaths and all that. But the Barker gang left him for dead and in fact he did die. And oh now they tell me, Sylvia come up north, we've got something for you, we'll make it up to you, you deserve Earl's share. So I take the train all the way up here and what do I get? Earl's share? Hell no. A baby sitting job."

She drank deep.

I lit her cigarette.

"They're users," she said. "They use, they discard. I'm not Mother Barker's first babysitter, nor will I be the last. These are the little geniuses Ma Barker raised, always using and taking. She'll cry and cry about Herman, but she don't mention the other one, spending life in prison for murder."

She rattled her ice cubes.

"Okay, I'm bitter," she said. "But I'm getting out before they ruin me entirely."

"I know the feeling," I said.

"Do you?"

A smile crept to the edges of her lips.

"So you're an understanding soul," she said.

I shrugged. "Maybe once in a while I figure something out."

"Do you use and discard, Michael? Are you going to use and discard me?"

I sipped my drink.

"I'll bet you will," she said. "You're a man aren't you?"

Her eyes went to the wall.

"Mother and I got the bigger room. No Murphy bed," she said. "Twins, thank god, I could not stand to sleep in the same bed as that woman."

She fixed me with a sleepy look.

"You know what's better than whiskey?" she said. "A back rub."

I grabbed the handle of the Murphy bed, and pulled it down.

"Ah," she said and unbuttoned her blouse. "Sleep, Mother Barker, sleep deep, sleep forever for all I care."

She removed her bra to reveal generous sagging breasts, and then turned away and flopped face down on the bed.

I kneeled over her and began to knead the knots in her shoulders.

She sighed. "You know you missed your calling," she said.

"I hear that a lot," I said.

CHAPTER FIFTEEN

I awoke to a light tapping on the door. Sylvia had turned into a cold, empty spot beside me in the rumpled bed. I slipped into a bathrobe and opened the door to see the elevator girl. She handed me a sealed envelope.

"Oh," I said, and found a quarter to tip her.

The note was hand lettered: *Meet at the Eagle Park Now.*

I shed my fluffy Commodore robe and dressed in a fresh-pressed dark blue suit and yellow tie. I calmed myself with thoughts that Swede Fanlund couldn't have made bail, and that the Eagle Park was a public place.

Without benefit of breakfast or coffee I strode two blocks to the cliff overlooking downtown. Atop that cliff was a small, grassy triangle park, lined with benches. In the middle stood a pedestal topped by a gigantic bronze eagle upon its nest. It its talons the eagle clutched a writhing snake, which it was preparing to drop into the mouth of its squawking young.

A sinister-looking black Plymouth sedan pulled up. Serious Bobby, playing chauffeur, popped out. He held open the back door. That was Big Ryan in the passenger seat. I got in behind him

Big Ryan's greasy hair actually touched the roof fabric of this low-slung car. The interior was all gray. A black shotgun stood, barrel up, clamped to the dashboard. Serious Bobby closed the door on me, lit a cigarette, and walked away toward the eagle.

Big Ryan sat back casual against the car door and adjusted the rearview mirror so he could see me.

"You should be under arrest right now," he said.

"I don't know what you think you've got on me, but it's a bad rap. You're wasting your time."

He gave the slightest shake of his head. "I never waste my time. Let me tell you how your day's going to go."

"Shoot," I said.

"In exactly one hour you will meet a man at the base of that eagle…" he pointed to it. "Right there. Unless you want to serve a long stretch in Stillwater for capital murder, you will help this man in every conceivable way. You will do what he asks without question or hesitation. After a few days he will release you from obligation. Then and only then will I consider your debt to society repaid."

He turned to stare directly at me.

"Questions?"

"Sure," I said. "But I'll keep 'em to myself."

He patted my forearm with his giant paw.

"That's the way," he said. "You *will* be compensated."

He turned, and all I could see was the back of his head.

"Anything else?" I asked.

"Out," he said.

I opened the door. It weighed twice what it should have, and I realized this was one of those new-fangled armored police cruisers. Serious Bobby threw me a veteran's salute as he walked around the long black hood and slithered into the driver's seat. Hands in my pockets, head down, hat low, I walked back to the Commodore.

When I entered the cafe, Ma Barker looked up from a platter of bacon, potatoes and eggs. She was alone. There was no avoiding her hungry gaze.

"Mother," I said, "does anyone call you anything besides mother?"

I sat opposite.

She plopped ketchup on her potatoes.

"Mister Powell," she said, "what are your plans for the day?"

"Oh," I said, "business."

"And what is your business?"

"Insurance," I said.

She leaned forward, speaking in confidence. "Miss Sylvia and I are headed downtown for shopping, and then to a bingo and then to the movies."

She speared potatoes and eggs on her fork and said, "Have you seen the one about the big old ape?"

"I don't keep up with the movies," I said.

She chewed, swallowed and said, "A big old ape takes over New York City, and nobody can stop it."

She had been sloppy with the lipstick, and looked like a daffy lady in an old folks' home.

I said, "I don't need the movies. A big ape has taken over Saint Paul, and nobody can stop it here either."

I signaled the waitress for coffee and a menu.

"I haven't seen Sylvia this morning," I said.

"She won't get out of bed, that one."

"Ah."

"Out all night."

I shrugged.

"It's indecent," she said, a strip of bacon held to her lips. She crunched.

"If I remember, you aren't a married man," she said.

"Divorced," I said.

Ma shook her head. She set knife and fork on her plate and wiped a tear from her eye. "My husband Arthur ran off with a floozy."

"I'm sorry."

"You remember my Arthur?"

"I do."

"Sober, he was such a well-dressed man. But he drank himself into a foolish state near every night."

The approach of the waitress halted that conversation. I ordered scrambled eggs, toast, coffee.

"And then he run off with a floozy. My boys chased him down, but he said he wasn't never coming home, no matter what they done to him. So ... it's hard being an old lady, lonesome like I am."

"You've endured many hardships, Mother Barker," I said.

"Being a mother is destitute on the heart," she said.

At about 10:30, suit coat over my arm, sleeves rolled up to welcome a warm day, I crossed Summit Avenue to the triangle park.

Nobody was at the bronze eagle. I sat on a bench where I could see both the eagle and the view of Saint Paul. The park was populated by idle youth, and we had plenty of those, and by mansion nannies pushing baby carriages well-shielded against the sun. I didn't have my pocket watch, but I felt acutely the passage of time, with a needling anxiety made worse by coffee jitters. I paced along the green-painted iron railing. Across from the park stood the University Club, a stone monument to its wealthy members, and a source of marginal employment to the men and women in white uniforms who occasionally popped out of its back doors.

Finally a light green Chevy coup pulled up to the curb and the driver discreetly tapped the horn. It was a jaunty car, with huge whitewall tires, a rumble seat, spare tire tucked near the door, chrome headlights perched atop the fenders.

I got in and sat beside George.

We shook hands like two businessmen. George wore a green open-neck sport shirt and white linen trousers. His hair was oiled and his face immaculately shaved.

"Big Joe Ryan sends his regards," I said.

"Who? Oh, that one. I detest working with coppers, but

sometimes it's a necessity, and this is one of those times."

He pulled into traffic without looking. A milk truck honked and swerved around us.

"They're so fundamentally dishonest, don't you find?" George said. "The police. The very summit of hypocrisy. Nevertheless!"

He held up one finger.

As we passed the Cathedral, a traffic cop waved us through the intersection. "Society, after all, needs someone to direct traffic. They're all traffic cops one way or the other."

We rolled up Marshall Avenue, the dividing line between black and white Saint Paul.

"Your Negroes are quite orderly," said George. "I commend you for that."

"You commend me?"

"In Chicago, the whites are losing all control."

I said: "What's on today's agenda?"

"Nothing much." He smirked. "Our only role in the unfolding drama will be communication."

"What unfolding drama?" I said.

I bit my lip. No questions.

A stop stanchion rose out of the street and George zoomed past it. He turned down a muddy alley and parked behind a brick apartment building, to which had been clamped rickety wooden stairs. We climbed to the third floor and entered the rear apartment.

It was clean, painted white, and spare. On the kitchen table sat a gleaming chrome toaster and a dull gray Corona portable typewriter.

"You're a high school graduate, I understand," George said.

I nodded.

"Have you used a typewriter before?"

I said, "It was a long time ago, but I took shorthand and typing in high school. Catholic school, you know. Those of us who weren't bound for college were trained to be clerks."

"Very good," said George. "Hang up your coat and let's commence the communications, shall we?"

I slipped my jacket into the hall closet.

"Can we open a window?" I asked.

"My asthmatic condition does not permit fresh air," he said, "not at this blooming time of year."

I visited the bathroom and when I came out, George was standing at the kitchen table, taking bites out of a piece of buttered toast.

"So," he said…

He lay the toast down on a coffee cup saucer.

"To the typewriter if you will. Take this down. Ready? Here we go: You must realize by now that your boyfriend is out of circulation."

I pulled back a kitchen chair and began typing.

"… that your boyfriend?"

"Indeed," said George. "That your boyfriend is out of circulation. No, back up. You must realize that this is not a joke as you had thought, and your boyfriend is out of circulation…"

I typed.

"It is imperative that you quickly gather $100,000 in 5s, 10s and 20s, pack said amount into a suitcase, and await further instructions."

He reached into his shirt pocket for a pack of Camels, withdrew a cigarette, and held it before his lips, as if he had come to a pause in thought.

"Let me see," George said, and ripped the paper out of the typewriter. "Excellent," he said. "All good writing is second draft, but you have the requisite clerical skills."

He lit the Camel, left the room and returned in a moment with a letter-size sheet of fine bond paper.

"Roll that in," he said.

It was a blank sheet, except at the bottom, where the name *William Hamm Jr.* was signed in blurry ink. As George paced and smoked, I re-typed the message in the blank space above Hamm's signature. When I finished, he stood over my shoulder reading and said:

"You misspelled imperative," he said. "See? It's R-A-T."

I typed x to blot out the word, rolled the platen, typed the correct spelling above.

"One more paragraph, if you will," George said. *"If you go to the police, we will get you and Hamm too."*

I typed that.

George folded the note carefully into a beige envelope.

"Now we wait," he said. He smashed a burning cigarette into a cereal bowl. Its ashes hissed in milk.

Without explanation, he creased the envelope, stuffed it into his trouser pocket, breezed out the kitchen door and clambered down the wooden steps. The shades were drawn so I couldn't see, but only heard, George start that Chevy coup in the parking lot. He drove off.

I wandered through the hallway and into the parlor. On a table meant to hold a telephone lay three books: two on landscape gardening and one by H.G. Wells entitled *The Shape of Things to Come*. I didn't know many people who read books, and among them, George was the only one to buy them in expensive hardcover.

I poked into the bedroom to see a bed made up neat and tight, with red satin cover. That well-made bed convinced me that George was a veteran, as he claimed. No man got through Basic Training without learning how to make a proper bed. A straw suitcase stood underneath two windows, shade drawn on both of them. In the closet were two suit-jackets and two shotguns, one double-barrel full length, one single-barrel and sawed off.

Whatever else he was, George was a good housekeeper. I

wandered into the kitchen and made myself toast with butter and jam, accompanied by a glass of milk. He had nothing else to dine on, except for cereal. I opened a fresh pack of Camels and smoked one, harsh on the throat. I pulled one of the shades aside and peered out at an empty, dusty alley. I tried to make sense of things.

Jack Peifer had joined three Chicago criminals to the Barker-Karpis gang, and now it seemed his purpose was to kidnap brewer William Hamm. The police, or at least Big Ryan, were in on it. So was Serious Bobby, who had scammed up an executive position at the Hamm Brewery. Serious Bobby was, among other things, bag man for County Prosecutor Irish Kinkead, and for every crooked badge in town.

My role was obviously typist and errand boy. But if the Barker-Karpis gang was now in the snatch racket, why did they need George? And Dad? And where was George's tubercular friend Monty?

I finished my meal and walked into the parlor. I turned on the radio. Cab Calloway was in town, and WCCO was playing his swinging bop music. KSTP was broadcasting farm prices. If William Hamm was in the hands of kidnappers, nobody out there knew.

In maybe fifteen minutes, I heard George's Chevy pull into the lot, and his footsteps running up the stairs.

"All right, Powers," he said, out of breath and flush in the face. "The trap is set. We await the rat."

He handed me the envelope that contained the ransom note. It was wrinkled and sweaty now, and on the front, in pencil, was scrawled an address.

CHAPTER SIXTEEN

My assignment was to get the ransom note to the Summit Avenue address scrawled on the envelope. I left George's with the note in my pocket and walked over to Selby to catch the streetcar. I rode it around the Downtown Loop, in the company of sweating shoppers, antsy children, and rumpled office clerks. I alighted at the Lowry Hotel. I walked a block to Herman's Haberdashery and bought a straw hat. I wanted to be remembered, if for anything, this straw hat. Back at the Lowry, that hat tilted over my face, I entered the back seat of a Yellow Cab.

I handed the envelope over the seat.

"How much to deliver that?" I asked.

The cabbie shrugged. He was a rough-looking mug of about 50 with a big, misshapen nose.

"A buck," he said.

I gave him two dollars, got out of the cab, and walked toward the river. Glancing around to assure there were no witnesses, I crushed that hat underfoot, kicked it down a sewer drain, and ducked into the alley behind Downtown Dutch's Paradise Pawn.

My second assignment was to report to an address near Macalester College, so I waited for the St. Clair streetcar and rode it lurching and sputtering to the big intersection at Snelling. One block past a gaggle of drug stores, grocers and dry cleaners, and just behind the college's football field, I found a big sturdy house at 204 Vernon Street.

Two boys on the street, both with leather gloves, were playing baseball catch under elm trees. They hailed me.

"Are you another new neighbor?" one kid asked.

I just waved friendly and mounted the stairs. I rang the bell and the shade lifted away from the door glass. The door opened and there stood Dad in underwear, clutching a bottle of beer.

He let me in. The house was hot and dark, a big Westinghouse fan blowing from one corner.

"George sent me," I said.

Dad took a swig from his beer.

"The message has been delivered," I said.

"Have a beer," he said.

"Gout," I said.

"Have one anyway."

From a galvanized ice bucket set on the dining room table, he fetched me a bottle of Hamm's.

I said: "George wants to know if you need any more from him."

"Powers, right?" he said.

"Yes."

"You don't know my name, do you?"

"Nope."

"Good." He swilled beer. He backed off to sit at the bench of a gleaming black Steinway grand piano. The piano was spread with a shawl, atop which stood three family pictures, people I didn't recognize.

"George can wipe his ass with that college degree," said Dad.

He sat, gray head down, leaning elbows into his thighs. He wore blue-and-yellow striped boxer shorts and had sweated nasty into a sleeveless white t-shirt.

"I can't wait to get out of here," he said. "Trapped."

"Well," I said.

"How do you figure in?"

"How do I what?"

"They keep cutting guys in, there's less to split, see? Do the arithmetic. Simple long division."

He took a tin ashtray off the piano, set it on the bench beside him and said, "First this guy, then that guy. And the women! Gee-ziz kee-riste. They don't know how to do anything but gossip and drink."

He hit a few keys, a clanging dissonant chord, while reaching for his pack of Chesterfield's.

"What kind of gangster goes around with a drunken golfing slut and his lunatic mother in tow? Recipe for disaster, if you ask me." He lit the cigarette with one quick stroke from a matchbook. "And they hate each other, the Mother and Paula. Hate the very ground the other one stands on."

He blew smoke.

"Thing is," he admitted, "these boys know how to rake in the dough."

He walked off to get another beer from the bucket, and add his bottle to a small standing army of empties on the lace tablecloth. On the way back to the parlor, he wobbled into the china hutch and bounced off, casting it an angry look, as if it had stepped into his path.

I said, "I'm a Saint Paul guy. I know my way around, I guess. That's why they picked me."

He sputtered tobacco and laughed.

"That ain't why they picked you."

I shrugged.

"Favor to Jack," he said, and blew smoke. "Whole thing's a favor to Jack."

He tapped ashes, missed the ashtray, hit the bench. His eyes, pale blue and fishy, were rheumy with drink.

"Doc is the one to watch out for," he said. "Oh brother, let me tell you. Stay clear of that one. Fred's greedy but Doc's just plain mean. Fred will kill you for a purpose, at least. Doc will shoot you for the pleasure of watching you die."

He nodded, affirming his judgment. He closed his eyes against the assault of his own cigarette smoke.

Outside, the faint ring of a bicycle bell sounded.

Dad squashed his cigarette.

"Here's the little drunk now," he said.

Out the half-shaded windows I saw two cyclists walking their bikes up the driveway. The steel gate to the backyard opened, and in went Paula, and Jack's woman Violet. She wore pedal-pusher pants with one vertical stripe down the leg, and a sweatshirt with arms hacked off. Paula wore white trousers and a sweaty pink blouse. Her hair was bobbed short and Violet's was cut even shorter, almost a boy's cut.

Dad had his finger to his lips, stood beside me at the dining room window.

"I wasn't telling you anything just now," he said.

The women walked through the back door into the kitchen, Paula first.

"Ah," she said when she saw me.

Violet looked away, as if she didn't want to see me here.

Paula opened the ice box and removed a crystal pitcher of lemonade, lemon slices floating on top. She set that at the kitchen table and Violet poured two glasses full. Paula fetched a flask of gin from the pantry and added a slug, but only to her drink.

"So," Paula said to me, "I keep seeing you around. Violet, do you know this character?"

"Slightly," said Violet, drinking from a frosty glass.

"He's a friend of Sam's," Violet said.

"Oh, a friend of Japanese Sam?."

"Horse racing," said Violet, and shook her head as if she pitied me.

"So," said Paula. She raised her glass to me. "You know the man's vices, you know the man. Now I've got you figured out

Mister..."

"Powers."

"Right. I knew I'd seen you around. Horse player. Okay."

She was a tiny woman, but with a beautiful figure, very attractive except for that smashed-in nose. Had some gangster flattened her face with a baseball bat? That's what it looked like. She poured me a glass of lemonade, gin flask poised over it. I shook my head.

"Another teetotaler," she sneered. She called into the parlor: "Fitz! Did you know this man is a teetotaler?"

Dad-Fitz limped in to the kitchen on a bad knee, bottle of Hamm's in one hand, unlit cigarette in the other. "Did I what?"

"He's a gambler," Paula said, "doesn't drink."

Fitz shrugged.

"I don't know," said Paula, and drank. "I can't place you. I've seen you somewhere, Mister Powers. Do you golf?"

"Yes," I said.

"Oh let's play," she said. "We need a fourth. You, me, Violet and..."

"George plays," I said.

Paula's lips curled. Violet laughed.

"George? George lectures," she said. "He tells the women how to play and then drives his own ball out of bounds. And cheats. Especially on putting, doesn't he cheat, Violet?"

Violet only smiled.

"The old foot wedge," said Paula, and kicked sideways, her feet shod in white sneakers with no laces.

"And don't even mention Monty," Paula said. "He's a pro, did you know that? A teaching pro. I've seen him drive par fours right up to the green. I'm not going to play with a smug bastard like that."

"Maybe we can interest Sam," I said. "He plays."

Violet wrinkled her nose, her head shaking in a no thank you.

"We'll find a fourth," I said. "I haven't played all year."

"Are you any good?" asked Paula. She finished her lemonade. "Six handicap," she said, pointing to her chest.

"From the women's tee," said Fitz.

"Shut up you old goat," Paula said. "You haven't played in years."

"I've got to get going," said Violet. "Nice to see you again, Mick. Fitz. Paula."

And with that she backed out the door.

"Well," said Paula, and watched Violet ride down the driveway. "The beauty queen. She's awfully regal, isn't she Charles?"

She turned to look at Dad-Fitz.

"Isn't she? Are you so dumbfounded by her beauty that you can't speak?"

Charles-Fitz-Dad waved Paula off, swigged beer, limped into the living room and sank into an easy chair. Paula shrugged. "I guess I'll have to drink alone, unless I can seduce Mister Powers. Will you violate your high code of ethics, Mister Powers, and have a spiked lemonade with me?"

"Sure," I said.

She stood on her tiptoes and kissed my cheek.

"You're too easy," she said.

"So they tell me."

"That's what they said about me, too, in Galveston, but they were wrong. Yes, I said Galveston. Have you been to that exotic island, Mister Powers?"

She mixed me a drink.

I said I was a stranger to Texas entirely.

"Well don't go in July, or you'll be sorry," she said, and handed me the frosty drink.

"Born and raised?" I asked.

"Oh God no. Please. I detest that town, absolutely. I ran boot. Yes, me, a tiny slip of a girl, and not quite twenty years old and I ran boot until they chased me out of town."

She smiled at some memory. "They couldn't take the competition. No girls allowed."

She held up her glass and we toasted.

"To Prohibition," she said, "it was fun while it lasted."

CHAPTER SEVENTEEN

I'm not necessarily against taking a rich guy's money, but that night at the Commodore, I couldn't sleep, or even stay in bed. The last Barker-Karpis venture I knew about was a bank robbery, and it had resulted in three men dead. Kidnapping was bad enough, but I worried that these gangsters would never release William Hamm alive. After all, he would be the best witness against them, and the Barkers had no qualms about silencing a witness. Even more worrying was the addition of Doc to the gang. I believed what Charles-Fitz-Dad had said about Doc. I had seen the emptiness of Doc's eyes, and was spooked by his soul-less gaze.

It was already warm at 6 in the morning when I knocked on Janie's door on the pretense of visiting my dogs. Snowflake and Hula Girl seemed stunned to see me, as if they had already adjusted to Janie, a new and better master. The dogs kept bumping into each other in their confusion. Any prospect Janie had of hiding her condition was gone. She was seven or more months in, and not gigantic, but unmistakably pregnant. She wore white painters trousers and a maroon t-shirt, and looked like she planned to spend all day at home.

"Major Hoople hasn't called you?"

"About what?"

"I figured he'd want all hands on deck. Even part time women reporters."

"Why?"

"The Hamm kidnapping."

"The what?" She turned to stare at me. "What did you say?"

"Little Billy Hamm's been kidnapped," I said.

"Since when, Powers? Come on."

"Mid-day yesterday. I guess the cops are doing a splendid job of keeping it out of the news."

Her mouth stayed open in big O for a long moment.

"You're not kidding."

"He is gone."

"Holy mackerel."

"Do you want the story?"

"What do you mean?"

"Do you want the story because I can roast it for you like a Thanksgiving turkey."

She grabbed a kitchen chair and sat, as if suddenly her legs felt shaky.

"Kidnapped? Really?" she said. "Nobody knows or somebody in the newsroom would have called me. Who took him? Why? Where did they go?"

"I've got two addresses. The Idlewild cabin on White Bear Lake Road where it meets Taylor. And 204 Vernon up by Macalester."

Her hands shook as she opened her purse and searched for pencil and notebook.

"And why are you giving me these addresses?"

If this had been a Harry operation, I'd have done anything to keep Janie out of it. Harry had it in for Janie. But Harry had nothing to do with this snatch. And he might not be displeased to see the Hamm kidnapping busted, and his rival Jack Peifer on trial.

"Feed those addresses to Goggles Thornton. Let him take it from there."

"The story of the decade and I'm to give it to Goggles?"

"Look, Janie, you can make a lot of money off this, but later, selling it to the detective mags."

"Why don't you tell the police what you know?"

"Because they're in on it."

She cocked her head at me.

"Come on, Powers." She slapped the notebook on the table. "You must be insane. Maybe Sigmund Freud can help you, but I can't."

"The police are in on the snatch. Take it from me."

"That's impossible. How could you possibly know?"

"That's the one question you can't ask me. But I know. Believe me, I know. Look, Janie, I'll feed you what I know, but on one condition. Let Goggles do the work up front. You work behind the scenes with the G-men. Yes. The Justice boys, in particular agent Roland Heater. You're not a detective. I feed you, you feed Goggles and the Feds. When it's all wrapped up and the bad guys are in prison, you can safely write the story for the national mags. "

She bulled past me and turned on the radio. I played with Snowflake's ears, which made Hula Girl nose in, jealous.

Both radio channels crackled with big band music. She turned it off, stood in the parlor doorway, spread her hands: "Nothing on the radio."

"There will be. Maybe, maybe the Daily News can pressure the cops to make an arrest. The gangsters are at one of those two addresses. At least they were yesterday."

"How could you…" she waved… "oh, never mind, I can't ask you."

"Hundred thousand ransom. Remember, let Goggles take the glory for now. You work quietly with the feds. That's the only safe way. Now get going. I'd poke my head into the newsroom if I were you. They're going to get a shock sooner or later."

I went to the city view windows of what used to be my apartment, and stood stroking my dogs, watching Janie hustle across the parking lot and disappear behind the streetcar tunnel. I felt some kind of tension leave my body, I could almost exhale it. I had put something dangerous in motion and yet, it soothed me. I felt that for the first time in years, I had done the right thing. If Janie was smart and careful, the Barker-Karpis gang would be put out of business soon. When they were safely in prison, and her baby was born, she could write an insider's account and be the hit of the detective magazines. She and her baby could live a couple of years on the magazines' dime. She'd need the dough, since an unwed mother wouldn't be exactly welcomed in the newsroom.

Maybe an investigation would lead back to me, but even if it did, I would trade what I knew for a soft sentence or maybe a disappearing act.

I reclaimed my couch, and while my dogs slept at the foot of it, fell into a delicious nap. I dreamed Janie had been crowned Queen of England and was visiting my beach hut in Havana.

I was to check in with George at noon, at our meeting place at the eagle. The first edition of the Daily News was to hit the newsstands at 1 p.m. I anticipated the biggest headlines I had ever seen. I tried to imagine George's reaction.

If I avoided that White Bear Lake cabin and the house at 204 Vernon, I might never be found out, even if others in the gang were arrested. The Barker-Karpis gang had many flaws, but one strong ethic: they never talked under interrogation. One of them, Larry DuVol, had taken a life sentence for the Third Northwestern cop killing, and except for one drunken slip-up, never uttered a peep. They were bad people, the Barker-Karpis gang, but very good gangsters.

George was waiting in his green coupe, idling beside the bronze eagle. I got in and found him eating a cheese sandwich on white bread. Between us on the seat was a brown paper bag.

"How," asked George, "are your driving skills?"

"Pretty good," I said.

"Let us commence, then," he said.

He lay the sandwich on its wax paper bag, dusted off his hands, and drove the car a couple of blocks, pulling over next to the Hill Mansion. This gigantic red-stone monstrosity, across from the Cathedral, had been built by a railroad robber baron, and was surrounded by hedges. George pulled the emergency brake, said, "You'll be driving," and stepped out for a stretch.

I took over behind the wheel, and when George plopped into the passenger seat he said, "You do know the way to Chicago?"

"Vaguely," I said.

"Follow my instructions, then. Wake me if you have to. You see, old man — get going will you? — you see something rather odd happened to me in the Army, and cut short my career as a pilot. It turns out I have a peculiar condition. The doctors are quite baffled. I fall asleep at odd times, for no known reason. This is particularly true at night, so… I take it your vision is acute, since you don't wear eyeglasses."

"Federal twelve?"

"All roads lead to Chicago," said George.

It was another blazing hot day, and we drove with the windows open and the wing-windows slanted to divert the slip stream. The asthma George claimed to suffer from did not seem to bother him now.

He turned on the radio. Jimmy Durante was singing, if that's what you call it, the song "Ink A Dink a Doo" on WCCO. On KSTP, some crooner, to the accompaniment of steel guitars, sang about his grass shack in Hawaii. This put me in mind of Peggy, too painful to contemplate, her life with a Navy officer, out in the middle of the Pacific. Did they have children now? That's all Peggy really wanted, not the Navy life, but children.

"No news," George complained, and snapped off the radio.

As we reached the outskirts of town we passed the massive brick fortress that produced Hamm's beer.

"It's a damn shame we won't get to the World's Fair on this

trip," George said. "I don't imagine you've been. It's a quite a wonder. But our venture today will be strictly business, in and out, highly efficient communication."

He reached behind the seat, came out with a bottle of warm Nehi orange soda, flipped the cap off with a steel bottle opener, and drank. He was already sweating into his high-collared white shirt.

"I'd offer you one," he said, "but two hands on the wheel at all times, that is my driving philosophy. Did you know that driving an automobile is the most dangerous thing we Americans do? It's as dangerous as flying. I don't suppose you've done any air travel."

I shook my head.

"Don't," he said. "Unless you have a very strong stomach."

He sipped from the soda bottle.

"Will King Hamm ever be restored to his castle? Right now, the outcome of our venture is in serious doubt. The police, you see, have tried to play an abominable trick on us. Their scheme was to hide a filthy policeman in the truck, and ambush us with a tommygun."

"What truck?"

"Why the Hamms beer truck in which the ransom was to be delivered. Apparently they have a policeman of rather diminutive stature, and they planned to conceal him beneath a tarpaulin."

"So they set a trap."

"It was doomed to fail. We have a copper on the inside, an informer, you see. High up on the police force. Didn't I tell you we were living in the age of communication?"

He drank soda. He sat back in silence. In a half hour, we reached the toll bridge that crossed the Saint Croix River into Wisconsin. As I slowed to pay the dime, George turned his head and stared out the passenger window, as if afraid to show the toll-taker his face.

We drove on. George was mostly silent, but sometimes

launched one-sided discussions of literature, opera or golf, exposing my shallow knowledge in all those subjects. Sometime around three we pulled into the blessed shade of a rest area near Black River Falls. There, at a picnic bench, George and I lunched on rubbery cheese sandwiches and warm orange soda. We had passed a dozen overheated cars on the highway, and two more were parked here, hood flaps raised, distressed families milling about.

George wore a gold watch, diamond ring, and that sweaty white linen shirt. He had long since removed shoes and socks. After lunch he went off to the outhouse, and returned with a lit Camel in his lips.

"Six or seven hours," he said, glancing at his watch. "Make that seven since we'll stay well under the speed limit. You'll be driving nearly the entire distance. You won't want me behind the wheel, unless you want to chance us rolling over into a ditch. I hadn't thought to ask, but you're not carrying a firearm are you?"

I shook my head.

"Good," he said, "because if you were, I'd have to request that you discard it." We got back into the car and drove.

By six o'clock we passed Wisconsin Dells, and George was asleep. At 7:30, when we reached Madison, the sun was behind us and the air finally began to cool. I pulled over at a rest stop near Beloit to use the outhouse, and George slept right through. He woke up, as if by magic, as soon as we crossed the Illinois line.

"When we reach this next big town," he said, "pull over." That was all he said, and made himself a wake-up meal of cheese sandwich and soda.

I pulled into a rest area just as the sun was going down. George asked me to step out of the car and turn around. He wrapped a black silk blindfold around my eyes, and guided me into the passenger seat.

"Just a precaution," he said, and for a few minutes he drove along a smooth highway and I, blindfolded, simply listened to the wind and the road noises. George turned on the radio, scanned the Chicago stations for news, and then snapped it off.

We entered some sort of town, to judge by the rougher roads and slower speed. We rattled across railroad tracks. Finally we parked. George set the brake, and led me, a tight grip on my forearm, stumbling along a concrete path. There I heard a man coughing, and a voice I knew to be Monty's said:

"Bad news, I take it."

"Nothing we cannot surmount," George said, and led me into a house. When George removed the blindfold I was in a cramped, smoky, chaotic kitchen, lit from a ceiling lamp above. At the table sat three men playing poker: Doc, Fred, Karpis. The table was crowded with empty beer bottles, playing cards, coins, bills and two revolvers, one black and another blue. On the sink drain-board lay mounds of dirty dishes, along with an open violin case that held a tommygun. Tall, gaunt Monty stood off to one side, red bandana to his face, coughing discreetly into it.

Doc was dressed in hunting trousers and a sleeveless t-shirt. Karpis wore a Hawaiian shirt. Fred wore no shirt at all.

"Shouldn't you be upstairs?" Karpis barked at Monty.

"He's asleep," countered Monty.

Karpis glared.

Monty, waving clouds of cigarette smoke away, turned and coughed his way out of the room.

We were in a house that belonged to some meekly employed individual. Much of the kitchen was occupied by an ancient iron woodstove. Cardboard containers that once held barbecued meats were strewn around the room. The furniture was bargain store cheap, the walls grungy. Resting in one corner was a beat-up rifle with a wooden stock. Though it was above 80 degrees outside, the windows were all shut, and the house stank of male sweat, cigarette smoke, and stale beer.

Karpis stood and stretched. From the top pocket of his Hawaiian shirt he drew a Chesterfield, but instead of lighting it, rolled it in his fingers.

"You've heard from our man?" Karpis asked.

"Oh, indeed," George said.

I, feeling sticky, washed face and hands in a dirty kitchen sink. George, Karpis and Fred stepped out the kitchen door and talked in a car parked in the alley. There, I presumed, George explained to them that the Saint Paul Police had tried to set a trap for them.

Doc fixed me with a glare.

"You don't look like no right guy to me."

I said: "What?"

He swallowed beer, slammed the bottle on the table so hard the coins jumped.

"You heard me," he said.

I said, "Yeah, I heard you but I'm not sure what you're talking about."

Doc laughed. Then he spit on the floor.

"How do I know you're not a double-crossing rat bastard?"

I said: "I've been in this racket since 1922."

"What racket?"

"The racket racket."

"Maybe you think you're a funny man but there's no jokers in this here deck. I don't like you. I don't like you around. I don't know why the college man brought you down here."

"Because," I said in a half-whisper, "he can't drive at night."

"Hell's bells, I've seen him drive at night."

"Not for any distance. He nods off."

"Well is that so?"

"It is so."

Doc twirled that blue revolver so it pointed at me. He didn't pick it up, just turned it, then squinted at me.

"Ain't you hot shit," he said.

"Okay."

"I live by the code," said Doc. "I don't take shit from man, woman or dog."

"You've been in some tough places, I understand."

"All men are created equal, except in this here gang," said Doc.

"Well, I'm leaving town when this is over, so you don't have to worry about me."

"Hell," Doc spat, "I ain't worried about you. Just don't think you're somebody, is all. Because you ain't somebody. It's me and my two brothers here, and we're tighter than three pups on one-titted bitch."

I was trapped with this lunatic. I couldn't walk out, because I was not supposed to see the hideout's exterior, or the town around it. I realized I had the blindfold in my hand and stuck it into my trouser pockets.

Doc sat back and asked: "If you was to pick a place to lam, where would it be?"

I said, "Cuba."

He nodded, as if I had said something wise. "I hear that's a hell of a town."

Some scraping noise came from the bedroom and Doc flinched, looked up at the ceiling. His finger went to his lips.

"He is scared like a rabbit," Doc said. "President Billy Hamm. We snatched us a soft one."

The kitchen door rattled and George, Karpis and Fred entered. George mounted the stairs that led to the bedroom. Karpis fetched a glass of milk from the icebox. Fred gnawed at a hog rib that had been stripped of most of its meat. Doc licked the end of a home-rolled cigarette and lit it in his lips.

George and Monty held a whispered conference at the top of the stairs and then George descended. He patted me on the shoulder like I was a favorite nephew and said:

"Splendid. I couldn't have chosen a better driver."

CHAPTER EIGHTEEN

George dozed while I drove back through the night to Saint Paul, arriving around 8 a.m. What was the exact purpose of his trip to the Illinois hideout? What did George accomplish huddling with Fred, Karpis and Doc? I only knew for sure that they feared federal wiretaps, and had made a pact never to speak on the telephone. My theory was that George, having learned of that police trap, was working out a new strategy with Karpis.

I drove hungry, stopping only when we were dead out of gas, without benefit of coffee or even water. George wanted to create the fewest potential witnesses. Only when we arrived at his hovel on Marshall Street did George allow me to go to the newsstand. Even then he insisted I use the Negro newsstand over on Rondo Street: Mister James News and Treats. The cops, he said, would never look for witnesses over there.

I saw the headlines from ten feet away.

WORD FROM HAMM KIDNAPPERS AWAITED

VEIL OF SECRECY THROWN
AROUND KIDNAPPING CASE

The Daily News story was written by Kevin Thornton, aka Goggles. It contained nothing but vague police evasions, and pleadings from Hamm's mother. If Janie had fed Goggles any of my info, it wasn't showing up in print.

I assumed Janie had visited the G-men, but whatever they were doing with her tips wasn't showing up either.

A sense of urgency overcame my usual caution, and I decided to claim my Terraplane down at Herb's. It was sitting underneath a tree, sticky with sap, and on the front door was a spatter of blood, Rico's blood, along with a bullet ding. My car had been parked just behind Rico's Studebaker that night at the Plantation.

The sight of that bullet ding filled me with a dizzying nausea, and I grasped the door post with a feeling I was falling over. I rolled down the windows to let all the hot air out, and then I took the car for a wash by Herb's boys. They had seen a few blood-splashed cars in their time, and in consideration of a big tip, could be counted on to shut up.

I drove my now clean shiny Terraplane across the Wabasha bridge and toward the animal stench of the stockyards. The McAmbly home was, like its neighbors, two stories of careless construction and peeling paint. What color paint it was impossible to tell. I mounted the rickety front stairs and rapped on the patchy screen door.

Maureen answered. She was a cute tyke with blond hair cut in a page boy. She wore a flowery sundress that covered all but her Irish-red face and bare feet. Her most recent birthday had been her 9th, and might have been her last, were it not for doctors at the Mayo Clinic.

"Little Mo," roared Billy from somewhere inside the house. "Who is that? What's he selling? Tell him to go away."

She turned to answer him: "It's Uncle Mick."

"So it is," roared Billy, drunk and stumbling onto the front porch. "Let that bastard in."

Maureen stepped aside and I greeted Billy, his breath beery from a handshake distance away. I followed him into a living room that was flanked with two built-in bookcases, one filled with the

Encyclopedia Americana and the other chock-a-block with Readers' Digest Great Books. On the wall above a beat-up Philco radio, a depiction of Young Jesus was nailed to the wall. Jesus was maybe 14, a profile in sepia, but for a golden halo. Behind that picture frame was a dried-out palm frond from some distant Palm Sunday.

Billy belched.

"Kind of early," I said.

"Don't bust my chops Mick, I just got off."

He led me into the kitchen where three Hamm bottles stood tall among the mess of breakfast dishes.

"Maureen," he yelled, and to me he said, "she's not supposed to play in the dirt." Then he lowered his voice: "On the porch, sweetheart."

He sat and put his head in his hands.

I said: "What's going on?"

"What's going on, are you nuts? The whole friggin place just exploded."

"Who's who?" I said.

"I'm home on a four-hour sleep break, that ought to tell you something. If these kids had a mother I wouldn't be home at all. They've got cots set up on the third floor. Nobody's going home until Hamm ..." he looked at me, suddenly suspicious. "What have you been up to? You look like shit."

He examined an inch of beer in the bottom of a bottle, drank it off.

"You're back on the sauce," he pronounced.

I said, "I've got news for you."

"Shoot."

I looked around to ensure no little ears were listening.

"I can hand them to you on a silver platter."

"Hand who?"

"The Hamm crew."

"Jesus Christ!" he exploded. He covered his ears with his hands.

He shot up, jarring the table so hard that all three beer bottles fell clattering into the mess of plates. He rushed out through the screen door and into the dusty back yard. I followed him.

There his son Kevin had drawn, in chalk, a strike zone on the neighbor's brick garage. A ripped-to-shreds baseball lay in a glove in the shadows. Billy picked up that glove and ball and said, "It cost a day's pay, and he leaves it out in the yard." He shoved his big hands into the glove and assumed a catcher's squat. He tossed me the gray wounded baseball.

"High and hard, Mick," he said.

I threw him a soft toss.

He stood up and threw the ball back.

"Mick," he said, "you know the story of Tay-dee Hurley, the Irish loafer, don't you?"

"Not really," I said.

"It's a story brought over by the old bastard, me accursed father, himself. Tay-dee Hurley drank, which is no sin in Ireland, but he refused to work, which is the greatest Irish sin of all. And then one day Tay-Dee came home to find his wife and children, put out by the bastard English landlord, and living in a tree."

He rolled the baseball toward the house.

"Living in a tree like monkeys," said Billy. "As a kid I wondered how Mrs. Hurley wedged her stove into that tree."

He wrapped his big ape arm around my shoulders.

"So shut the hell up, Mick. Now and forever. I may be a drunk but I'm all those kids have got. The difference between me and Tay-Dee Hurley is fifty-five bucks twice a month from the Saint Paul Police."

He let go his clasp.

"I can't afford to miss a paycheck. Hell, a hundred thousand, that's hardly a whisker off Billy Hamm's chin."

I drove away feeling foolish. I had thought to offer Billy the chance to be a hero and earn a promotion. I had come away with a lesson in police politics. I drove from the worst neighborhood in Saint Paul to the best, straight up Summit Hill to the Commodore. I asked the desk girl to ring Sylvia, only to find that she and Mother Barker had checked out.

I surprised the breakfast waiter by demanding a shot of whiskey, bolted it down, and took the elevator to my room. I set the alarm for 11:45 and for the next two-hours, entered a sleep that was a jangly as if I'd been holding an electric wire.

At noon I waited at the eagle. And waited. And waited. I retreated to the shadow of a scraggly young tree. That shot of whiskey had left me with a bad taste and a ravenous appetite. Yet I dared not leave, even for coffee a block away at the Commodore.

At somewhere past 1:30, George drove up in his green coupe. I got in and he smelled sickening strong of aftershave. His face looked sunburned, like he had spent the morning tanning in his yard.

"Limber your fingers, Powers. Crack your knuckles, old boy. We are going to write a masterpiece of the genre."

He executed a U-turn and drove back to his shabby apartment. In the kitchen stood that Corona, alongside sheets of paper, three of them signed at the bottom by William Hamm.

"Practice makes perfect," George said.

I sat in a wobbly wooden chair at the typewriter, and rolled in a blank for the draft.

"We are wise," he dictated, "to your filthy little tricks. We hereby demand that all coppers be pulled off. Further, the money must be delivered in a car with the doors and trunk lid removed. You will... no, you *shall* hang a lantern in the trunk so we can verify that no one is hiding inside. Prepare the cash and await further instructions. If there is any more double crossing we will experience the pleasure of hitting you in the head."

As I finished typing he lit a Camel and looked over my shoulder.

"It makes me nervous," I said. "You looking over my shoulder like that."

He walked to the kitchen window, opened it a crack, blew cigarette smoke out it in a lazy stream.

I handed the note across the table and he pitched that cigarette out the window. He studied the note and said, "Take out filthy."

"Okay."

He handed the note back to me.

"It's pejorative, don't you think?"

"Sure," I said, but I wasn't certain what he meant.

"After all," he said, "we're attempting to secure their cooperation."

I typed up the note, wondering what game Serious Bobby was playing. He was Big Ryan's errand boy and a Hamm's consultant, and that was a double-cross in itself. But had he helped police plan their tricky but failed ambush? That would make it a triple-cross at least, and I began to see the logic of Billy McAmbly's choice: Stay on the sidelines and be satisfied with an honest paycheck.

With the ransom note sealed in an envelope marked CONFIDENTIAL, George and I walked up Grand Avenue, which was thick with Saturday shoppers. We stopped at an ice cream parlor, ordered vanilla cones, and ate them at a picnic bench in a shadowy alley.

George wore a white coat, white trousers and panama hat, and he held that dripping cone in a white handkerchief as he licked it. He obsessively checked to see that the envelope was secure in the silken inside pocket of his jacket.

"I'm exiting of this racket," he said. "Toots sweet."

"What?"

"Have you not even a smattering of French? Good God, man, where did you do your service in the War?"

"Fort Dix," I said.

George smirked.

"If you don't like this racket," I ventured, "Why did you get in?"

"The fellows promised me I could be the Minister of Communication," he said. "They needed a certain sophistication. They are, after all, creatures of the backwoods."

George crunched the last of his waffle cone and said: "You see, they put my king in prison. The kingdom of Chicago is going to pieces. Wars of succession and all that. All the Italian princes want to be king. Think of me as a knight, offering his services to another principality, while things in his homeland settle down."

"I see," I said. The summer heat was melting the ice cream all over my fingers.

"A gentleman is not a gentleman," George said, looking with disgust at me, "unless he has a handkerchief."

I licked my fingers.

"You see, Powers, this is easy money. It's like making a small fortune while on vacation. And in our business, the communications business, there is almost no risk of injury. Non-violent, and entirely civilized. You see?"

So, he was claiming to be one of Capone's boys, I thought, as I followed him out of the alley. I didn't know whether to believe him. We circled around quiet residential blocks to where his Chevy coupe was parked, drove along Grand, pulled over on a leafy side street. At the end of the street was Rosedale Drugs.

George handed me the envelope folded in half.

"Go have yourself a soda in a booth. Leave this envelope in the booth."

"Leave the ransom note in a booth?"

"Right away," he said.

"I can't," I said. "They know me. The kid in there knows me. I robbed the joint once."

George glared at me, angry, skeptical, frustrated. He snatched the envelope and, a vision in gentleman's whites, sauntered across the shaded street. In ten minutes he crossed again, dodging a streetcar this time, and arrived sweating at the coupe.

"Find a public phone," he commanded.

I drove the alley and parked behind a dark tavern. He indicated I should follow him inside. In the dark interior near the men's room were two public phones. He dropped a nickel into one of them and barked, "Stand between me and the door."

I stood so that no one in the bar could have seen him from their stools. I picked up the phone speaker just to look right. George behind me said, "This is Mr. Robert Pearson. I was just in your store and I'm afraid I left a letter. Would you please see if you can find it in the rear-most booth."

After a long pause, in which he kicked the wall softly, he dropped another nickel and finally said into the phone: "No, I did not say lighter. I said letter. Look again, my good fellow."

In another minute he said, "Deliver that letter to me, Mr. Robert Pearson, at the address written on the envelope, and I will have a good tip for you. As soon as humanly possible, please."

And then he hung up.

And then he sighed.

"Communications," he muttered.

CHAPTER NINETEEN

When I next called for Janie, I had the .45 in the glove box, but it wouldn't do much in combat with the Barker Gang's machine guns. So when I drove her to White Bear Lake, we zoomed past the Idlewild cottage at highway speeds.

But the cottage was shut down.

It was just sundown of a very warm day. We parked in town and waited twenty minutes. We engaged in kidnap speculation, but I was only half paying attention to the conversation. This snooping was dangerous, but Janie was determined, and she had to make a living somehow. If I could persuade her to have patience and let the G-men do the heavy work, she'd be okay.

Or so I told myself.

We drove past the cottage again, slowly this time. There were no cars parked there, the windows shut tight even after a brutally hot day. The kidnap gang was gone.

"Of course they're not there, they're out kidnapping people," Janie said. "Do you know who the landlord is? I'm going to have Goggles call him right now."

"I do know who the landlord is, but if Goggles calls he'll tip off the gang."

"How do you know who the landlord is unless you have something to do with this?"

"Let's just get out of here," I said.

We drove in silence, Janie pouting. When I'd had enough of that

I said: "I know somebody who arranged for the summer rental, okay? What else do you want from me?"

"Names. I need something specific, that's what the federal men want."

"It's Fred Barker, Doc Barker, Alvin Karpis and three guys from Chicago."

"Six men in all."

"Plus Serious Bobby Pearson and Big Joe Ryan."

"How about President Roosevelt? Is he in on it too?"

"I don't send you down dark alleys, Janie."

She cranked the window and warm evening air blew her hair back.

"Let's say you're right, what's in it for you, Powers? If you're implicated in this thing…"

"A guy doesn't like to be used," I said. I kept to myself that I planned to turn stool pigeon on the whole rotten gang.

When we got to Saint Paul I took a hard left on Snelling. The shops on the avenue were closing, the taverns coming to life for a long twi-lit Saturday night.

I hit the accelerator and sped until we reached Macalester College, turned at the football field and cut the engine. I drifted around the corner and parked on a leafy, darkening street. We sat while the overheated engine ticked and clucked.

"This is as close as we dare," I said. "Four houses in. If you want to walk past and check it out go ahead. I don't think they'll be suspicious if a pregnant woman walks by. But I can't be seen. Don't ask why, I just can't."

"What am I looking for?"

"There's a guy in there, maybe 60, tall, beer belly, gray hair, mustache, limps a little. I don't understand what role he plays. But they left him behind. Maybe he's the babysitter for the girl. She's Fred's girl Paula, sporty dresser, can't miss her, a tiny woman, reddish blond hair cut in a page boy, smashed in nose. There may be more, but those two for sure are waiting it out right here."

Janie grasped the door handle.

"I'm going for a walk."

"Be quick, be subtle," I said.

She closed the door without even a click.

I watched her walk, lime green purse slung over her shoulder, wearing shorts and a floppy shirt. Head down, eyes ahead, she walked past the kidnappers' lair and into the bushy entrance to the college. I swung the Essex around and met her on Grand Avenue.

"What did you see?" I said when she got into the car.

"Woman sitting on the screen porch, smoking, maybe drinking a beer."

"Accompanied by…"

"Nobody."

"Did you get a good look at her?"

"Nope. Too dark. So what do I have to take to the G-men, Powers? A woman drinking beer? It's legal, remember?"

"That's the kidnap house."

"I thought you said it was out in White Bear?"

"It's both. They used both. It's a big gang."

"Drive me to the federal building," she said.

I left her at the federal building, then zoomed up the hill to Myrtle's place. I had to rap loud on the door to cut through the music. She was blasting a Duke Ellington tune, *Buy Yourself A Broom and Sweep the Blues Away*.

"What do you want?" she said, and slipped into the hallway, guarding the entrance against me.

"You've got a gentleman caller?"

"I don't know any gentlemen."

"I came by to ask you to the late show."

"What's playing?"

"King Kong."

"I don't need to pay admission to see an ape."

"My treat," I said.

The music ended in a horrible hissing-scratching that caused Myrtle run into her living room. She lifted the needle arm from the record and said:

"Saturday night's the worst."

"For what?"

"The blues."

I kissed her.

"That don't help," she said. "It only makes it worst. See the problem with you men is, you think you can solve everything. You got a formula for everything, and when that don't work, you whip out a gun. You think you can fix a girl's blues with a night at the movies, or dancing to an orchestra. But it don't work, I tell you. See, when a girl is ruint, she's ruint. Cinderella's coach was a rotten pumpkin all along."

She retreated to a window seat. The sundown cast a halo on her frizzy hair, her sad chubby face. She fiddled with a joint from a candy tin, but didn't light it.

"I want to marry you, Myrtle."

"No you don't."

"Yes I do."

She shot me a hard look.

"To keep me from testifying against you?"

"Because I'm lonely and you're lonely. Why should we both be lonely when we really like each other?"

She lit the joint. There were still darkish patches where Rico had squeezed her throat.

"Like?" she said.

"Like."

"Not love."

"Well…"

"Please say it's not love," she said.

"Okay," I lied, "it's not love right now."

She blew smoke.

"I don't want it to be love ever."

"Myrtle…"

"I fell in love once. It was the worst thing what ever happened. Love ruint me."

She crossed her legs and sat back against the woodwork. "Where would we live? Not that farm out in the boonies."

"Here," I said.

"Too many memories," she said.

"I can get my apartment back in January."

"Nix, I don't climb four sets of stairs."

"Havana."

"In Cuba? Are you nuts?"

"We go there for a long honeymoon, miss the damn winter, come back in spring, start over fresh."

"Doing what?"

 I shrugged.

"Michael."

"I wouldn't mind being out of the country for a while. Things are getting hot. The hillbillies are running roughshod. Bank robbery, that's handled by the local cops. But a snatch, they're playing against the G-men. I've been wanting out for a long time. Havana. Six months, if you don't like it, Chicago."

"You've been to Havana, I take it."

"Nope."

"How much Spanish you speak?"

 "Adios and a couple of other words."

"Well that's a dandy plan you have there Señor Powers."

"Filben needs a man there. Or he will soon. Slots."

"Mick, do me a favor, don't mention this harebrained scheme again. I'm not marrying a man whose best source of income is the race track."

I sat down heavy in an ornately-carved dining room chair. Myrtle seemed able to work something out of every man, but had never asked me to buy her a thing, except for the occasional dinner. I took that to mean something. I watched Charles and Amelia flutter, yellow and green flashes of wing. Myrtle snuffed out her joint. She was barefoot, dressed in a long purple shift. She gathered that glowing material around her. She waved the smoke away from the parakeets.

"It makes them act goofy," she explained. "There's nothing worst than a doped-up bird."

She put her head in her hands. Her shoulders, exposed, seemed like magnets for my hands. I gave her a soothing rub, or thought I was doing so, until she shrugged me off.

"My father was a harsh man," she said. She looked up at me with wet eyes. "He didn't mean it. He loved us all really. He was a hard-shell turtle, all soft inside."

She bit her lips hard.

"No, that's a lie, Mick. He was a bastard bully, mean from head to toe. Forget it, Mick. There's nothing left for people like us. We might as well get drunk and see that ape movie."

CHAPTER TWENTY

After we saw King Kong climb the Empire State Building, we rushed out of the Paramount ahead of the crowd. There were about 2,000 people in that theater, many headed for the Terrace Cafe at the Lowry. On Saturday night there would hardly be a table free. I palmed the hostess a buck and she squeezed Myrtle and me in behind a potted plant. It was like watching the orchestra through a jungle. The rubes began to pile up at the entrance just as I ordered our cocktails.

It was approaching midnight but the heat of the day hadn't gone anywhere. The big overhead fans managed merely to waft hot air over the crowd. Norvy Mulligan's Orchestra did its best imitation of "Night and Day" and "How Deep is the Ocean" and it took only half a gin and tonic to get Myrtle dancing with any man who could move his feet.

Which left me at a palmy table drinking ginger ale. I wandered out to the open deck and stared down at the street. A white carriage led by a plodding horse weaved through the last of the night's auto traffic. Punks who aspired to be gangsters roamed the streets, drunk and laughing. A rich man's long dark Lincoln pulled into the Lowry garage beneath me and out stepped the driver, Tommy Filben.

I ran down the stairs. Tommy, dressed in white, red tie knotted even in this heat, was waiting at the glassy elevator.

"Just the man I wanted to see."

"Do I owe you money?" Filben joked.

"Take a walk," I suggested.

"Is this going to end badly for me?" Filben asked, a sly look in his eyes.

Certainly he had heard the rumors about how Rico had met his end. The police may have been clueless but the gangsters knew everything.

"Come on, Tommy," I said, "smoke with me."

We crossed the street to the Saint Paul Hotel, skirted its garden and sat on a bench in Rice Park. A faint breeze stirred the leafy trees, water burbled in the big fountain behind us. I filled my pipe and offered Filben the leather pouch.

"Havana Gold," I said.

He sniffed it.

"If you get my drift," I said.

He retrieved a tiny bent pipe from his suit coat pocket, filled it with tobacco and lit it with a gold lighter that was shaped like a pen. We smoked like a couple of professors pondering an ethical dilemma. I said: "So how do you like Havana Gold?"

Filben shrugged. "I suppose you'd like to get out of town," he said. "I don't blame you, seeing as who you're running with."

I blew smoke.

"And who might we be referring to?"

"Come on, don't kid me."

"Square up, Tommy."

"You square up," he said, blinking against his own smoke. "Where the hell is Billy Hamm?"

"How should I know?"

"Yeah well," he sat back against the bench. "Take a look over your left shoulder, what do you see?"

I said, "Lights."

"Yeah, in whose offices?"

"Department of Justice."

"Your gang isn't messing with the local constabulary now. J.

Edgar's boys work hard and they can't be bought."

"My gang?"

"Yes, Shotgun George and the rest."

I rapped my pipe gently against the bench.

"Shotgun George?" I said.

"You know very well," Tommy said. "The character you're running around with. I'm stupid to be seen with you."

"Shotgun George…"

"Ziegler," Filben said. "Don't play dumb."

"I wish I knew what you were talking about."

"You might have heard of a little incident a few years back? The Saint Valentine's Day Massacre? Powers, you can't be as dumb as you pretend to be."

"Shotgun George Ziegler…"

"Shut up when you say that name," said Filben, looking around at a dark empty park. The white carriage creaked around the corner and the horse stood restless while a drunken young couple stumbled out.

"This guy George," I said, "had something to do with said event?"

"Everything to do," said Tommy.

"Meaning he's…"

"Yeah, the little Chicago Italian, the one with the scarred face, the one who got in trouble with the taxman? Yes. These Chicago fellows are awful high rollers for a humble Saint Paul horseplayer to mix with. Don't you think?"

The young squire who'd been in the carriage stopped to ask Filben for a light. His girlfriend, dressed in lace, seemed wary of us, and maybe she should have been. When they walked across the street to the Saint Paul Hotel, Filben said, "He's going to get lucky tonight."

"So, Tommy, you're telling me…"

He looked around before whispering: "Capone's lord high

executioner," he said.

"That guy? George? Come on, he's an opera buff."

"So was Capone, although I don't know what kind of performances they put on in the Atlanta Pen."

"Shotgun George."

"Named after his preferred methodology," said Filben. He twirled that tiny pipe between his fingers. "How did you get mixed up in this, Powers?"

"I wanted to see you about that, Tommy."

"Oh did you?"

"Slots."

"What about them?"

"Cuba," I said.

"It's almost as hot down there as it is in Saint Paul."

"I'd be happy to run a bag for you down there."

"Would you now? Christ almighty, at this time, there is no bag to run. At this particular moment, the political situation on that lovely island is somewhat unsettled."

"I heard there was riots."

"Worse, until the matter is settled, we don't know who to bribe. There's a fellow named Batista who's vicious enough, but I wouldn't bet him to win just yet. In this race, the horses that place and show will be executed at the finish line."

"Keep me in mind."

"Powers, whoever snatched Billy Hamm has made a dreadful strategic error. Up until now the G-men were focused on a little hamlet called Chicago. Your friends are attracting national attention. I don't know about you, but I'm quite comfortable answering to the Saint Paul constabulary. They're a very understanding bunch but you can't say the same of our friends across the road..."

He pointed his pipe at the Federal Building.

"Beware," he said. "If the Feds don't get you, the Shotgun will."

Filben didn't want to be seen entering the Lowry with me, so I sat on that dark bench and watched him go. I glanced over my shoulder at the G-men windows, second floor. I tried to fit Filben's information into what I already knew. Al Capone had a hit squad of "American Boys" who did his dirty work. These fellows were assumed to be behind the Saint Valentine's day massacre, unsolved these past four years. But even if Filben was right, and George was a Capone executioner, what was he doing on a snatch job in Saint Paul? And who was his friend Monty? And the old man I now knew as Fitz? Why had Jack Peifer joined these Chicago mobsters with the Barker Gang for the purpose of snatching William Hamm?

I couldn't wrestle it into anything that made sense. The carriage driver cracked his whip and he, horse and gilded white carriage moved into the darkness. I ambled back toward the Lowry with a feeling of doom. However the kidnapping turned out, with Hamm dead or restored to his castle, I was dispensable. I knew all the actors, yet wasn't part of the gang. If Shotgun George had mowed down a garage full of Chicago gangsters, what fate awaited me?

So when I rejoined Myrtle at the Lowry I was distracted and she was gulping her third gin and tonic.

"Your buddy Tom Filben sashayed in," she informed me, appraising her eye makeup with the aid of a pocket mirror.

"You don't say. Let's go home."

She put down the mirror, surprised.

"The orchestra's coming back for another set," she said.

"Home," I said.

"Well you're in a swell mood."

"Not feeling well," I said.

"Oh, well in that case." She stood and put her hand to my forehead. "Poor darling, you have a fever. Let Nurse Myrtle cool you down."

She held the icy cocktail glass to my cheek. "You know if you drank more you'd feel better."

"I don't think so."

"Okay, well," she snatched her purse from the table. "I always go home with the sap who brung me. Ready?"

We took the elevator down to the garage, but already I was overcome by fear of the dark. I was not in the habit of carrying pistols to the movies, and so was feeling defenseless.

"What's the matter with you," said Myrtle, tugging me in the dark. "Something you ate?"

My legs felt about as mobile as stone pillars, and I was sweating heavy. When we reached my Essex I fumbled for the keys, got in, and breathed deep. Myrtle lit a cigarette and I zoomed out of the garage.

"Take it easy," she said.

Looking into the mirror as I drove, I detoured across the Wabasha Bridge, pulled over in the mud flats as two cars rolled by.

"What kind of dope are you smoking?" Myrtle asked.

"You ever heard of a guy named Shotgun George Ziegler?"

"Can't say that I have," she said.

"Saint Valentine's Day?"

"What about it?"

"Chicago?"

"Say what you mean, will you?"

"Never mind."

I put the car in gear, performed a squealing U-turn, and drove back over the bridge toward the city lights.

"Myrtle, I've been in love you for years," I said.

She flicked her cigarette out the window, over the railing, and into the dark Mississippi.

"If you were sane, Mick, I'd take that as a compliment. Sentimental, maybe, but a compliment anyhow."

"In case something happens to me, I wanted you to know. I want you to remember me fondly. Because if nobody remembers you fondly, why then, your life wasn't worth living at all."

"You don't say."

"They're going to get me."

"Who?"

"The boys."

I made a turn on Third and drove along the river toward Seven Corners. There, men and women, mostly young, wandered, dressed for the tropics, among taverns, flop houses and dice parlors.

"They're not going to get *me*, are they?" Myrtle asked.

"You know better than that." I was about to suggest that women were off-limits to gangsters but there, below us, was the very pier where Sadie and Rose had met their flaming fate.

"Lucky me, I don't know nothing," said Myrtle.

My spunky Terraplane climbed Cathedral Hill, up and away from the low doings of downtown. As we passed the wide stone steps of the Cathedral of Saint Paul, Myrtle said: "How much money you got?"

"More than a thousand."

She slapped the dashboard.

"Drive west."

"If I bail now I'm a hundred percent dead. If I stick it out until the end, I have the smallest chance in the world."

"To…"

"Collect my share and split for Cuba."

"Oh."

"See with my share, I don't need Filben. I'll have a couple of years worth of dough to spend in Havana."

"Your share," she said.

"I'm up to my waist in the swamp now, I might as well catch a fish while I'm out here."

"Don't take me home," said Myrtle.

"You want to come back to the Commodore with me?"

"Hell no. Drop me at the Barking Dog, I'll call a cab."

"Why? Oh. You don't want to be seen with me."

"You're a danger, Powers."

I took that in, burning with resentment. One day she couldn't live without me, the next day she didn't want to be seen in my company. I drove in angry silence to the Barking Dog, the beer garden that, until a few months ago, had been a speakeasy disguised as a pet shop. Behind its high walls, people were having a loud, and now legal, beery time.

Myrtle got out of the car, then leaned into it, filling the passenger window.

"Take my advice and split town," she said.

She turned away and leaned back in.

"And wherever you end up, Mick, call me with an offer."

She winked.

"You never know."

CHAPTER TWENTY ONE

The Sunday editions of all the papers contained news that a
second ransom note had been delivered. All the accounts were
vague and conflicting on details. The Daily News story was written
by K.F. Thornton, and contained no hint of the information Janie
had about the gang's hideouts.

The newspapers engaged in wild speculation about the identity
of the kidnappers, all of it wrong.

I bought the papers at Blind Benny's as they were delivered in
bundles off big dirty trucks. A half dozen curious citizens milled
around the newsstand, sleepless like me, and wanting to know the
latest details of this sensational crime. I walked back to the
Commodore with the papers under my arm, read all the accounts
closely over coffee in the cafe. I waited until after seven to phone
Janie at home, and got no answer.

I drove over there and let myself in, to a rousing greeting from
Snowflake and Hula Girl, but Janie wasn't home. I took the dogs
for a walk around the Cathedral grounds. Early Mass was letting
out its shirtsleeve crowd. It was already 80 degrees and sweaty, and
today, the newspapers warned, would be the hottest of the year.

I returned the dogs to Janie's apartment and stood looking out
the open windows as the sun bore in. A nervous wakeful night
caught up with me and I lay on the couch, the one I had purchased
back in my married days. With the dogs panting on the floor, fell
into an exhausted nap.

I awoke to the scrabbling of eight dog paws on bare wood

floors. Janie stood at the open door, a young man hiding behind her.

"Powers, what are you doing here?"

I rolled off the couch and offered the young man a hand. He was tall, of medium build, with a pale, bad complexion, blue eyes, and crew-cut blond hair. He smelled faintly of stale beer and held a bottle of Hamm's in one hand. He wore a Hawaiian shirt over ratty white shorts. His face was flush from embarrassment or the heat or a beer binge, I couldn't tell which.

"This is Chaz," said Janie, fixing me with a hostile stare.

"I came over to walk the dogs and fell asleep," I explained. "Be leaving now."

I crouched to caress the dogs.

"Behave now," I instructed them. I rubbed Hula Girl behind the ears. "Especially you, sassy miss."

"Powers," Janie said, "it's okay. Chaz knows."

"Chaz knows what?" I said, as if the young man wasn't standing right there swilling beer.

"Everything," Janie said. "He's a neighbor, across from 204 Vernon. He knew all along they were gangsters. Tell him, Chaz, don't be afraid."

"We knew they were gangsters," Chaz said. "My mother. She's always home. She noticed. She kind of, you know, keeps an eye on the street."

"She noticed what?" I asked.

"Across the street," Chaz said, "none of them ever went to work. Nobody left in the morning and came back at dinner time."

"Chaz is helping me," Janie said. "He's a witness."

I picked up the front section of the Daily News and rattled it.

"You're writing something for the Daily News?"

She nodded.

"No no no no no. After. Only after these mugs are in prison."

"Powers…

"If you're writing for the Daily News, what happened to your story, then?"

"The desk ate it."

"What does that mean?"

"I wrote my story as a sidebar. Thornton read it over my shoulder, then stormed into Major Hoople's office, screaming that my story had no legs. The Major said give it to the desk, and let them massage it into the mainbar."

She raised her hands, helpless. "All the good stuff disappeared."

"But it's all true," said Chaz, "Every word. The kidnappers lived right across the street from me. I'm a witness."

He raised his hand. It seemed this was a momentous time in his life, as if he were in court with one hand on the Bible, the fate of men hanging on his testimony.

Back at the Commodore, I ordered a big Sunday breakfast and re-read all the news. Department of Justice men were focused, all right, but on some other crime. In Kansas City, gangsters trying to free a prisoner had ambushed G-men. Two local cops and two G-men were dead. J. Edgar Hoover fumed and thundered from his federal throne in Washington. The kidnapping of Billy Hamm was, by incredible luck, no longer the top priority for G-men. Edgar was now focused on this shootout they were calling the Kansas City Massacre.

I began to hope I could squirm out of this thing alive. With Serious Bobby and Big Ryan playing their roles, and the G-men distracted, this could play out fine. Hamm would be home safe, Jack would have accomplished his purpose, whatever it was, and the kidnappers would scatter. The Saint Paul cops would, as usual, bumble until the story blew over. I could move self and dogs to Havana, or maybe just Miami. Myrtle could join me or not.

These hopes bolstered my nerves as I met George at noon at the eagle. He was standing in his vanilla suit, hands in pockets, overlooking the city as if he were considering buying it all. Yes, I had seen the shotgun in his car. But it was still hard to believe that this cultured, educated man had pulled off the most notorious gangland murder of my lifetime.

"Well, sport," he said, "we're on the move. One last errand."

"Shoot," I said, and then bit my lip.

"A bit of spy craft," he said. "This afternoon, if all goes well, mechanics in the Hamm Brewery garage will be outfitting an automobile for our special purpose."

"All right."

"They will remove the doors of a coupe, and the trunk lid as well. Your task is to make certain that no little copper hides in the trunk. True, a man friendly to our cause will be driving, but he has not attained the level of trustworthiness we would like to see. So you..."

He patted me on the shoulder.

"Shall be an agent of trust. When our driver leaves that garage he must be alone in the car and followed by no one. It's up to you to ascertain this. You will communicate your assurances. Then you will be compensated and we will say farewell."

"Exactly how will we communicate?"

"There is a spot in Herb's Garage reserved for you. It is now occupied by an orange traffic cone. After you make your observations, you will park head in, if all is well. You will back in and face out if anything has gone wrong."

I nodded.

"Head in, all is well. Backed in, something's wrong. Is that clear? If all is well, Herb will have an envelope containing your compensation. If things have gone wrong, meet me here immediately for further instructions."

"Okay."

"Clear?"

"Clear."

"Head in, all is well. Backed in, something's wrong."

"Got it," I said.

"I look forward," George said, "to never seeing you again."

"Same here," I said, and shook his hand.

I returned to the Commodore, lounged in their shady yard, and lit my pipe. How exactly was I going to spy? The Hamm Brewery, even at the gates, would be swarming with cops. I might get a wink from Serious Bobby, but Big Ryan was running this investigation and he'd handcuff me on sight.

But a hapless female reporter from the local paper, hanging around to question the cops, that wouldn't seem out of the ordinary. That her belly was bulging with child could only make her seem more harmless.

I called Janie.

"What are you doing right now?"

"Uh, sleeping," she said.

"At noon?"

"You can't seriously be calling to ask about my sleeping habits."

"I'm calling with a tip. Right now, at the Hamm Brewery garage, they're outfitting the ransom car. They're ripping the doors and the trunk lid off. It's going to be driven straight north on Highway 61 until the drop signals are given. Take your notebook over to the Hamm garage, and call me at the Commodore. Call me when the car leaves. I need to know if the driver's alone, if they try to hide a cop in the car, and whether the cops follow the car."

She didn't respond.

"Janie? You can get in with your press credentials."

"I'd go if I could get a photographer to drive me. None of them works Sundays. That's why the Monday paper is so dull."

"Take your friend what's his name."

"Chaz? He takes his mother to Mass on Sundays. He's very devoted to her. He's all she's got left. Michael, I don't want to drive right now."

"Because you might have to go to the hospital?"

"I'm afraid of that, yes. I don't want the police to take me. I don't want my baby delivered in a police car."

"You've got a press camera, haven't you?"

"Sure."

"I'll be over."

I drove the Terraplane and parked in my old spot, just outside what used to be Janie's basement apartment. I ran up the stairs, fedora in one hand. While she fed the dogs I posed in the mirror, hat slouched over my head, her yellow press card stuck in the ribbon. If I could keep well away from Serious Bobby and Big Ryan, I might get away with it. The camera was a bulky, heavy thing with a flash unit the size of my head. I yanked the cord, which cut the connection between flash and battery. I practiced slipping in a film plate, and then we were off.

The drive to Hamm's took less than ten minutes, Janie looking grim, notebook and pen held tight to her big belly, as if they might blow away in the hot slipstream.

"What have you found out?" I asked.

"A lot," she said.

"About?"

"White Bear," she said. "I canvased the neighbors. I asked at the cafe. People noticed."

"I thought you were going to let the feds investigate."

"The neighbors said the "family" was obviously a bunch gangsters. Lots of cash, flashy cars, lots of drinking. Strange. They said a short, chubby old lady was sitting on the porch every day. A gangster mom, I suppose."

"Ma Barker," I said.

"What's she wanted for?"

"Having awful children. Did you get to 204 Vernon?"

"Not yet. That's what Chaz ... he worked at a print shop, but he's been laid off and so he goes over there sometimes and runs errands. Not that the gangsters ever let him into the house."

"He ran their errands?"

"Mowed the lawn mostly, and fetched booze and groceries. The blonde with the smashed in nose? She drinks like crazy and tips the same way. Plenty of beer and ice delivered. Men and women coming and going night and day. Not a normal family at all."

"See?" I said.

"Coming and going at all hours is not a crime."

We pulled in at the gates of the Hamm Brewery. Two cops I didn't know, outfitted in Saint Paul's forest green uniforms, slouched against the gate. The older one, tall and bald underneath his peaked cap, leaned in and leered at Janie.

"Help you, miss?"

"Daily News," she said. I flashed the yellow press card that had been in my hat.

"Sorry," the cop said, and shook his head. "We're in the middle of a police investigation."

"That's why I'm here," she said.

"You can just turn around right there," he said, and pointed to a muddy lot.

"Don't make me call my editor," she said.

His partner, a big-nosed dark fella, eased into the shade of an oak tree.

"Can you tell me?" I said to the bald cop, "have they let any press in there at all?"

He shrugged. "Sorry, can't give out no information."

I got out of the car and grabbed my camera. I stepped back and pointed it at him.

"You are officer…"

He put up his hand like a big stop sign.

I snapped the picture.

"Look," I said, "let's have a conversation in the shade. We're all baking out here."

While Janie sat in the Essex, I walked the bald cop over to his shorter partner. Even in their short-sleeve uniforms, they were sweating under those nasty caps. I said: "Such a hot day, you boys could use a beer after your shift's over."

One cop looked at the other.

"Let's see," the bald cop said.

"Ten cents a beer," I said, "you boys probably have a lot of friends, let's make it fifty beers apiece."

"Make it a hundred," said the little cop.

I palmed them both a ten dollar bill.

"You were distracted," I said. "A couple of nosy reporters slipped through while you were dealing with an unruly crowd."

"I don't see no unruly crowd," said the little cop.

"Look harder," I said.

He shrugged, put the tenner in his trouser pocket, and said, "Okay Lou."

"Hurry up," said Lou. "I'm not going to open the goddamn gate for you."

I opened the gate just wide enough to slip the Essex through. Down at the bottom of a muddy hill, at the wide doors of the big garage, maybe a dozen people surrounded a coupe parked under the eaves. Inside that garage were beer trucks in various states of disrepair, and police cars parked by cops desperate for shade. I parked in the shadows of the garage and stayed in the car, slumped, fedora over my face. I recognized Serious Bobby, Big Ryan, Chief Dahill, Lieutenant Charles Tierney, and the tall lanky bespeckled Irish Kinkead, county attorney.

Janie approached the crowd of cops. Dressed in red shorts and a floppy, lacey white blouse, she looked pitifully pregnant. This would rouse the sympathy, I hoped, of all those middle-aged, law enforcement males. She stood in front of Irish Kinkead, whom she knew from her days on the county beat. They talked. Kinkead smiled. I had never seen such a thing, Kinkead's Irish eyes smiling.

Big Ryan paced around the ransom car, like a lion deciding how to attack a wounded gazelle. The doors of this car had been take off and set aside against the garage wall, and two mechanics in dirty blue uniforms worked on the trunk hatches. Serious Bobby, dressed like he was at a banking confab in Panama, jawed with the tiny wiry detective Charles Tierney. This Tierney was the cop who had volunteered to ambush the gangsters, except that the plan leaked. So there actually were brave cops willing to do their duty in Saint Paul. Strangely enough, Tierney's partner was the criminal-in-uniform Big Joe Ryan.

Chief Tom Dahill squatted, inspecting the headlights as a mechanic tested them. I lay the camera on the driver's seat and sat back. A dusty breeze whipped into the garage. I slouched the hat over my face, and even with all that was happening in front of me, felt the gradual, irresistible call to the dark regions.

I woke up when Janie slammed the door and sat beside me, beads of sweat on her forehead and upper lip. Serious Bobby, at the wheel of the doorless coupe, drove past an armored car that had pulled in while I slept. Cops opened the brewery gate, Bobby drove that coupe out, and it disappeared behind a brick wall.

"He's alone?" I asked.

"Uhm-hmm," said Janie. "Except for two suitcases full of cash."

"What time is it?"

She checked her watch. "It's 4:35. You napped? Some newsman you are."

I fired up the Essex and joined a procession of police cars creeping toward the gate. None seemed in any hurry to follow the ransom coupe, and outside the gate, all turned south toward the police station, while the coupe headed north.

"When did they deliver the money?" I asked.

"I don't know, a few minutes ago, while you were in dreamland."

"What did you find out?"

"They're just going to let the ransom go. They're going to play it safe until they get the Hamm back."

"What did Irish say?"

"Oh, he's thundering about offering a big reward for the kidnappers."

"Oh is he?"

Janie said: "I believe you now Powers. They're not fooling me anymore. They're all guilty."

"Maybe not Dahill and Tierney, but Irish and Big Ryan are in on it. Bobby too."

"Powers, they're as guilty as sin. Now I know why the Daily News will never break this story. Too many big shots would be exposed. Who knows how deep this goes?"

As she wrestled with an idea I had accepted a long time ago, I dreamed of the beaches of Havana. They had beaches, didn't they? Yes, and some kind of sea wall? I had seen pictures in the Saturday Evening Post. I could almost feel the luxurious sand between my toes as I walked the beach. The warm waters lapping up around my ankles. The call of the sea birds.

I dropped Janie at the apartment and zipped downhill to Herb's Garage. I got out of the coupe to remove an orange cone from a parking spot. Then I slipped the Essex in, nose first, and shut her down.

Nose in.

Success.

I took a deep heavy breath.

It was over. The ransom would be delivered and Hamm returned safely. The ransom was far less than the family could have paid, and so what was the purpose of the kidnapping? I had doped out an answer. Hamm would be returned safely because Jack wanted him back, intimidated.

That way, it would be Jack calling the shots at the brewery, with his man Serious Bobby in the executive suite. This wasn't a kidnapping as much as the ultimate shakedown, with Jack serving notice that the Hamm's Brewery was under gang control, as it had been during Prohibition.

I walked into Herb's office and there was the man himself, in greasy overalls at a metal desk piled with paperwork and auto parts. He looked up at me, bald, bespeckled, tired and said: "How'd you park?"

"Head in," I said.

"Well you took all day. Thanks for ruining my Sunday."

He handed me a manila envelope. It was sealed with red wax and much smaller than I had imagined it would be, only letter size. I had expected a bundle of cash, but this envelope weighed barely an ounce.

"Thanks," I said. "Sorry Herb."

"Get out of here," he said.

If Shotgun George was out to get me, it wouldn't be here, not at gangland's favorite garage. Gangsters needed Herb's Garage, and the less public attention it got, the better. I walked uphill toward the Cathedral, envelope in my pocket. With every step I imagined more danger. As cars passed me, I imagined one might pull over, and the barrel of a shotgun stuck out a window would be my last sight on this earth.

As I approached the great Cathedral, I wrestled with my fears and the shattered remnant of a Catholic conscience. No I wasn't proud of my participation in a kidnapping, but it hadn't exactly been voluntary. No harm to the victim, I tried to convince myself, except that he would be rattled for a while. He was a multi-millionaire, and really wouldn't miss the ransom. I expected the envelope would contain one or two thousand-dollar bills, enough to give me a year's head start in Havana.

Now, uphill and out of sight of Herb's garage, I sat on the Cathedral's stone steps. Surely they wouldn't gun down a man on

God's stairway. I ripped open the envelope.

Out fell two tickets to The Barber of Seville.

CHAPTER TWENTY TWO

I could feel doom closing in on me. I had served my purpose in gangland. Like Arthur Dunlop, like Sadie and Rose, I was now disposable. I never dared return to the Commodore. I let myself into Janie's apartment and hustled the dogs down into the car. Unarmed and protected only by two 25-pound canines, I drove to the edge of the Macalester campus and turned on Vernon Street. No one was stirring at 204 Vernon. I knew the gangsters wouldn't be there, but imagined it might have been swarming with cops.

I walked around to the back of Chaz's house and knocked on the kitchen door.

A stooped old lady parted the door's window curtains. I might have been the Grim Reaper himself to judge by the look on her face. She faded away, and then Janie opened the door.

She stepped out. She was sweating, her hair tied back, and she looked pale, like she was enduring a bout of nausea.

"What?" she whispered.

"I'm leaving for Wisconsin and I advise you to do the same," I said. I sounded stern, even to myself. Janie put a hand to her forehead to ward off the blazing sun. Charles appeared at the doorway and called out: "Mister Powers, would you like a beer?"

"Not right now," I said.

"Michael," Janie said. "I have a doctor. He practices at the Anker delivery room. He's not going to drive to Wisconsin to deliver my baby. I'm not going anywhere."

"Then stay here," I whispered, "with this lug…"

He appeared right behind her, encircled her, protective, with his hairy arms. One hand lay over Janie's belly, the other clutched a bottle of Hamm's beer.

"Chaz," I said, "no matter what she says, keep her here for a while, until this thing blows over. And don't go volunteering yourself as a witness. The cops can't and won't protect you, believe me. The two of you, lay low. Stay home. Keep out of it. In a couple of weeks it'll all die down, and this girl…"

I touched Janie's sweaty cheek … "has other priorities. Listen to me, Chaz. I know what I'm talking about. Lay low and shut up."

He swigged beer.

"Can you do that?"

"Sure Mister Powers," he said. "Hey I heard you once held up a bank with a tommygun."

Sometimes an overblown gangster reputation comes in handy. I said: "The same tommygun I'll use on you if you don't stay home and shut up."

I winked at Janie. I patted Chaz on the shoulder.

With the dogs in the car panting, I drove away from the city, the sun going down behind me. I didn't take a deep breath until I was across the St. Croix River and into Wisconsin. Near midnight, exhausted, I rented a tourist cabin near the train station in Minoqua. In the morning I drove the last hour, turned the key in the Eagle River farmhouse, and felt safe for the first time that summer.

I stocked up on groceries and bought a Remington 12-gauge lever-action shotgun, along with four boxes of ammo. It took me all Monday to test fire the shotgun in the woods, clean up the house, install the screens, and get the electric and water running. The kick of that shotgun bruised my shoulder, and on Tuesday I drove downtown to the drugstore for liniment, and to buy the Saint

Paul papers, a day late at twice the price.

The Monday Saint Paul Daily News screeched:

HAMM FREED;
HUNT TO FIND ABDUCTION GANG STARTS

There were photos of Hamm, hair oiled, cheerful, standing with Irish Kinkead and Big Ryan, who were pretending to be his saviors. Kinkead proclaimed that his investigation would "never cease until all those responsible have been brought to justice."

In Tuesday's papers, Janie's story burst into the news, but to my relief, carried no byline.

HAMM KIDNAP GANG LAIR
BELIEVED TO BE IN ST. PAUL

I cursed Janie. Her need to be a newshound had outweighed her common sense. At least her editors had kept her name off the story, which identified 204 Vernon Street as the kidnappers' lair. In the story, neighbors and merchants described tenants who had suddenly fled at 2 a.m. on the night of Hamm's release. The descriptions of the men were contradictory, but everyone had gotten the unmistakable Paula right: attractive, petite, bejeweled blonde, crushed nose.

Nowhere in any account were mentioned Shotgun George, or his connection to the Saint Valentine's Day Massacre. Chicago criminals Monty and Fitz-Dad were also left out. In a separate story, Irish Kinkead as county attorney offered a reward for anyone who would squeal on the gang.

That was a trap Kinkead was laying for the naive. Certainly he would squelch any evidence that led to the Barker Gang. But he would now get a hundred tips and use them to muddle the investigation.

In the Wednesday papers the "Vernon Avenue Mystery House" was explored, again in a story that must have been written by Janie Vetter, but again without byline. The landlord had been questioned by reporters and police. The man he described as his tenant was Fred Barker, who had rented under an alias.

That story died as quickly as it arose, to be followed by a story about Big Joe Ryan, leading a raid on a cabin that was supposedly the kidnappers' hideout. Master of misdirection, he managed to terrify a mom and daughter on vacation, and to produce headlines that further muddled the case. The day after that, the main news story speculated that the kidnappers had fled to Wisconsin. A day later, the Hamm kidnapping was no longer worthy of Page One.

I'd seen this kind of thing before. Crime reporters depended on cops. That meant, in Saint Paul, that crime news was whatever Big Joe Ryan said it was. Big Ryan could turn crime news on and off like a faucet. No cop dared speak for the record when Big Ryan wanted silence. The Hamm Kidnapping was about to sink into the dark depths with the other unsolved Saint Paul crimes. The Federals would keep quiet too, not eager to highlight their inept investigation.

I settled in for a long summer of barbecuing, reading, swimming in the lake, walking the dogs in the woods. I had plenty of repair work to do in the farmhouse, because last fall my sister Mona had torn it up in search of Aunt Doris's hidden money. When Mona finished ripping up floorboards and drilling through walls in the house, she attacked the barn and chicken coop.

I'm not much of a carpenter, but I got advice and sometimes even help from my closest neighbors, Pastor Dan and Wendy. They were taking a year's break from saving souls in Africa. They rented a lakefront cottage that was a ten minute walk from the farmhouse, down a path through the woods. That wild end of the lake belonged to my cousin Cindy, a single woman who had moved to Milwaukee in hopes that the doctors there could cure her of a crippling disease.

Pastor Dan and Wendy could have no possible connection to Midwest gangsters. They were friendly, honest souls and seemed eager enough for company. I visited them at Cindy's cottage almost every day for coffee. They rarely spoke of Africa and seemed grateful to be spending a cool, quiet summer at Snipe Lake. I began to re-acquire a wardrobe in quick, furtive visits to downtown Eagle River. Wisconsin lake country was full of vacationing gangsters from Saint Paul and Chicago, so I spent as little time in public as possible.

Two days before Independence Day, a Yellow Cab rolled down my long gravel driveway. As the dogs yelped and lunged, I kneeled at the windows and aimed the shotgun through the screen. The cabbie got out, stretched, and opened the back door. Myrtle, holding his hand, wedged herself out of the cab.

The driver set out a carpet bag and a suitcase. I was a stunned, shotgun-wielding human in a dog insane asylum, the inmates barking, leaping and yowling. I lay the shotgun on the kitchen table as the taxi U-turned, clipping off a piece of my aunt's favorite rose bush as it spun away.

Myrtle, in sun dress and bonnet, waved.

I banged out the screen door, angry and delighted.

"What the hell?" I said.

The dogs circled Myrtle, sniffing.

"Try to give a girl the slip, will ya?"

"How did you get here?"

"With great difficulty," she said. "Are you going to give me a hug, like maybe you were glad to see me?"

I embraced her. The dogs leaped on us both.

"I'm kind of hot right now, Mick," she whispered.

"Let's go to the lake."

"No, the other kind of hot," she said.

"Oh."

She grabbed her earlobe to show off a diamond earring.

"Kleinsmidt's accused me of walking off without paying. I managed to squirm away from their goon. They sent their private dicks over to roust me, middle of the night. I can't stay home, got to cool off."

"Minneapolis," I said. "You should've known better. You can't get a fair shake over there. The cops sometimes enforce the law."

"Do you have a gin and tonic, Mick? Can I stay?"

"Of course you can stay."

I carried her bags into the kitchen.

"No limes," I warned her.

"I don't care for fruit," she said. "Too squishy."

"Jewelry now, you're branching out."

"It ain't as easy as furs," she said. "The old switcheroo don't work, see. You got to have good running legs. It's try it on, snatch and run, that racket."

"I don't think I have tonic, either."

"How about a martini?"

"How about gin and orange juice?," I said, and grabbed the icepick from above the icebox.

"Myrtle, is anybody asking for me?"

"Nope," she said. "You're forgotten. We're all going to be forgotten, some sooner than others, that's all."

She lit a Pall Mall, covering its end with red lipstick.

"You could call a girl once in a while."

"You heard anything about Shotgun George Ziegler?"

"Nope."

I chipped enough ice for a dozen drinks, and filled a porcelain bowl.

"How about the hillbillies?"

"Reno, I heard."

"Reno."

"The Hamm snatch, it's cooled off, Mick. Nobody gives a

damn. Beer is flowing out of that brewery, money is flowing in. It's like the whole damn thing never happened."

I snapped my fingers. "Clean," I said. "That's what happens when you cut Big Joe Ryan in on your action. It's the best insurance policy money can buy."

I delivered the drinks to the kitchen table and looked her over. "I assume you brought a bathing suit."

"You know I like it nude."

"Well, it's complicated Myrtle. We have neighbors in Cindy's lake cabin now. Summer renters."

"They got something against nude?"

"He's a preacher man," I said.

"They're the horniest kind," said Myrtle.

In the Daily News July 4th editions, Janie had broken through with a snippet of truth, although it carried no byline. Her story identified the tenants at 204 Vernon as the Barker-Karpis Gang, whose principal members were Fred, Doc and Karpis. Still, the story made no link to the Hamm kidnapping, merely noting that the gang's leaders were wanted for two murders: "Pop Anderson" and a sheriff in Missouri. Nobody yet linked the gang to the triple murder in that Minneapolis bank robbery, or the Burned Ladies of 1932.

At first, I seethed with anger. The most dangerous thing she could have done was identify the Barker-Karpis gang. I was perplexed, because her due date was right around July 4. Was she writing stories from the hospital? But after I thought it over for a while I began to realize that, for the first time, the Daily News was naming suspects who were under Big Ryan's protection. That suggested that Big Ryan's grip on the city, and the police department, was getting shaky. Where the G-men onto The Deal? Were they the ones feeding the Daily News?

Myrtle was at the farm barely a week when the countryside

made her restless. She had taken the train from St. Paul to Minoqua, and now began hinting she'd like a ride back to the station. I argued that she was too hot to go back home, that the jeweler's private cops were more dangerous than the Minneapolis Police, and that she'd be safer to wait out the summer.

I didn't say I wanted her company. If I told her that, she'd have thought I was trying to con her.

I bought her a phonograph, two albums by Goodman and two by Ellington. I provided good London gin and tonic. I grilled steaks, although I didn't care as much as she did for beef. Twice I rented a boat and took her out on the chain of lakes, but all she got out of it was a sunburn. On a Sunday night, as the sun went down over Snipe Lake, she began to crack.

She stood sloppy drunk, arms spread in the farmhouse door, wearing denim shorts and a t-shirt, her curly hair a mess.

"I'm drowning," she said.

"In gin," I said. "I'll make coffee. Sober you up."

"I got no use for sober," she said. She turned on me, a ferocious look on her face: "You! You and your goddamned dogs."

She said it so loud, and so mean, that Snowflake approached her on his belly, while Hula Girl crawled under the easy chair.

She kicked Snowflake. He yelped and scattered.

"Hey," I said. "Kick me if you want, but leave the dogs alone."

"I hate you, you rotten sober Irish bastard," she said.

I stood to shield her out of the room. She backed onto the rickety porch and threw her gin glass against the farmhouse wall. It shattered.

"What did I do to you, Myrtle?"

I stepped outside and closed the door behind me. She backed off the porch, fell to her knees, steadied herself with her hands, and rose. Her knees got cut bloody by glass shards.

"Where's your love?" she snarled. "Where's all this love you're talking about. Where is it? You hand me a bottle of gin and call that love? In a bottle of gin? Is that where it is?"

"What are you talking about?"

She ran barefoot for the forest.

At the firewood pile she fell. I strode over there, stretched out a hand to help her up.

"You're buying me, Mick. Like every other man, you think I'm for sale. A slab of meat and a bottle of gin and you own Myrtle's soul. Well I've got news for you, you fool. Myrtle's on to you. Keep your money in your pants, tiger, because this woman is not for sale."

She rose to her feet without my help and muttered: "I'm going to learn how to drive and then I'll keep going until I run out of road."

She sniffled and dabbed at her nose.

"Learn to drive," she repeated. She took her cigarette lighter out of her t-shirt pocket, sat at the firewood pile, and set a splinter of kindling ablaze.

"I'm going to burn these goddamn woods down."

"No, you're coming into the house with me. You're going to drink coffee until you sober up. In the morning, if you want me to put you on a train, I'll do that. If you want to learn how to drive, I'll teach you."

"I'll teach myself."

I stepped on the tiny blaze to extinguish it, and helped her up. I walked her stiff back to the farmhouse, sat her in a kitchen chair, and boiled water for the French press. She sat gloomy, silent, head propped in her palms.

I pushed a cup of coffee at her.

"The Professor," I said. "He's your excuse to live in the past. But it's a past that never was. It wasn't so smooth as you pretend, between you and the old con man. He conned you like he conned everybody else. When he ran out of bribe money, the cops took him to prison, and left you flat broke."

She only moved her lips.

"Right?"

"Fuck you Mick."

"You're still being conned."

"I'll slap your face if you don't shut up."

"I'm finished," I said. "Said my piece. Tell me what you want in the morning."

"I could ruin you," she said. She arose and leaned over the icebox to retrieve the shotgun. She slammed it on the kitchen table. "Go ahead and shoot me like you shot that Wop."

I felt like lightning had struck me.

"He was choking you, Myrtle. You had the bruises for weeks."

"Ah, go ahead. You want to shut me up, brave boy? You're such a big, tough gangster. Put me out my misery. See if I care."

I grabbed the shotgun, strode into the living room, buried it underneath the mattress of the day bed. The dogs scampered upstairs, cowering.

Myrtle had her head down on the kitchen table. I rubbed her shoulders and she began to whimper. I kept rubbing and Hula Girl, curious, put her little black muzzle around the corner of the stairway. Snowflake, maybe inspired by her bravery, peered over her shoulder.

"Sleep, Myrtle," I said, "it will all make sense in the morning."

I settled in downstairs, on a lumpy mattress on top of that shotgun, with only the dogs for company. Myrtle took a long shower, and wrapped in towels, plodded up the stairs exhausted. I helped myself to the last of the gin and ice, and fed the dogs scraps of barbecued steak. Half drunk, I fell into a deep sleep. Sometime in the night the dogs awoke me with furious barking, an eerie glow at the windows. For one stunned moment I knew nothing, and then realized the farm was on fire.

CHAPTER TWENTY THREE

I ran out of the house. The barn was on fire, so was the tall grass and the woods beside it. Greedy fingers of fire reached across the lawn for the chicken coop. The dogs ran in panicked circles yelping. The firewood pile was smoking, the blaze spreading beyond it to the forest, the wind blowing flames and swirling smoke away from the house and toward the lake. I pounded up the stairs to the sleeping loft, tendrils of smoke leaking through the screens.

"Myrtle!"

I flung on the light to see an empty, rumpled bed. I ran downstairs, sure she must be in the kitchen. From underneath the mattress I grabbed the shotgun, ran out the kitchen door, stunned to find that someone had stolen my Essex. The dogs led me in retreat from the flames, smoke and heat. Up the driveway we ran into the forest night, the fire crackling and the trees moaning behind us.

We ran down the dark forest path under a moonlit and smoky sky, a fearsome blaze at our backs. Snowflake and Hula Girl paced me, stopped to look back, ran again. A frightened doe popped out of the forest, changed her mind, and bounded back into the dark. The dogs led me through a patch of heavy ferns and into the backyard of Cindy's lake cabin. The lights were blazing inside and as I struggled, breathless, toward the patio, lanky Pastor Dan opened the kitchen door.

"We've called the fire department," he shouted.

In the driveway behind the cabin, I saw my Essex. Behind Pastor Dan stood a trembling Wendy. I realized I must have presented a frightening sight, a shotgun-toting man in t-shirt and skivvies. I turned to see the forest behind me going up fast, with a roar like a locomotive. Wendy grabbed my arm and said we should get in the car and drive off if the fire got closer.

Myrtle sat in their living room, drunk, on the couch, babbling hysterical.

We stood along the lakeshore for hours, me and Dan and Wendy and the dogs, as Myrtle slept snoring on the couch and the volunteers of Vilas County put out the fire. The burnout lasted until after the sun had risen through the pines. The firemen had run a hose all the way down to the lake, and used a pumper engine.

In the choking early morning smoke I walked to the edge of the forest. The trees near our barn had burned to stumps, the charred barn had collapsed, the farmhouse was only scorched but surely ruined. The chicken coop was a blacker spot on blackened grass. The windows of the farmhouse had popped out, black tongues marred its white paint, which had bubbled in the heat.

After we finished the smoky, grim inspection, we returned to Dan and Wendy's, and made coffee. Myrtle slept. The sheriff and fire marshal visited the kitchen, took my name, and I told them what little I knew. Pastor Dan loaned me shirt and trousers. I looked over my Essex, and in the back seat saw Myrtle's suitcase and carpet bag. I put the dogs in the car and that was when Myrtle woke up. She gaped at Dan and Wendy as if they were monsters and ran out of the cabin.

I caught up to her on little hummock overlooking the lake. She was heaving into the ferns.

When she recovered, sunk to her knees, she wiped her lips with her sleeve and looked up at me.

"I don't know what got into me. I panicked, Mick."

I held out a hand to her.

"I was drunk," she said.

I walked her back to the Essex. The dogs were cowering in the back seat, windows open to a hot wind. The awful stench of burned forest blew in on the westerlies.

"You got any gum? Awful taste in my mouth."

She fished for gum in her purse, and finding none, her trembling hands lit a cigarette.

"I didn't know you could drive, Myrtle."

"I can't drive."

"You did."

"I don't know how. I was out of my mind."

She blew smoke.

"Didn't know what I was doing," she said.

I let her into the Terraplane and drove down Highway G, away from the charred farm and into a bright morning, through a green forest, past a gentle flowing Wisconsin River.

"What?" Myrtle said.

I shrugged.

"You're blaming me?"

"I didn't say a thing. Guilty conscience?"

"I was drunk asleep you bastard."

"I'm putting you on the train."

"I was asleep. People don't start fires in their sleep."

"It's done, okay? The farm is ruined. Go away."

She pitched the cigarette furious out the window.

"I can't believe you're blaming me."

"This is a good time for us to break up."

"We were never a couple."

"No hard feelings, then," I said, but I had plenty of them. They were kept in check by the knowledge that Myrtle was a witness to Rico's last moments.

"You are a son of a bitch, that's what you are," she said and tapped out another cigarette. "Man, will I be glad to get away from you."

"Ditto," I said.

"And that goes double for me."

The Chicago and Northwestern line at Eagle River offered no direct service to Saint Paul, but did run to points south and Chicago. One of those points south was Waupun, where Myrtle's Professor was locked up. It was three hours until the next boarding, and when I bought her a ticket to Waupun, the station was empty except for a cranky young clerk.

"Cheer up. Be glad you have a job," I scolded him.

He waved at me like I was a pesky fly.

Myrtle and I sat on a wooden bench outside the station, me holding the dogs on a leash. Snowflake stayed as far as he could from Myrtle. We said almost nothing for a long time. Across the street, tourists in skimpy clothing shopped for moccasins, trinkets, swim suits, home-made fudge. The moccasin shop had set out fake totem poles for that authentic North Woods experience.

I tied up the dogs, crossed to Bev's Diner and ordered scrambled eggs and toast to go, along with cardboard containers of coffee. We ate breakfast picnic style under the shade of a willow tree where Eagle River meets the lake. We watched small boats carrying fishermen, or day-trippers on excursion. For a moment there, I forgot I had just been ruined.

"I guess it smoldered all night," Myrtle said.

"What smoldered all night?"

"My little play fire."

"Little play fire!" My anger alarmed the dogs. I had a mad vision of pushing Myrtle into the swirling river.

"Or maybe somebody drove by and threw a cigarette out the window," she said.

"Somebody who? Myrtle, that barn is two hundred yards from

the road."

"I don't know," she said. "Maybe you did it, smoking your pipe. Did you ever think of that?"

She wore a pink dress, fluffy and belted. She adjusted it, as if the belt were itching. "What time do the taverns open?"

"Never," I said.

"My mouth tastes just awful."

She sipped coffee, poured it out on the grass. The dogs circled behind me, Hula Girl whining. Snowflake bumped me.

"So this is how you get revenge," I said.

"Revenge for what?"

"That's what I'd like to know."

"You got insurance, don't you? Trees grow back, you know."

I sat in the grass, hunched into myself. Myrtle wandered down the banks of the river, walked back and said: "You don't have to wait with me, champ."

My eyes fixed on the jeweled rings on her fingers.

"You saved all your own clothing and jewelry, I noticed."

"I told you I panicked."

"And you let me sleep with the woods on fire?"

"I don't know what I did, Mick, I was crazy drunk. I was drunk on gin and panic, I tell you."

She kneeled on scabby knees and then lay in the grass, looking up at me, curly hair, eyes pretending innocence.

"I'm sorry it happened, Mick, but I didn't do it."

"Maybe it was a raccoon," I said. "They get drunk and start fires all the time."

"Aren't you a riot," said Myrtle

She rolled over and looked at the sky.

"Just leave me," she said.

"You're going to be okay?"

"Yeah."

"You've got enough money?"

"Who's got enough money?"

I took a twenty out of my wallet, crumpled it into a ball, let it float down. It landed on the belly of her pink dress.

"Keep the change," I said.

The balled bill blew off her dress and into the grass. The wind picked it up, blew it into the river. It floated like a tiny boat.

Myrtle eyed me as if suspecting I might push her in. She waded into the river and retrieved the money.

After she insisted twice more that I leave her at the train station, I did. She set her suitcase and carpetbag on the concrete platform and blew me a kiss. I drove back to the farm to view the charred wreckage, just to plant it in my mind, my North Woods refuge no more. I couldn't even camp in a tent here now, the charred smell was so strong, and the mud from the fire hoses so deep.

In my tourist clothes, with crackers and summer sausage to get us through the journey, I drove self and dogs all day back to Saint Paul. I imagined Myrtle in Waupun State Prison, visiting Professor Banks, her one true and only love. Maybe if I was lucky she would stay in Waupun. In Saint Paul, she was a danger to me.

I drove five hours until I reached the East Side bungalow occupied by my sister Kelly and her family. It was late on a summer evening. Gary, her husband, was out drinking beer after a long day of delivering coal.

"Gary works that hard in the summer?" I asked.

"Cheaper to stock up now." Kelly said. "Everybody's got to save the nickel."

"The girls?" I asked.

"They're at Camp Hooray."

"Hooray?"

"That's what all the parents say when the kids leave for camp."

She lit a Viceroy. Until I showed up, she had been enjoying a rare quiet moment.

"I was wondering if I can stay on the couch tonight."

After a double-take she said: "Oh you can stay in Veronica's room. Neither of them will be back until Sunday."

"How's Aunt Doris?"

She shrugged. "Still bitching about being alive."

I looked out the window, where Tallerico's porch jutted out toward the street.

"What's happening at the Tallerico's these days?"

"Bunch of punks. His nephews. Turned it into a party house. Just what I need. Ronnie and Lizzie go over there. God knows what goes on." She blew smoke toward the ceiling. "They never arrested anybody for his murder, did they?"

I shook my head.

Kelly sputtered. "This town, I'm telling you."

"How's Gary."

Shrug. "He likes his beer. Have you got luggage?"

"Not really"

"No?"

"I don't think we should tell Aunt Doris."

"Tell her what?"

"Her farm burned to the ground."

A sick grin crept across Kelly's face. "Did you say burned to the ground?"

"Not much left," I said.

"How the hell did it burn to the ground?"

"Forest fire, I guess."

"Oh my God, it burned? To the ground?"

"Didn't I just say that?"

"I can't believe it burned to the ground. Just like that?"

I opened the refrigerator and poured myself a drink from a bottle of Altwasser Ginger Ale. I looked across two yards to the empty dog kennel behind the Tallerico house. I was glad I got the bastard before he got me, and before he choked the life out of

Myrtle. But I was sorry, too, because someday I would have to explain that Mortal Sin at Saint Peter's Gate.

"We're not going to tell her," I said. "Doris. It won't do her any good to know. We'll just file an insurance claim and then…"

I turned to Kelly.

"Maybe we'll build a new farmhouse with the insurance money?" I said. "We'll see."

Kelly shook her head.

"What?"

"Nope," she said. "No insurance."

"What do you mean?"

"No fire insurance. We never had it. Insurance, yes, but not for fire. They wouldn't write it. They won't insure a house heated only by a barrel stove, not any more. Property, liability, yes, but we never had fire insurance."

I set my ginger ale on the gingham cloth.

I said: "So we're going to inherit 40 acres of charcoal?"

"I guess that's it." She shrugged. "Life sucks, doesn't it? My God, what are we going to tell Mona? She'll have a fit. Who the hell started a fire in those woods?"

That night I slept in my niece's lumpy narrow bed, or I should say I lay there pleading for sleep. I heard Gary stumble home late, but did not rise to greet him. I lay there wondering what I would do now, with my hideout in ashes, with a crazy Myrtle liable to blab the secret of Tallerico's killing, with the Barker Gang and Shotgun George looking to dispose of me, and a chance that Swede Fanlund would soon be discharged from the Hennepin County jail. The inheritance I had counted on was now reduced to ashes. My Derby winnings were already half gone, and in the respectable world of post-Prohibition, I had the same lousy job prospects as ten million other guys.

Sleep? Not a chance.

CHAPTER TWENTY FOUR

"What's a snitch worth these days?" I asked.

Heater mouthed his cheroot. "Depends. The Director is no spendthrift."

"No I didn't think so."

"What's your gist?"

"My gist?"

"You know what gist means, don't you?"

"Sure I know what gist means."

"Well let's go." His cheroot dangled in his mouth. "Gist."

"Hamm kidnapping," I said.

"We might come up with a little cash."

"I want a federal job in Havana."

"Doing what?"

"That's up to you. Enough to live on, that's all I want. Something in diplomacy, maybe. Department of State, right? I can type. Not fast, but I can type. Clerk's job would be fine with me."

"I regret to inform you, Powers. I can't snap my fingers and produce federal jobs."

"I regret to inform you that your agency has no clue in the Hamm thing."

"As far as you know."

"I know pretty far."

"Oh do you?"

"I know the way to Cuba."

"Tell me one thing I can check," said Heater.

"Idlewild Cottage, White Bear Lake."

I had my story ready: How, in complete innocence, I had rented that cottage for myself for the summer, and then subleased it to some Chicago tourists after I'd hit a losing streak at the races.

"Idlewild Cottage," Heater said. "That's been in the newspapers."

"Who paid the rent, that's the key."

"All right, who?"

"Somebody I know."

"I can't check that now, can I? Unless you give me the name."

"The ransom notes," I said. "Corona portable, pica type."

His face darkened. He rested that cheroot in glass ashtray, delicate.

"Okay, Powers," he snorted. "Corona pica. Maybe. Maybe that's something."

"Hasn't been in the papers, has it?"

"No it hasn't."

"Then maybe I do know something."

"Maybe you do."

"The original ransom note had the word *imperative* misspelled. It was x'd out and spelled correctly above."

Heater, for the first time, looked at me seriously.

"I might need immunity from prosecution," I said. "Look, there are guys in this town who want to see me dead. If I'm seen leaving this building, the date of my execution might move up. I'm taking a chance, here, Heater. I need immunity, I need Cuba, I need cash."

The enormous windows were thrown open to a hot day, the big floor fan blowing. The birds were singing across the street in Rice Park. Truck drivers were gathering over there, the first stirrings of a Teamster strike. I imagined I might see my brother-in-law Gary out there.

While I gazed at the park, Heater typed a memo.

"I didn't know G-men could type."

"A most essential skill," he muttered.

I felt grateful to the striking Teamsters. With this gathering crowd, I was less likely to be noticed by whichever clerks Harry and Jack paid to spy on the federal building.

"Fifteen bucks a week for four weeks," he said. "How's that?"

"You're kidding. In return for dope on the Hamm kidnapping?"

He shrugged. He typed.

"Havana," I insisted. "If all you can get me is a one-year temp job, I'll take it."

"Jobs are scarce, Powers."

"So are convictions."

"Jenny," he called, and when a tall girl in a blonde bun and gray business suit answered, he handed her note.

"Clegg at Headquarters."

She nodded and left with the note.

"I didn't ask Washington about compensation," he said. "We'll get to that. Tell me more."

"Kidnap hideout," I said. "You're way off. Not Wisconsin, like it said in the papers."

"Draw me a map."

"My map leads to Havana," I said.

"Okay, I promise, I'll try," said Heater.

"Capone connection," I said. "You're missing that. Saint Valentine's Massacre, you're missing that too."

"How about the Lindbergh kidnapping, can you tie that in?"

"I'm not joking, Heater."

"So we should be looking in Chicago?"

"Too late for that. I'm not coming down here anymore. Meet me tomorrow, Pilot Knob, the cemetery, four p.m. Get me Havana and I'll get you the kidnappers."

Downstairs in the park, I found Gary at the edge of the crowd and used him for cover in the angry mingle that passed for a labor rally. We edged away from the crowd and up to Seven Corners for a beer. I told him thanks for the stay and I'd be moving out tomorrow. Where I was going, well, I told him, I had to keep that a secret.

CHAPTER TWENTY FIVE

The gangster-infested hotels of Saint Paul were not a smart option, even for a temporary stay, but I did know one desperate landlord with a cheap place. I needed no credentials to rent from Mrs. Holy Reardon. She gave thanks to the Virgin Mary when I offered her $25 for a one-month stay in the basement apartment that used to be Janie's.

It wasn't easy finding renters in a city with 50,000 men unemployed.

Janie's apartment was sort of an underground prison. The dogs were gloomy until I shoved a kitchen table underneath the two barred windows that let in the only light. Then they had a view, except when blocked by Mister Holy Reardon's Oldsmobile, parked just inches from the window. But I was seeking obscurity, so that was fine with me. The apartment was sparsely re-furnished by the Reardons, including a crucifix over the doorway and a poster pasted to the door that rendered an Irish proverb:

IF YOU WANT TO KNOW WHAT GOD THINKS OF
MONEY, LOOK AT THOSE HE GAVE IT TO

I soon learned to live with the pipes overhead, which cracked and groaned with hot water. I made peace with the tiny, two-burner stove. I signed up for adult school, Spanish lessons, starting in

September, just in case I wasn't in Cuba by then. At the Saint Paul
Public Library, a kindly librarian helped me determine that it was
no problem bringing dogs to Havana, as long as they had their
shots. I applied for a passport and had my picture taken.

I heard nothing from Agent Heater at Hoover's Department of
Justice. The Hamm kidnapping investigation sunk beneath the
waves of other news. A phone call to Heater went unreturned, and
I didn't have a phone in that basement, so he couldn't call me.

I found a new and better race-book downtown, in an upstairs
room over a tavern. There I could play my game while not
bumping into Pat Reilly. After Belmont's last race one Saturday, I
ran into my brother-in-law in the tavern downstairs, drinking with
his brother Teamsters. He said my sister had been looking all over
for me. Aunt Doris was dying.

Our destination was the Mother Mercy Home for the Aged.
Kelly and I tiptoed into Doris's room, as if maybe the dying
shouldn't be disturbed. I brought coffee in cardboard cups, and a
hunk of the crumb cake Doris had always been fond of. But she
was asleep, breathing lightly, a gray head, wrinkled skin, and skinny
form under blankets on this warm muggy evening. A nun had taken
the crucifix from the wall, and set it near the shaggy pillow that
cradled Doris's head.

"So..." said Kelly.

"So we're not going to tell her, right?"

Kelly shook her head. "No reason for her to know," she
whispered. " I've got to get out to Eagle River to see it for myself.
How long does it take a forest to grow back?"

We sipped coffee. I took two modest chunks out of the crumb
cake.

Kelly said: "You remember your first trip out to that farm?"

"Oh yeah."

"The wooden dollhouse she had for me?"

"I remember my chrome six-shooter and white cowboy hat."

"Wisconsin cowboy," said Kelly. "Mona sunk the rowboat, remember?"

"I was always hoping to meet an Indian in the woods. You know, my whole childhood, I thought Doris owned that lake."

"She thought so too. Between her and Cindy, they were like the twin goddesses of Snipe Lake."

"She was flabbergasted when the Chicago tourists showed up with their speedboat."

"Oh, she loathed those people," Kelly said, then stroked Doris' gray hair.

Kelly arose, looked up and down the hallway.

"Where the hell is Mona?" she said. "I called her."

She returned to the bedside and lit a Viceroy. She blew the smoke away from Doris.

"She always hated cigarettes," she said.

Doris's body jerked, as if a jolt of electricity had come up from the bed. Her eyes fluttered open and she smacked her lips.

"Thirsty," she murmured.

From a big sweating tin pitcher on the nightstand, Kelly poured water into a glass that had a built-in straw. She held this up to Doris's parched lips. Kelly dropped her cigarette to the floor and stepped it to death with the sole of her blue high heels.

"Drink more, Doris," Kelly said.

Doris made a face like a disgusted child being ordered to eat broccoli. Kelly withdrew the water.

"Tend my farm," Doris said.

Kelly and I exchanged glances.

"Feed my chickens," Doris said.

She hadn't had chickens there in years.

Kelly patted her veined, spotty hands.

"Don't worry about the chickens, Aunt Doris, we're taking good care of that farm."

"Keep the goddamned deer…" she muttered, and tried to rise, and fell back.

"… out of the vegetables."

She licked her lips.

Her eyes fluttered closed.

She smiled, she coughed, she exhaled as if choking on air. A strange papery gasp emerged from her throat. I held one hand, Kelly held the other.

"I'm going to get the nurse," I said.

Doris went still, eyes shut, mouth slightly open.

"Don't bother," Kelly said. "Let her go. She's done with this world." Kelly fixed me with a wet-eyed look. "I sure wish I believed in God and Heaven."

The moment of death is not so obvious but I knew when a tremble rippled through me, when my throat felt like I'd swallowed a lug nut, when Irish tears flooded my eyes and Yankee determination held them there, I knew the old gal was gone. That wasn't her, lying there helpless. The real Doris was the dynamo who'd supported a declining husband as hard times deprived him of work and spirit. Doris, who survived a hundred blizzards, and raised a crop in among the dark pines, on cheap land no other farmer wanted.

"That's that," said Kelly. "That's a life."

I kissed my aunt's forehead. I felt, on my lips, I can't explain it, like kissing granite.

"Goodbye, good woman," I whispered. "Safe journey to Jesus, now."

Kelly glared at me, the look you give a traitor.

"I don't know why I said that," I muttered. "Moment of truth, I guess."

"You of all people," said Kelly. "The woman's an atheist."

I shrugged.

"Doesn't matter now," I said. "She was good to us all, that's what matters."

When Doris hadn't drawn a breath for five minutes or so, I went for the nuns. They had called the priest that morning to give Extreme Unction, and were not surprised. They adjusted her covers, as if to make her comfortable in the afterlife. One of the nuns lit a big candle and placed it on the service table. Another handed us rosaries. We kept a short vigil, we prayed a decade of the rosary, and then we retreated to sign papers in a dark, stuffy office.

Although her death occured in a home attended by nuns, and was met with crucifix and rosary, Aunt Doris had turned against the Church and wanted no funeral. Kelly and I arranged for cremation, and held a tea-and-remembrance for a few friends and family. We handled the details. Mona's part was to show up late at the funeral, drunk.

The will giving Kelly, Mona and I an almost-worthless farm went to probate, and would be tied up for months. We once imagined the farm was worth $15,000, but who could assess its value now? We had counted our inheritance before it hatched.

So now it was as depressing as it was lonely, just me and the dogs in the basement apartment. The one thing that cheered me up was the birth of a baby boy to Janie. I had been distracted by the fire at our farm, by the death of Aunt Doris, and only caught up with Janie three days after the birth of her child.

It had not been an easy birth and they both were still in Anker Hospital. When I visited, little Dane Vetter, pink and squalling, lay under blankets in a bassinette in a room with a dozen other babies, kept safe from us germy folks behind mammoth, and sparkling clean, windows. Janie, confined to bed rest, looked pale but healthy. I held her limp, sweaty hand. She still wore her grandmother's wedding ring.

Every topic I could think to bring up was sensitive: How much did her parents know? Had she heard from Larry in prison? Was

Dead Like Lazarus / 204

Chaz a serious suitor? How did she plan to support this child? I certainly didn't want to bring up any gangster news. So just to have something else to talk about, I told Janie a few highly selected details about the fire at Eagle River. I didn't say Myrtle had set it. But I did say Myrtle and I had broken up after the fire.

Janie asked me to crank the bed up. She looked saintly, with her pale skin, the white sheets. She was a vision topped by brilliant red hair, piercing green eyes.

"She loves you, Mick," Janie said. "A woman can tell."

"We have our differences," I said. "She's pining for an old lover."

"I doubt that," Janie said. "She's testing you, and you're failing the test."

"How's that?"

"You don't *need* her. She can sense that, and it's driving her crazy. A woman wants to be needed. Not just loved. She wants to be important. She doesn't want to be a castoff, a second thought, a bit player. You know how I can tell she loves you?"

I cleared my throat.

"She's insanely jealous of me," Janie said. "Even though she knows we're not an item, she does everything but growl when she sees us together. That's because she knows you like me, and she wants to be number one in your heart."

"Maybe you're right," I said, and patted Janie's hand.

"Don't patronize me, Mick."

"It's just that…"

I poured Janie a glass of water out of a sweating enamel pitcher.

"You've been burned," she said, and drank.

"In more ways than one. It takes time for a forest to grow back, Janie."

She looked at me, perplexed, then sighed. "Oh," she said, "I so much want to take my baby and get out of here."

I had been avoiding every Near Occasion of Gangster Sin, and everybody I knew except Kelly and Janie, but I hadn't played a round of golf all summer, and that was my excuse for calling Sam. What I really hoped for was not a round of golf, but a hint of gangster gossip.

I phoned him from a booth near Blind Benny's newsstand.

"How about a round at Como tomorrow?"

"Nix," he said. "What are you doing in town?"

"What do you mean, what am I doing in town."

"Ah…" the phone went dead for a minute, and then after a fumbling noise, Sam said: "You know about Swede."

A shudder went through me.

"What about Swede?"

"He's here."

"What do you mean, here? At the Hollyhocks?"

"Over at the bar."

"He's out?"

"Obviously," Sam said.

"How the hell…"

"Oh, he's been out a week, ten days, maybe longer, I don't know. He's cursing your name. He's asking around about you."

Sam lowered his voice. "He's dead drunk now if you want to take him."

A long silence followed.

"How drunk is he?" I asked.

"Babbling. Drink spilling. Talking too much and too loud."

"Already?"

"Been here since lunch," said Sam.

"He's not with any friends?"

"He's got no friends."

"How did he get out?"

"Case fell apart," said Sam. "Don't you read the Minneapolis papers?"

"Well, I was out of town," I said. "What's he want at the Hollyhocks?"

"Information he's not going to get. I'm going now. It was nice not talking to you."

Click.

I was holding a dead phone. I went into Manny's Bar, newly opened like so many opportunist taverns, and ordered a Coke. I stood with only myself in its darkest corner. I had a big decision to make and only a few minutes to make it in. I had cost Swede Fanlund parts of his fingers when I'd left him unconscious and freezing. I had put his buddy Rico in the ground. Swede probably suspected I had framed him for the Third Northwestern robbery. This man was going to kill me. His honor was at stake.

And now would be my best chance. Why was he at the Hollyhocks? He was probably trying to connect with Jack, but Sam had told me emphatically that Swede "had no friends." Which meant Jack wanted nothing to do with Swede.

The bastard might never be this drunk and vulnerable again. I told myself it would be good riddance to a nasty hit man, a man who enjoyed burning people out, a sadist and a psycho. He had killed and torched Rose and Sadie, hadn't he? That went against the gangster code. Women, children and innocent bystanders were safe around honorable gangsters.

Swede Fanlund deserved to die.

I drained my Coke and called for a refill. The other end of the bar, near the Seventh Street windows, was filled with noisy college students. I envied them. They would be growing up in a better world, the jobs would come back, the gangsters would fade into history.

Swede must die, I tried to convince myself. And if so, I had to leave this bar within ten minutes, and stalk him in the shadows of the Hollyhocks.

On the other hand there was the risk I would be seen. That

somebody would identify me or my car. The dinner crowd was already there. The casino upstairs attracted gamblers all night. I began to lose courage, or gain sense, whichever it was.

And if Heater could get me to Cuba, I could leave Fanlund and all this behind. Let Fanlund stew, some other gangster would knock him off soon enough. I would be walking Snowflake and Hula Girl along the Malecon, salty waves splashing.

Let the Swede live. Do the easy thing, Powers, it's what you've been doing all your life. I slurped up that Coke, walked uphill to my dungeon. Looking over my shoulder for Swede's blue Pontiac, I strolled the dogs, and locked myself down for the night.

CHAPTER TWENTY SIX

Little Dane Vetter was quiet in his crib, underneath the sunny windows, as if he were being blessed by the Cathedral. A bag of fresh-scented cloth diapers lay on the kitchen table. Alongside it, a stainless steel bottle holder was sunk in an enamel tub of warm water. I poured coffee for Janie and myself.

Dane coughed, uttered a cry, then gave a contented sigh.

Janie pulled the bottle out of its holder, shook it to release drops of milk onto her wrist, and approached the crib. She sat on a kitchen chair. Arm through the crib slats, she eased the bottle's nipple into the baby's mouth.

I sipped coffee and said: "I don't want to be nosy Janie, but I can't help but wonder."

"About?" she said over her shoulder.

"Money."

With her free hand she bunched her hair behind her. It was hot up there. The morning breeze had died. I promised myself I'd buy Janie a gift, a Westinghouse fan for the baby.

"I hate to bring up money," I said.

"Freelancing," she said. "At least for this year, then we'll see."

"Can you make a living from the detective mags?"

"They've got the money," she said. "If you've got the lurid stories."

I wanted to keep Janie away from the truly dangerous stories, the ones about the Barker-Karpis gang. Who knew where they were, and whether they would return to Saint Paul. Just as dangerous was Shotgun George and his Chicago friends.

"Jack Bevans," I said. "You know that story?"

"Remind me," she said, distracted, focused on feeding the baby.

"Editor of the Twin Cities Reporter. You know, lurid and sensational news. And then what? He kills his own wife and chops her up."

"So? What's the angle?"

"Murdering journalist puts himself on Page One."

"Oh, I don't know."

"What's wrong with that?"

"Maybe that's an inside story. I'm looking for a cover piece."

"What do they pay for a cover story?"

"Up to $500," she said. "If you've got a strong story and pictures."

I whistled.

"But the Jack Bevans story," she said, "isn't going to make the cover. I mean, we're talking about a national magazine, they want it big, they want it bloody, they want it sexy."

"The Hamm case is neither bloody nor sexy."

"A hundred thousand bucks, and a clean getaway" countered Janie. "That's sexy."

"So, two, three cover stories a year, and you could make a living."

"Conceivably. And there are a dozen magazines."

She picked up Dane, put him on her shoulder, and began patting his back. The baby's blue eyes swam in his head, as if he were dizzy, looking down from the great height of five feet above the floor.

"I need the Hamm Kidnapping," she said. "That's the most sensational crime ever to hit Saint Paul. That will push all those New York and Chicago blurbs right off the cover."

The baby burped.

"Too dangerous," I said.

"And you know all about the Hamm kidnapping, Mister Gangland," she said. She challenged me with a mean look. I realized in that moment she wasn't a girl any more. She was a mother lion protecting a cub.

"I can't ..." I said, but even as those words left my lips, I realized Janie had to make a living somehow. An unwed mother would never be welcomed in the newsroom. Even if she were to get married, making a living wouldn't be easy now. Married women who worked were scorned. It was assumed they were taking jobs away from family men.

"I guess I can help," I said. "I guess I have to. But only if you hold up your hand to God and promise to stand behind the G-men when you write it. You can only write about cases where they've already made an arrest."

"I swear," Janie said.

"Turn to face the Cathedral."

With the baby making cooing noises on her shoulder, she faced the great copper dome.

"Swear on the Blessed Mother."

"I, Janie Vetter ..." she said.

We left Dane in the care of Mrs. Holy Reardon. I reminded an anxious Janie that Mrs. Reardon had raised 6 children from infant to adult, and lost not a one of them. Janie dressed Dane in shorts and a navy shirt and delivered him to Mrs. Reardon, kissed him all over, and began to tear up.

When we got into the car, she said: "We've never been apart before."

As we drove away, she turned to look at the apartment building and noticed the shotgun lying across the back seat.

"Rifles? Are we going to a wild west shootout?"

"It's not a rifle, it's a lever-action shotgun. On second thought, we should bring the dogs."

I circled back into the parking lot, darted into the dungeon, freed Snowflake and Hula Girl. Both leaped into the back seat, panting, squirming, happy, and made themselves comfortable despite the shotgun.

"Just so you know," I said. "It could be dangerous to be with me. A guy might be looking for me, a Chicago criminal named Shotgun George Ziegler. He's connected to the Capone Outfit. He's medium height, blonde, and dresses like a prince. He might come after me himself, or he might send his goons. I have no way of knowing whether they're after me or not. But they could be."

"Why?"

"Because I know certain things. Also, you didn't tell me Swede Fanlund was sprung from jail."

"I didn't know. You might have noticed I've been distracted over the past few weeks."

"Yeah, well, Swede's out. So being around me could be double dangerous these days."

She bit her lip.

"Okay, then," I said, "it's against the code to murder a bystander, so you'll probably be okay. But that's why the shotgun. Let's take our doggies for a ride."

A rainstorm rolled in as we drove out Fort Road, the windows fogging over, barely cracked open. The temperature and humidity were tropical, the rain a drizzle. Janie wore white pedal-pushers that ended at her knees, and a red shirt emblazoned with a white W, for University of Wisconsin. Over her shoulder was a rough leather handbag for notebooks and pens.

"So what happened," I asked, "with Major Hoople and the 204 Vernon story?"

"It was a weeklong struggle to get even that sad remnant of a story into the paper." She sighed. "Goggles went in to the Major's office and tried to lobby it off the front page. He said his job was tough enough, without a freelancer embarrassing every cop in town. So Major Hoople chopped the heart out of that story."

At Fort Snelling we crossed the Mississippi on the Mendota Bridge. Overlooking all was the grassy hill that river men had named Pilot Knob. On one of its slopes was a ruined Catholic church from pioneer days, and a small cemetery. Here, Rose Perry had been buried last year, after being torched on the docks of Saint Paul.

We drove in, parked underneath a dripping oak tree at the top of the hill, and waited. We let the dogs out. Hula Girl romped in the rain, while Snowflake stayed dry near the tree trunk.

"Shotgun George what?" Janie said, flipping open her notebook.

I spelled Ziegler for her.

"Golfer, opera buff, landscape gardener, executioner."

"Give me an example."

"Saint Valentine's Day Massacre."

"A serious example."

"Oh I'm serious. Add the Hamm kidnapping."

"Why would someone from Chicago kidnap William Hamm?"

"I'm still trying to work that out. Here's our man."

Agent Roland Heater drove a government clunker, a black Ford that could hardly make it up the hill. I reached over the back seat, flung open the door, and called the dogs in. Heater drove up until his auto was inches away, then cranked down his window.

"Who's this?" he asked.

"Janie Vetter, she's a newswoman."

"Get rid of her."

"No chance."

Janie piped in: "Background only."

Heater shook his head.

"Heater," I said, "let me tell you, this girl knew about 204 Vernon when the Barker Gang was still there. The cops wouldn't take her seriously. The Daily News editors won't listen either, so she's writing for the magazines. She's hot on the Hamm story and she stays."

Heater threw his cheroot to the ground.

"No quotes," he said. "I was never here."

"No quotes," Janie said.

"You will identify your source as a man familiar with federal investigations."

Janie locked her notebook and pen in her purse.

"Havana," I inquired.

"Progress," said Heater.

Rain blew in on his $5 government suit, and he raised the window a bit.

"You've got nothing for me, I've got nothing for you," I said.

"Government work is scarce these days," said Heater. "I'm working with an export guy in Havana."

"A spy," I said.

"Let's call him a friend in the harbor. He's got a warehouse job he needs filled. It ain't much. Night watchman. Apparently it's a bunch of thieves down there."

"How solid is this?"

"Solid. We make an arrest, the job is yours. Gotta pay your own way down, though."

"Word of honor?"

"We make an arrest off of your information, yes, word of honor. I will get you something in Havana. If not this, something."

I pointed at Janie: "She's going to write an article eventually. For the national mags."

"Write all you want," said Heater. "Leave me out of it."

I said: "Heater, there's a Saint Paul cop behind this whole thing. A traitor in your midst. During the Hamm snatch, he copied down your playbook and sent it to the gang. He was sitting right across from you in the strategy meetings. You know him as Big Joe Ryan, dethroned police chief."

Heater waggled his hand as if that wasn't important.

"You want me to make the arrest for you, too?"

"Where's the evidence?" he said.

"He's too shrewd to leave evidence lying around. But he spends ten times what he earns. That's the kind of thing that put Capone in prison, right?"

"Maybe you should be talking to the IRS."

"His man about town, Serious Bobby. All of a sudden he turns up as an "consultant" at the Hamm Brewery. His previous job was gangster bag man. Funny how he was chosen to run the ransom money. Get him in the back room and step on his toes."

"For the record," said Heater, "we don't do that kind of thing."

"Who are you kidding?"

"Keep going," said Heater.

"The snatch team was Fred Barker, Alvin Karpis, Doc Barker. The ransom note writer was Shotgun George Ziegler, once employed by Al Capone and lately a resident at White Bear Lake. Ziegler had a couple of hangers on, an old guy named Fitz and tubercular skeleton named Monty."

"Where did they hold Hamm?"

"Illinois. Somewhere in Illinois. Somewhere east of Rockford and west of the lake."

"Obviously west of the lake."

"Half hour or more east of Rockford on crappy roads."

"How do you know this?"

"Can't say," I said. "Small town, I think. Home to a railroad yard, lots of locomotive noises, whistles, bells."

"Can't give me an address?"

"Wish I could."

Heater stroked his chin, nicotine-stained finger over dark mustache, brown eyes hooded.

"Who set it up?" he asked. "Who's the finger man?"

"That information will come to you," I said, "via telegram from a happily employed man in Havana."

"Give me something I can corroborate."

"Try 204 Vernon," said Janie.

"I didn't know this was a three way conversation," said Heater.

"You know now," I said.

"Two days after Hamm came home," Janie said, "the cops took my tip and raided 204 Vernon. Actually, Mister Heater, the cops were afraid to go in. They milled around. They were afraid of the big bad machine-gun gang. The owner showed up and the cops boosted him through the windows, rather than go in themselves. That's what kind of shameful police force we have. The owner found his tenants had fled. The cops came in and raided, all right. They raided the refrigerator for beer and sandwiches. A few days later they got around to dusting for fingerprints, and all they found was their own."

"All right," said Heater. "My agency was distracted. We had this bad, bad thing in Kansas City. Our own men were killed. Edgar was beside himself. He still is."

"Well now," Janie lectured him, "you can catch up. The landlord at 204 Vernon knows now who he rented to: Fred Barker."

"Which doesn't make Barker a kidnapper."

"Fred Barker skipped town hours after Hamm was released. You can bring him in as a suspect, can't you?"

"Where is he?"

Janie gave a helpless shrug and looked at me.

"At full force," Heater said, "the Division of Investigation has got six field agents in Minnesota. We're working with a police department that actively opposes us. There's a hundred million people milling about this great nation of ours. I can't just snap my fingers and find this one particular bad actor."

"Reno," I said. "I heard they're in Reno."

"You heard."

"A rumor," I said.

"You know how many rumors I hear during a day's work?"
He looked at his watch.

"Ultimately," I said, "it all leads back to the finger man.
Everybody in town knows his name."

"And he's the same man," Janie said, "who picked up the
Burned Ladies last spring, on the night they were murdered."

"We got a package for you Heater," I said. "Gift wrapped with a
nice big bow on it. J. Edgar's going to throw you a bear hug when
you bring this in. You'll solve the Hamm snatch and the Saint
Valentines shootout and the Burned Ladies all at once. You're
going to jump two pay grades and get transferred to an easy job in
Washington. I want Havana, she wants the story for the detective
mags."

Heater used a handkerchief to wipe his fogged windshield.

"Next time," he said, "no girl reporters."

"She's a mother, not a girl. And there will certainly be a next
time, Heater, because you'll find out we're giving it to you straight."

He rolled up the window and drove off, leaving behind a
gagging, blue exhaust.

CHAPTER TWENTY SEVEN

I lived quiet in my dungeon. When I could shake my paranoia, it was a pleasant summer. I spent a lot of time on the roof patio with the dogs, barbecuing, loafing, reading newspapers and magazines. I'd watch the sun light up the Cathedral's stained glass windows. When I was on the roof, no assassins could approach unseen.

My luck with the horses was up and down. My expenses were few. I had a phone installed just so Agent Heater could call me.

He didn't.

I didn't want people to know I was in town, so the only gangster gossip I heard came from Janie. She visited the newsroom twice a week to relieve the boredom of caring for a baby and to hear the latest rumors. She told me that the Swede trial had been dumped when witnesses began to falter, and Swede's alibi held up. Some rumors now had Swede leaving town for Chicago. Others said he'd been seen around Saint Paul. Nobody seemed to know for sure.

Every once in a while, I visited my old apartment to help Janie on her expose. It might, we realized, be turning into a book. I read her beginning pages, and we talked. Janie said that freelance writing was the ideal occupation for a new mother, since she could work whenever the baby slept.

I reminded her I was never to be named as the main source for her story. Her book would begin with the murders of Sadie and Rose in the spring of 1932, cover the North American heist, the deadly Third Northwestern robbery, and would end with the

Hamm kidnapping. The bomb it dropped was to recognize the Barker-Karpis gang as culprits in all those crimes, with the help of their friends in the Saint Paul police.

If she sold the book, she planned to move to New York, for her own safety. She had raised her sights from the detective mags, and was aiming respectable, for Harper's, the Atlantic, or the New Yorker, using the magazines as bait for a book deal. She was writing patiently to New York, seeking an agent.

On a late summer Sunday I grilled hamburgers and sweet corn on the rooftop, and we enjoyed lunch under a red-striped beach umbrella. For desert, she made sweet milky iced coffee. Dane, dressed only in a diaper, and drunk on baby formula, snoozed under the shade of that umbrella.

A sweaty Janie sat back and waved away a mosquito.

"Ralph Tallerico," she said, and across the table handed me a police report. It was rubber stamped in red: HOMICIDE.

"Do you have a theory?" she asked.

"On what?"

"Who killed him and why?"

I shrugged.

She tapped the police report.

"Your friend Myrtle was there."

"Yup," I said.

"What's happened to her?"

"She blew town," I said.

Jane threw me a skeptical look. "Have you heard from her?"

"No."

"Then how do you know she's alive?"

"I just know."

"How?"

"I would have heard if anything had happened to her."

"Do you have any idea where she took off to?"

"Chicago."

"Chicago?" Janie said. "Why, that doesn't make any sense." She grabbed the report and re-read it. "Didn't she tell the police that Tallerico's killers were Italians from Chicago?"

"I guess."

"Was it one of those Chicago thugs who tried to choke the life out of her? Doesn't it seem strange that she would pick up and go there?"

She sipped coffee.

"You know what I think?" she said. "I think Myrtle might have set Tallerico up. That's why she took off."

"Bad theory," I said.

"Why?"

"Because I know who killed Tallerico and Myrtle had nothing to do with it. She was an innocent bystander. Tallerico was trying to force Myrtle to put one of her friends on the spot. She refused. He tried to strangle her. That's my theory."

"Who shot him?"

"I told you at the beginning, I can't tell you everything."

"You also promised not to lie."

"I'm not lying. Rico was a murderer, and got gangland justice, and just leave it at that, Janie, a mystery. It had nothing to do with Barker and Karpis."

She cleared her throat.

"You're not worried about Myrtle?"

"She can take care of herself, believe me. Look, she's a mixed up woman whose heart got broken and never healed. She was raised by a brute, and finally found herself a gentle man. But he was a con man who got slammed into prison and she started lifting furs to make a living. That's Myrtle. That's all."

"Okay, back to the Hamm kidnapping."

Although there was no one else near, she whispered: "Jack Peifer. Motivation?"

"Shake down the Hamm brewery for years to come. There are

very few breweries that survived the last 13 years. Prohibition cleared the battlefield. Do you know how much cash that operation will throw off?"

"What I don't get is the Barker gang, you know, who do they work for, Harry or Jack?"

"It's a contest," I said. "Like a boxing match. Harry versus Jack for champion of Saint Paul. They compete by dreaming up jobs for the Barker-Karpis Gang to pull. Harry set them up a Minneapolis bank job, Jack counterpunched with a snatch job. Barker-Karpis, they're professional. They're a rarity. Fred's the ruthless killer, Karpis has the brains. They do as they please, leave bodies behind, and get away every time."

Janie sat back and tapped her pencil.

"Focus," she said.

"Big Ryan, he's the hub of the wheel, master of The Deal. None of it works unless he can offer police protection. Whether the mastermind is Harry or Jack, Big Ryan is the security guard."

She chewed her pencil.

"I'll have to talk to him."

"Big Ryan? He may carry a badge but he's a dangerous gangster. I'd talk to him last, when I had a book deal and was ready to skip town. Or maybe wait until you settle in New York and call from there."

She looked off at the Cathedral.

"Maybe," she said, and gathered her manuscript into a leather briefcase. "New York. It seems so far, far away."

That meeting with Janie was on a Saturday, and on Sunday morning, the newspapers made me sick.

The Department of Justice in Chicago, led by some bastard named Melvin Purvis, announced to the press that they had made an arrest in the Hamm kidnapping. Their suspect was Roger Touhy, Chicago bootlegger and main rival to Capone's Outfit.

Arrested along with him were several henchmen, none of whose names I recognized. The G-men in Chicago promised "severe" interrogation to solve the Hamm kidnapping.

But I knew for certain that neither Roger Touhy, nor any of his henchmen, had even a remote connection to the Hamm kidnapping.

I called Agent Roland Heater

"I'm sorry," said a female, "Mister Heater is not in, but I can take a message."

I threw the phone against the wall.

When I picked it up it had no dial tone.

I had paranoid visions of Swede watching my car, so I slouched up Selby, hopped a streetcar, got off at Snelling and took another streetcar to a drugstore near Macalester College. From its phone booth I called Heater.

Not in.

I walked around the block of grocery stores, dry cleaners, soda fountains, taverns, hardware stores. These were the places Janie had canvassed to build her case against the Barker-Karpis gang at 204 Vernon. I couldn't believe, I couldn't work out, how it was possible for the G-men to arrest the wrong gang. On what evidence?

I sat on a bench along with two gossiping college girls waiting for a streetcar. I cursed myself for always doing things the easy way. I should have taken the Swede out when I had the chance. Havana might as well be on the moon now.

From payphones near campus I called Heater and called him and called him. Finally after suppertime, I took the streetcar down to the Federal Building, got off at Rice Park, and there saw his window lit up. I slipped in to the side door and ran up the stairs of the nearly empty building, footsteps echoing. I pounded on the clouded door that said U.S. Department of Justice and after a while Heater answered.

"What the hell!" I said.

Finger to his lips, he invited me in. We were alone in the steno room. A teletype clattered as the only noise.

"What happened?"

"Keep your voice down," Heater said.

"What the hell?"

He held his hands out as if to calm the waves of anxiety rolling off me.

"It's Chicago's case now."

"What does that mean?"

"Purvis figures he's got the bad guys."

"He does not have the bad guys."

"Purvis enjoys the confidence of the Director," Heater said. "Apparently, I do not. It's Chicago's case now. They're behind it. They've lined up their own prosecutors. They'll put on the show."

"But they've got the wrong guys."

"So you say."

"I know."

Heater shrugged. "I'm out, Purvis is in. Look, I don't know what they have, but it must be pretty good evidence if..."

He sat on the stenographer's desk.

"Oh, hell, Powers, it's just you and me here. They took Mister Hamm down to Chicago. In an airplane. He had a look at these guys. He fingered them. It's not a shabby case if they have the victim's ID."

"He's mistaken. Witnesses make mistakes."

Heater shook his head, maybe in disgust, maybe in sympathy.

"We've got our agents down there building a case. We've got Chicago police helping us."

"What about Havana?" I asked.

"You gave me bad dope."

"I've got to get out of town," I said.

"I can't get you a federal favor unless your information leads to an arrest. In this case, it did not. However sincere you appear to be,

Powers, you must be simply mistaken."

"I typed the ransom notes!" I shouted.

Heater smiled.

"Corona pica."

"Sure, Powers. Or maybe that's a lucky guess. Maybe you're trying to pull one over on Your Federal Government, and get a free ride to Havana." He patted me on the back. "People love to confess to the splashy crimes," he said.

He held open the door. "Do go gently into that good night, Powers."

"Imperative," I reminded him. "That word, crossed out in the ransom note."

Heater looked at me, pity in his dark eyes.

"We'll be in touch," he said.

The week the Touhy Gang was charged with the Hamm Kidnapping, Janie went into a dark funk. Her dreams of authorship were trashed, her confidence shaken. Her theories, and mine, about the Barker-Karpis Gang were looking wrong. She fed, changed and cuddled Dane, she drank a lot of coffee, she developed a sudden, odd fascination with cheap Hollywood magazines. She stopped typing her manuscript. She rarely left the apartment. She quit visiting the Daily News, where she felt unwelcome, even by her old friends.

I sometimes saw Chaz come to visit Janie and the baby. Not that he was the greatest husband material, but Janie needed somebody, almost anybody right now. She had dedicated so much time to work that she'd never developed much of a social life. The men in the newsroom made dirty jokes about her now, I was sure, and the women were embarrassed for her.

With my escape routes cut off, to Havana and Eagle River, I, too, spent a lot of time in my apartment. Being in the basement with only one door and two barred windows, it was just the bunker

I needed if it came to a gun fight. I had no idea what Swede Fanlund was up to and was afraid to ask around. I followed the preparations for the Touhy trial strictly through the newspapers. I didn't expect a call from Heater. He was too savvy to stand on the tracks in front of a federal locomotive. The Touhy gang had been hustled to Saint Paul and were sweating it out in the Ramsey County jail. The Barker-Karpis Gang was blowing the ransom in Reno.

I had one last play in this town. There was a chance the justice system would actually work, and the Touhy gang would be judged not guilty. If so, Heater would be sent scrambling, and might be desperate enough to renew Havana talks with me.

However, Havana had broken out into political riots. It was so crazy in Havana that August that the United States sent gunboats to the harbor. Marines landed to protect Americans. Bombs were going off all over Havana. The rooftops were full of snipers. Every day, it seemed, another rival militia claimed to be in charge. I read this news with the contradictory notions that I had missed my chance and that my life had been spared by Fate.

William Hamm's apparent identification of the Touhy gang mystified me. Newspapers offered varying speculations on the strength of the case: One day the prosecution of Touhy was first-round knockout. The next day the case was in tatters. The way I figured it, witness identifications were often shaky. People made their IDs under pressure from prosecutors and cops. After all, honest witnesses had mistakenly identified Swede as being among the robbers at the Third Northwest.

So wary and alone, except for visits upstairs to Dane and Janie, I waited for the trial, scheduled for November. Depending on what happened, well, if Havana was in full revolution I might give Key West a try.

I don't know how Swede got hold of me, but it wouldn't have

been that hard. I usually parked my Essex two blocks up Selby, on the other side of the Cathedral. A check at Herb's Garage would have revealed what kind of car I drove. I had lived in this apartment building for more than ten years. Neighbors knew me as the divorced fella who walked two dogs, one black and one white. Fanlund could have been simply cruising the neighborhood and seen me. At any rate it didn't matter, because there he was, a week after Labor Day, standing on the sidewalk between me and my basement apartment. He wore a light trench coat, fedora, shiny shoes. He kept his hands in his trench-coat pockets.

"Well, well, well," he said. "Shaky Powers."

The dogs scrabbled into a defensive position and Snowflake bared his teeth.

"Swede Fanlund," I said.

"I've been looking for you," he said.

"Well, you found me," I said.

I was not carrying a weapon, to my immediate regret.

"I'm happy to bump into you," Swede said. "We got a score to settle."

"Oh do we?"

"When you leave a man for dead in a frozen alley, you'd better hope he dies."

He pulled his right hand out of his pocket, the middle and ring fingers just ugly stumps.

"I still feel 'em," he said. "Even though they're not there."

"Look, Swede…"

"I heard you was at the Plantation the night Rico died. I would have been there to buy you two a drink, except I was locked up. Shame isn't it. Somebody set me up. Otherwise…"

He shoved me with that mutilated hand.

"Who set me up, Powers?"

I didn't know what to do. I might try a sucker punch but surely he was armed.

"Just toying with you, Powers. I think you owe me. What do you think? I think I deserve something out of you, Powers. Some kind of payback. I hear there's a reporter going around asking questions about me. A kid, a little girl, working for the Daily News."

"I don't know where you get your information, Swede, but it stinks."

I stopped myself from saying Janie no longer worked at the Daily News. The connection to the newspaper may have made Swede reluctant to target her.

"My information stinks?" he said. "Smells all right to me. Nobody wants to cross the Daily News, they can bring a lot of unwanted attention. But I don't like this girl poking into my business and neither should you. You're on borrowed time, Powers."

"We all are," I said.

"So borrow a little more," he said, "and get this bitch off my case."

I bit my tongue.

"I could use you, Powers."

"No you can't, Swede."

"You've been seen at the Federal Building. Some people would find that interesting. Could be your dogs are going to need a new master."

He crouched, and Snowflake backed away from his touch.

Hula Girl raised her lips in a snarl.

"Good doggies," he said. "Get that reporter girl off me, and we'll see how it goes for you. Rest easy, Powers. If anything bad happens to you, I'll take care of your dogs."

CHAPTER TWENTY EIGHT

"You must realize he knows where you live, Janie, and you know what he did to Sadie and Rose."

She flashed me an angry look. "Who told him, that's what I want to know?"

"Could be anybody. Anybody you talked to. Anybody you interviewed."

"The cops," she said.

"That was our theory on Sadie and Rose. The cops leaked on them too. Swede doesn't know you're on the outs with the Daily News, but he'll find out. Once he realizes you don't have the protection of the Daily News, you're disposable."

I walked into her bedroom, my former bedroom, and yanked from her closet a straw suitcase. I lay it flopped open on the dark wool bedspread.

"Pack," I said. "You're getting out of town."

"And where exactly am I going?"

"Back to what's that town? Back to your parents."

In the living room, Dane gasped in his crib. Janie looked toward him, then back at me.

"Mick, I haven't been there since Christmas."

"They don't know?"

Her face flushed, she shook her head.

"They'd be so disappointed in me."

She walked to the bedroom windows, looked out, anything to

hide the emotions welling up out of her heart.

"They sent me through college," she said. "They were so proud."

"Well, you have to tell them sometime."

"Of course," she said, and sniffled. "Just not now."

"Other relatives, or maybe friends, in Wisconsin you could stay with?"

"Move in on somebody with a baby?"

"I'm grasping at anything, Janie. How about Chaz?"

She walked to the dresser, nervously fumbled with a rosy pink jewelry box.

"His mother…" she hesitated. "She can be a problem. Do I have to come out and say it?"

"I'm not a mind reader."

"He's not ready for fatherhood right now."

"Does he love you?"

She nodded. She looked at herself in the mirror and then said with certainty: "He does. He's hardly more than a boy, but I believe he does love me. But he's never had a good job, and he doesn't have any job now. We've only known each other for three months. He can't take on an instant wife and baby."

"I'm the caretaker of a home," I said. "Deep in the woods of Wisconsin. Hours and hours from here. It's a beautiful home, right on a quiet lake, surrounded by 160 acres of land that's in my family. It's owned by my cousin Cindy, who's sick and lives in Milwaukee. All summer this home was occupied by a missionary family. Just this week, they've gone back to Africa. Why don't you and Chaz take a vacation there, together, spend some time getting to know each other, just you, him and the baby."

"We can't just…"

"A nice September vacation. This is the loveliest time of year up there. No tourists, no mosquitoes, the lakes are still warm. Stay a couple of weeks and let things settle down here."

Janie walked to Dane's crib and looked down at his sleeping innocence. Letters of the alphabet, painted bright, and carved from wood, were strung across the crib rails. Janie spun those letters as she stared at her child.

"We'll see," she murmured, utterly focused on the baby. "Let me talk to Chaz."

That evening I drank beer with Billy McAmbly. He had sworn off taverns. They charged too much, and at taverns, cops were often challenged by drunks. Billy's beer marathons were restricted now to office, backyard, and kitchen.

So we drank in the backyard. A pit fire brightened, but hardly warmed, the October night. We ate fire-roasted hot dogs and drank Altwasser, both sale items at Essenmeyers. Billy was half in uniform, wearing cop boots and striped trousers. His gut was busting out of his plaid hunting shirt.

"I feel bad about the kid reporter, that's all," I said, and crushed an empty Altwasser can. "I thought you hated canned beer?"

"Cheaper now by the case," he said.

"She staked her reputation on the dope I gave her," I said. "It wasn't wrong, Billy."

"I know very well it wasn't wrong."

"I cannot put it together," I said. "The G-men added two and two and got five. The Touhy gang doesn't even know where Minnesota is."

"It's broken, the ladder of justice, every rung. You can hardly survive in this damn town unless you realize that."

He threw his head back for a look at the crystal stars.

"Do you believe there's men on Mars, Mickey?"

I wiped a dab of mustard off my white shirt.

"Probably not."

"Me neither," said Billy.

"But I'm a horseplayer."

"What does that mean?"

"There are no sure things, Billy. Might be little green men up there, sitting around a wood fire, drinking beer made of the purest Mars water."

The McAmbly children were inside the house, listening to Amos and Andy. The radio was so loud we could hear it through the slammed shut windows.

"Turn it down!" shouted Billy.

They couldn't hear him.

"They'll end up with hearing aids, all of them."

"Well I've got to solve," I said, "my Swede problem."

With a steel opener, Billy punctured a can of Altwasser and got sprayed. He licked his dripping hand and said: "Strategy?"

"I can run," I said. "But Florida, Arizona and Chicago are out. Too many gangsters in all those places."

"Check," said Billy.

"Gunfight at high noon, that won't work. He's too tough, he's too wary, he's survived Chicago, he's walked down all the dark alleys."

"Believe that," said Billy.

"I could hire a couple of brutes to do my dirty work."

Billy took a long, loud sip from the punctured can. Over in the rail yard, a train made a booming coupling that rippled down a line of freight cars.

"Why aren't you dead already?" Billy said. "Answer me that."

"Probably because Swede can't be sure that I don't have a halo from Harry. He's asked around, he's still not sure, and if he wastes one of Harry's men, he'll never work again. At best. And at worst…" I waggled my hand.

"So, buy a halo."

"It's fifty a month. Either that or I go back to doing Harry favors, and you know where that leads."

"How about your buddy Sam? Can't he plead your case with

Jack?"

"Jack's not the best man for protection. Even so, he too would want favors in return. You either pay off or run favors. Nothing's free in this town, Billy. You step off the sidewalk, and you're up to your knees in the mud. It ain't like the old days. Bootleg money's dried up. Used to be a bag man could pay his rent in this town, but it ain't the innocent days anymore."

"I'll take care of Swede for a thousand bucks," said Billy.

I laughed.

"I'm serious," he said. "I've got kids to feed, and it takes me almost a year to earn a grand."

He looked over his shoulder at the bright lit windows of the house, maybe worried that the children might overhear. In a lower voice he said: "Swede's got it coming anyway."

"I'm not going to put you on the spot, Billy."

"Spot hell," he said. "I've hated the bastard since high school. Dark alley, uniformed cop, a convicted felon, who's going to squawk?"

"I wouldn't think you had it in you, Catholic Billy. You still pray the rosary, right?"

He drank off the beer, tossed the can, hiss, into the dying fire.

"Catholic for the kids," he said. "Strictly for the kids."

"You haven't done anything like this before, have you? Hell, I shouldn't ask."

He shook his head, pulled out a five-cent cigar and lit it. "I'd hate to see you run, Mickey. Running's no good. You're always looking over your shoulder no matter where you go."

He blew smoke rings that danced in the firelight breeze.

"Look at me," he said. "Do I have a nickel in the bank? Do my kids wear anything but hand-me-downs? I've got a model-A Ford that's been overheating all summer, needs a new radiator I can't afford. I want to send the kids to school with the nuns, Brian especially, as wild as that boy is. I kept my hands in my pockets for almost twenty years, as the detectives lived high off bribes."

"I'm couldn't pay a thousand anyway."

"You're trying to chisel me?"

"No I'm saying, a thousand's a fair price but I can't get up the scratch."

"Horses going lame on you?"

"I'm not gambling much Billy."

"There's always the installment plan," suggested Billy.

People say crazy things when they're drunk, and that's how I wrote off Billy's proposal. But I couldn't help thinking about it as I drove back to my apartment that evening. I pulled up a block short in fear of the Swede. After ten minutes of quiet on the dark street, I let myself out and unlocked the trunk. There lay my Remington shot-gun, post-surgery. A fellow at Murray's Rod and Gun had taken nearly a foot off the barrel. That operation wasn't legal, and like so much in this town, had required a bribe.

Sawed-off shotgun concealed in my suit-jacket and clutched under my arm, I stayed as much as possible away from bushes and garages. Turning down a muddy alley, I was drunk alert. Swede Fanlund lurked in every dark spot in my imagination.

The real Swede was sitting on the picnic bench outside my apartment, in the half glare of a streetlamp. My eyes searched for a weapon, but saw none. Swede wore a clean, pressed blue workman's uniform. He was smoking a cigarette, casual, relaxed, like a man without a care.

"Shaky Powers," he said. "Been waiting for you."

I drew my shotgun and pointed it at the muddy ground.

"Oh, I come in peace," he said.

"Speak or get out of my way," I said.

"You don't have the nerve," he said. "For cold blood."

"What do you want, Swede?"

"Congratulations," he said. "You know Union Depot is

watched, don't you? The red-haired reporter, I see she got her baby out of town. She took a big lug along for the ride. That was wise, very wise."

Mrs. Holy Reardon peeked past the window shade. For a moment I prayed she would call the cops, but then came to my senses. What was I thinking? This was Saint Paul.

"So Powers, you done good, getting that nosy bitch out of town. Now why don't we come to a gentleman's agreement?"

"What are we agreeing on?"

"Last winter, some bastard knocked me out in an alley…"

"I heard you slipped."

"As I was saying, knocked me out in an alley and I lost two fingers to frostbite. Ever have frostbite Powers? Very painful. Even after the docs saw off your fingers."

"Sorry, Swede," I said, despite myself.

He laughed.

"Hospital bill, lost income, eight hundred dollars," he said. "Fair is fair. I'm only asking for what I deserve. There's gotta be justice in this world."

Our eyes met, fierce.

"Oh I see," I said. "This is a shakedown."

"I look at it more like an insurance settlement. Look, you hustled the girl reporter out of town, I appreciate that, I owe you for that. You done good, you deserve a break. Let's call it seven hundred, and we're even. No more hard feelings."

He stuck that mutilated hand at me, wanting a handshake.

I let it hang in the air.

He shrugged. He stood up from that picnic bench and bowed, cigarette bobbing in his lips.

"We've got us a simple, fair financial settlement. Think it over, Mick. I give you three days. Which is more of a chance than you gave me, when you left me for dead."

I pointed the shotgun at him.

Swede smiled. "Hey, I don't blame you. If I was you I would have finished me off back in that alley. You had a good poker hand. You didn't have the balls to play it."

"Out of my way," I said.

"As you wish."

Acting gallant, Sir Swede backed into the shadows.

I walked backward down the steps to my apartment, expecting gunfire from the shadows, but as I opened the door I realized no shootout was coming. My dogs leaped up on me. I lay the shotgun on the coffee table and gave them both love rubs. But my hands were trembling.

I knew Swede's game now, I knew why I wasn't dead. He intended to shake me down for every dime I had, and only then dump my corpse in the river.

CHAPTER TWENTY NINE

The Touhy Gang came to trial in Saint Paul just as Americans turned vigilante in response to kidnappings. It had been a more than a year since the Lindbergh baby had been found dead, with no suspect credibly charged. Kidnapping that year was like the measles. Some of the cases were big, the victims rich, like this Oklahoma oilman Urschel. He'd been snatched by Machine Gun Kelly. But most of the kidnappings were pulled off by copycat amateurs. They targeted even college students and children, with chump change demanded as ransom.

The G-men, newly empowered by federal kidnapping laws, arrested Machine Gun Kelly. They convicted him in a quick, clean trial that was the Lindbergh Law's first success. The Feds sent him to Alcatraz, the newly opened draconian prison.

But nothing seemed to stop the kidnappings. In San Jose, California, the son of a popular merchant was kidnapped, and a mob broke into the county jail and lynched two suspects.

That sort of madness had spread to Saint Paul by November, when the Touhy gang went to trial. Angry crowds gathered downtown, day and night. Inspired by the San Jose vigilantes, the night crowds brought deer rifles, rope and torches. Some vigilantes pitched rough tents in Rice Park. One construction worker drove a bulldozer down Market Street, threatening to crash the jail. Furious citizens began mailing neckties to Roger Touhy, an invitation to hang himself in jail.

It took every cop and deputy in town to stop the lynch mob. Even out-of-shape Billy McAmbly was recruited for the police redoubt. It was assembled out of lumber and sandbags on the library steps overlooking Rice Park. The crowd taunted and stoned the cops, screaming for blood: *Let us have 'em!*

Even the federal government was intimidated. They sent in extra marshals, and switched the Touhy trial from the federal building to the Ramsey County Courthouse, which could be reached from the jail via underground tunnel.

After two riotous days of the Touhy trial, my just-repaired home phone rang with a call from Sam Tanaka, inviting me to drive to the Hollyhocks.

It was a Saturday, and with the trial on weekend break, Saint Paul had become a ghost town. Sixty thousand people were crammed lunatic in a stadium watching the Badger-Gopher football game. Everybody else, it seemed, was at home or in a beer hall listening to the game on the radio.

Despite the easy drive, I was squirming with worries. This certainly wasn't an execution in the making, not with Sam involved, but Jack had dreamed up some use for me now. Whatever it was, I wouldn't be able to say no. Had the trial of the Touhy gang emboldened him? Did he believe he was untouchable now? Did he have another kidnapping in mind? If so, I concluded, I would gather Snowflake and Hula Girl, point my Essex south, and never return.

Sam was in his favorite place, the garage, flushing the radiator of Jack's olive-green Packard, getting it ready for winter. The Gophers-Badger game, beamed on WCCO, rattled the speakers of his humble radio. After wiping his hands with a rough cloth, Sam extended me a soiled hand of friendship.

He sighed, hands on hips, and stared at the mansion where his master served up steaks, gin and games of chance.

"He is not himself," Sam said, and shook his head. "Perhaps we should go for a walk."

We crossed Mississippi Boulevard where it overlooked the river. A path of half-frozen earth wound among boulders, fallen leaves and frost-killed plants. Using rocky footholds here and there, we reached the sandy beach. Sam wore a leather jacket, and removed it, overheated on this mild and sunny day. We had the river beach to ourselves. We sat on the trunk of a fallen tree that, in the next flood, would be taken by the river.

"The Master," Sam said, "gets himself into fixes, have you noticed?"

"Yeah, maybe."

"He builds twisting curves into the track-bed, and is surprised when the train goes off the rails."

"Speak plain, Sam."

"For instance. He married a beauty queen half his age. She might have married any number of legitimate, wealthy, athletic men. A lawyer, perhaps, or a young banker. Or an older, wealthy man, one of the Alt cousins, perhaps, or the Bremers. Jack built a nightclub business that attracts just such men. And then he fumes and drinks in jealousy, because the men his casino attracts hover around his wife."

He took off his driver's cap, folded it into his back pocket.

"You're going bald," I said.

He ran his hand over his hair.

"Here is a man who shot himself in the privates, remember. A self-inflicted wound. I could site other instances where the Master has caused his own troubles, but some things are better unmentioned. You're a survivor, Mick. You've been playing the game a long time."

"In our world, there's only two things that matter," I said. "Making money and staying out of jail."

"More than two things," Sam said. "There is family, and there is honor."

"Honor. Yes, honor, and speaking of honor, Swede Fanlund wants to bleed me of every dime, and then snuff me. I'm not going down that road, Sam. If I'm going to go, I'll go honorably, man to man. I'm not going to try to buy my way out. It wouldn't work anyway."

Sam grunted.

I weaseled. "You could help me, though, Sam. You could put out the word that I'm Jack's nephew."

"Even when you aren't?" His one eyebrow was raised. "Too dangerous."

He skimmed a rock on the river. It flew like a bird, like a bird catching a fish and bounding away. And then it sank. Like the stone that it was.

Sam approached the remains of a beach fire, kicked idly at it with his high polished boots.

"Feed the feds," Sam suggested, hands in the pockets of his tweed trousers.

"I tried that, Sam."

"What do you mean, tried?" Sam asked.

I realized what I had admitted, and to whom. Now that I had let it out, I tried to finesse it.

"Oh, you know, I just, they tried to shake me out, one time, that's all. And I felt them out, too, you know, just to see what kind of deal they offer."

"In return for what?"

"Just in theory, Sam."

He walked away from me, up the beach. I kept up.

He said over his shoulder: "What did they want from you?"

"Cars, you know, crossing state lines. That's all they're interested in. Well, okay, kidnapping nowadays, but who's in the stolen auto racket, that's what they were probing and I said you know, what if I fill you in? And they made a lot of noise about helping your country, and it was a Depression and we needed patriots to help the government."

"I don't believe you, Powers."

I sighed. "Feed them who, Sam? Who should I feed the G-men?"

"Harry."

"Feed them Harry?"

"Right."

I stuttered.

He said: "I know you have been with the G-men, Powers."

"I admitted that."

"The Touhy case is a sham, we all know. When their case goes sour, the G-men will reopen their pitiful investigation,. When that happens they should be looking at Harry."

"So you want me to go in there and poison the well?"

"Convince them that Harry is the source of all evil, and in particular, that he's the finger-man in the Hamm kidnapping."

"That would be a big favor to Jack, wouldn't it?"

Sam nodded.

"A very big favor," I said. "Risky. If Harry found out, I'd be dead the next morning. You realize that. So if I did Jack this tremendous and dangerous favor, what is he offering as a reward?"

"Swede will be neutralized."

"So if I make the G-men suspicious of Harry, Jack will take care of Swede?"

Sam heaved himself up on a boulder, began swinging his legs over burbling water.

"This water, Mick, that's passing under my feet? Soon it will be in Saint Louis and the next day it reaches New Orleans. Then it goes out to sea. Once it reaches the sea it will be too late."

"To be clear, Sam, you want me to point the Feds at Harry if they reopen the Hamm case."

"This river has been carving this canyon for a million years,"

Sam said. "But men, we have very little time allotted to us. This misdirection with the Department of Justice is the one thing you can offer Jack. He doesn't want your money…"

"Not that I have any."

"As I see it, you are out of options, Mick."

He walked toward the stony cliff. In a natural rock cave, kids had been writing on the walls for years in chalk and paint. Their artwork nearly covered an official, stenciled sign, in white paint, that said: NO FIRES. We stood in the shallow dark cave and looked out at the muddy rushing river.

"Certain things make sense to me now, Sam."

"Enlighten me."

"Maybe you know, and maybe you don't, but the kidnappers used a cottage out at White Bear Lake to plan the Hamm snatch."

"Agreed."

"I'm the one who rented it. Jack sent me on that errand."

He shrugged. "Perhaps."

"He didn't send you because you're too valuable to him. I was disposable. And I still am."

"In the end, we all are disposable."

"So if I talk to the Feds about that White Bear Lake cottage, they'll discover that I rented it from the owner."

"Odds are great they never will," said Sam.

"But if they do it sends me to Leavenworth."

"There is only one witness to your rental. We have located that man and made him promises. Even if he weakens and bears witness against you, you can say that you rented the cottage at Harry's direction. Look, the federals want a Hamm finger man. They don't care how they get him, or even whether he's guilty. They only want a conviction. If the G-men cared about lying witnesses, the Touhy boys would not be on trial."

"I don't want to go to any prison for any length of time."

"If you do Jack this favor, it's likely the G-men will never connect you to the case. They have not demonstrated a stunning competence, have they? But if by longshot chance they charge you, you will have the best legal representation. You will be out on bond the same day. Jack has many friends among the judges. He knows how to steer a case. Come to the Hollyhocks any night, and you will see those judges. They rarely lose at our tables. The odds are always tilted in their favor."

"Dangerous," I said. "Risky for me."

"Not as risky as dodging the Swede."

"If I turn rat on Harry…"

"Mick, we will get you out on bond. You will take up residence in some sunny, warm place of your choosing, with enough cash to relax for quite a while."

"Really?"

"In addition, the Swede will be neutralized. We've been friends a long time, Mick. This is the best deal you will ever be offered."

He put an arm around my shoulder.

"We can both get out of this cave," he said, "you toward the tropics, and me toward the rising sun."

CHAPTER THIRTY

That evening, I called my cousin Cindy's phone out at Eagle River.

Janie answered.

"Just checking," I said into the mouthpiece. "How's it going?"

"A little chilly," she said.

Misunderstanding that, I gave her directions on finding a stash of firewood.

"Well, not that kind of chilly," she said.

"Oh," I said.

"We'll work it out," she said, in a whisper. "I can't talk right now. I'll call you."

I had barely hung up the phone when it rang. This was my sister Mona.

"Guess what the fire marshal told me," she said. "Pain in the ass, I've been calling him every day."

"Total loss?" I said, "that would be no surprise."

"Nope."

"Come on, Mona, don't make me guess."

"Deliberately," she said. "Set."

"What do you mean?"

"Accelerant," she said. "Probably gasoline. It was soaked in the bushes around the side of the house. It was just a lucky wind that sent the fire racing toward the barn. Otherwise…" I could hear her blow smoke, "we wouldn't be talking, because you…"

"Otherwise, bullshit. Swede Fanlund."

"What are you talking about?"

"Swede Fanlund. Don't bullshit me, Mona. You know. The guy you were playing kissy face with in the Green Lantern."

"Kissy face?"

"Nice choice of men," I said.

"I danced with him. Once. And for your information, Mister Judge and Jury, I went home alone that night."

"Uh-huh."

"And for your further information, he kept asking about you. Wondering how you were doing. Hadn't seen you around town in a while. He was worried about you. He was a friend from back in Sacred Heart, right?"

"That's one way to put it."

Mona hung up on me.

I took the streetcar to the Saint Paul Public Library. Only the riverside entrance was open. The steps that faced Rice Park were barricaded by cops and deputies. Vigilantes, the unemployed, the curious, the thrill-seekers, the half-soused, all milled around a chaotic Rice Park campgrounds. They followed the Touhy trial by listening to the rumors coming out of the courthouse.

With the help of a librarian I found that, according to the Minneapolis Tribune, Swede Fanlund had been released from jail three days before the fire at Eagle River. So he had shagged Myrtle. He had followed her to Union Depot, and maybe onto the train. Or perhaps he had learned her destination from the ticket clerk, and driven to Minoqua. Either way, Swede Fanlund, pyromaniac. And I had blamed Myrtle for the fire.

I sat at a library desk, confused in head and heart. I owed Myrtle an apology. But short of calling every hotel along the Chicago Northwestern Line, I had no hope of finding her. And there was little chance, anyway, that she'd register under her true name. I realized that Swede was determined not just to kill me, but to wear

me down to nothing before he pulled the trigger. I rolled up my
sleeve and looked at that cigarette scar, as deep now as when he
had burned me a quarter-century ago.

A dull roar outside the library windows built to a full-throated
cry of a thousand savages. I stared out the third floor window,
overlooking cops and deputies as people swarmed out of office
buildings, hotels, taverns, cafes and the courthouse itself. In a flash,
Rice Park was overflowing with a riotous mob.

The cops began lobbing tear gas bombs into the crowd. Some
people retreated, some charged the barricade, to be repelled by
nightsticks and rifle butts. A fire-truck in front of the Hotel Saint
Paul began to deploy hoses, two lines of firemen blasting the mob
with water. Banshee screams filled the air. Rocks and sticks flew.
Teargas drifted. Cops in gas masks, riding horses, appeared like a
panicked cavalry from behind the Wilder Charity Building. German
Shepherds in the canine unit, held fast on the steps of the Federal
Building, howled for blood. A motorcycle cop crashed into a fire
hydrant, and went over sideways. Some in the mob helped him to
his jackbooted feet.

I sneaked out the riverside entrance. A man sweating in a parka,
goggle eyes behind thick lenses, stopped me to say: "Did you hear?
Not guilty!"

I heard. I heard again and again as I rushed uphill toward my
basement bunker. There I hid in the dark with the dogs. My life
was now reduced to zero options. The Hamm kidnapping
investigation would be reopened. The G-men would eventually
trace it all back to rental of that cottage in White Bear Lake. One
way or the other, I would be on the spot. The Feds would work me
for a plea deal. Unless I lied, unless I set up Harry and took the
focus off Jack, Swede would be waiting in the dark for me.

Shaky Powers.

My enemy the Swede had named me well.

As I cowered in my bunker apartment, a taxi pulled up to the lobby doors. All I could see in the dim reflection of headlights was a vague glimpse of trousers and boots alighting. I listened to somebody climb, fainter and fainter, up the stairway. I waited, trying to think clearly. Janie was out in Eagle River. My sister Kelly would never waste money on a cab. Sam would arrive in Jack's Packard. Reilly owned a truck. I could not imagine who was up there. I calmed my riotous dogs with shelled peanuts. It took a couple of minutes for me to catch a normal breath. I grabbed my sawed-off Remington and pushed out into the night, then through the lobby and up the stairs.

The penthouse door to my former apartment was flung open.

I saw a flash of red hair.

"Janie Vetter," I said, out of breath.

She glanced at the shotgun.

"I'm not a burglar, you know."

I closed the door behind me.

"What are you doing here?" I demanded.

"I'm on the lease, remember?"

But I could see what she was doing. Two cardboard boxes and a straw suitcase lay on the living room rug.

"You came back for your things."

"Brilliant observation, Michael."

Despite the cool weather, it was hot in there, her face sweating, the city-side windows cracked open above whistling radiators. On the dining room table lay a canvas basket. I peered in to see Dane, under blue blanket, happily sucking on a detached bottle nipple.

"Where's Chaz?" I asked.

Janie looked at me like a wise schoolteacher answering a dumb boy's question.

"With Mrs. Lax," she said.

"Who's Mrs. Lax?"

"His mother."

"Oh," I said. A dread silence followed.

"So, you're taking the baby and going to … "

"Waunakee," she said.

"Home," I said.

"Until I get my bearings."

She brushed her hair back. I could see the disappointment, worn into what used to be a girl's face.

She looked around. "So I guess you can have your penthouse back, free rent for a month."

I walked to the city windows. It wasn't that I wanted to see the view, I just didn't want to look at Janie right then. I didn't want to share her failed dream. I'd had enough of my own.

"Once I've gathered my things," she said behind me, "I'll be picking up Dane and taking a taxi to Union Depot. And I don't need an armed escort, in case you were thinking …"

"I was thinking one last drink on the roof."

"It's kind of chilly."

"Irish coffee," I said. "It will warm you up, keep you safe on your journey. Don't use the baby as an excuse. You can have one, just one, last drink with me."

I descended four stories and into the dungeon. There the dogs watched as I made two Irish coffees, with genuine smuggled Jameson, cream, and fresh-ground coffee. The idea of moving out of this dungeon, and up to the penthouse, even if temporarily, cheered me. Whatever else happened, my last days in Saint Paul would be lived in style.

Although without Janie. I realized, making those drinks, how much I would miss her energy, youth, optimism and cheer. It felt like I was sending a daughter off to a fate unknown.

I was adding an extra trickle of Jameson to the cups when a clattering auto pulled in front of the barred windows. It took up the spot reserved for the landlord, Mister Holy Reardon. I found a tray for the coffees. I shelled peanuts so the dogs could have a rooftop treat as well.

Mister Holy Reardon mounted the stairs, or so I assumed. But the license plate that nearly touched the window bars was wrong. I had been looking at Holy Reardon's auto for months now, and this wasn't it. I approached the windows with a growing dread. Parked there was a dark Pontiac.

I grabbed the shotgun. I marched bold up the stairs, dogs scrabbling behind. The door of my former penthouse apartment had been flung open. I stalked from room to room. I was calm. A wave of courage had welled up from deep within, and replaced all fear.

But the penthouse was empty. Janie's suitcases stood upright and packed, but that was the only sign of her or Dane.

I climbed the stairway to the trap door and with the butt of that shotgun, pushed it open. The dogs circled Swede Fanlund, barking and snarling. Janie, eyes big, face alarmed, sat in a lawn chair. Under it, protected by her legs, was a squawling, howling Dane.

Swede, between me and Janie, turned to me, hands in his overcoat pockets.

"Away from her, Swede," I ordered.

Swede backed up.

"What did he do to you, Janie?"

"Nothing," she squeaked.

"Good enough," I said. "Keep your hands in your pockets, Fanlund."

The snarling Snowflake nipped at Swede's ankle.

Hands in his overcoat pockets, Swede backed away.

Hula Girl charged him and pulled up short.

Swede eyed a fire escape ladder that dropped down the Cathedral side.

Snowflake made another lunge and Swede's left hand flashed out of his overcoat. He pointed something dark at me but before I knew what it was, my finger twitched.

I was flung backward. The world went pure white and my ears rang as if someone had punched me in the head. Swede Fanlund staggered backward, tottered at the wall, and fell over.

Dogs howled.

A woman screamed, a baby wailed.

I strode to the low brick wall and peered over. There, five stories below, on frozen earth and dead grass, lay the twisted form of a man in an overcoat.

Janie, hands holding her head, appeared at the wall, looked over, and held on to it, dizzy.

"Michael," she said in a low, strangled voice. "Did that just happen?"

I took the shotgun and bounded downstairs to my dungeon. I grabbed my Army .45, and a wad of cash, quickly packed a suitcase, leashed the two dogs, and fired up my Essex. Janie had gone around the side of the building, carrying the basket with Dane in it, to inspect the body of Swede Fanlund. But I didn't need to. I backed out of the parking stall and Janie ran up to the car window.

"I guess I'll see you around, kid," I said. "Give my regards to Crumley and the Bulldog. Tell them anything you want, I don't care. Good luck to you Dane," I said to the baby. "You'll grow up in a better world."

I pulled out of the parking lot, feeling strangely calm about whatever darkness lay ahead. With one last glance at Janie and her baby I drove past the Cathedral, into the maw of downtown, and just squeezed that car down Filben's alley.

I kicked at Filben's office door until it opened, bulled in and flailed in the dark until I found the button that raised Filben's electric garage door. I eased the Essex in, knocking aside a clutter of wrecked slot machines.

I closed the door. I spent the chill night in the back seat of my car. Hula Girl and Snowflake each claimed a spot in the front seat.

I slept like the cold cold dead.

I awoke stiff when the garage door began to clank open. In my imagination Crumley and the Bulldog stood there. Mocking looks distorted their cynical and delighted faces, with Crumley dangling a giant pair of handcuffs.

But no.

Tommy Filben stepped in, with a surprised look that turned into a laugh.

"Whole town's looking for you," he said.

He inspected the door I had kicked in.

"That'll cost fifty bucks," he said.

I let the dogs into the alley and slapped the rear fender of my Essex.

"I came to offer you an advantageous trade," I said. "This beautiful Terraplane for any reliable car you've got."

"With legit plates, I take it."

"Right."

"How about a new driver's license?"

"Do I get to pick the name?"

"Under these circumstances, no. If you want one this morning, you'll have to take from my stockpile, and those by the way, cost a little more."

He held one finger up like a lecturing teacher.

"Crime is expensive."

"How expensive?"

"Well, on top of your trade-in, I'd say two hundred bucks. And forget about the door you so rudely broke down. The door, I'll throw that in."

"Deal," I said, and peeled bills off my roll.

"Here doggies," said Filben at the damaged door. "You ought to consider getting rid of them," he said as the dogs scampered in, looking to me for breakfast. "Everybody in town knows you by those dogs."

I shrugged. "They're going with me, I'm never coming back, Tommy."

"Sure," he said.

"I suppose Cuba is out."

"Cuba is bullets and bombs these days. Christ almighty, it's a crying shame."

"Well," I said. "The USA is a mighty big land."

"So it is. Say, I'm going up to Herb's now, to look over the fleet. I'll be back with your not-so-new car in twenty minutes. You obviously can't be seen in so-called civilization, so…"

"Can you bring coffee and maybe some rolls on the way back?"

"Am I dressed like a butler?"

The phone in his office rang.

"Don't answer that," he said. "It's probably my wife. Nobody important calls at this hour of the morning."

And then he was gone. The phone quit ringing. It was cold in that warehouse and a little warmer in the office, so with the dogs I retreated there.

I sat in Filben's big oak chair, worrying about what kind of jalopy he would return with, and how far it would take me down Federal 12 before it broke down. The dogs, restless and hungry, sniffed the walls for mice.

The phone rang.

I ignored it. I toyed with one of the slot machines that were set up on a long table. The phone kept ringing. It annoyed me to the point that I left the office and lugged my suitcases and weapons out of the Essex. I gave it a final brush-out with a whisk broom, and slammed the door for good on the best car I'd ever own.

I realized the phone had stopped ringing only when it began again.

I marched into the office and commanded the phone to shut up. It did not. I picked up the receiver and gently set it on Filben's desk.

"Hello!" I heard a tinny voice say. "Is someone there?"

A female voice.

"Tommy are you there? Pick up, will ya?"

I recognized that voice.

"Tommy I been calling you since yesterday. I know you're there."

I picked up the receiver.

"Myrtle?"

"Mick?"

After a pause she said: "What are you doing there?"

"I'm in the market for a new car," I said. "Where are you?"

"Wisconsin," she said.

"Wapun?"

"I'm miserable out here," she said.

"Did you see the Professor?"

"What's left of him. There ain't much, Mick. They've unmanned him in there. Where's Tommy?"

"Doing me a favor," I said. "How are you?"

"Lousy," she said.

"Myrtle," I said. "I owe you the biggest apology in the world."

"Yeah? Don't hurt yourself now, apologizing. For what?"

"You didn't start the fire. You didn't burn down the farm. I know who did it and it wasn't you."

That was greeted with absolute silence, except for phone static. Then she hung up.

I was left staring at the receiver.

Waupun, Waupun, how many hotels could be in Waupun? Or maybe she was calling from a drugstore. The call had taken less than three minutes, and it meant nothing that I'd heard no operator come on. She could be at a gas station, a tavern, anywhere.

I made up my mind to at least try, to drive to Waupun. That would take five or six hours. I could make it by dinner time.

I paced the room. Tommy was right about the dogs, they were

recognizable, and I locked them into the little office with me. I fumbled into my jacket for pipe and tobacco. I lit up.

Hula Girl whimpered for breakfast.

Snowflake lay, resigned, muzzle over paws.

I blew smoke, watched it curl to the ceiling.

I replayed and replayed in the movie of my mind, my final moments with Swede Fanlund. It was very bright and silent. Flash flash. He staggered backward. His hat flew off. His face looked as if he had walked into a surprise party, delighted, angry and suspicious all at the same time. I saw no blood. His black automatic pistol fell to the tar roof, and I wondered whether it was still there. Had shotgun pellets, or pure surprise, sent him over the wall?

The phone rang.

It could be the police, I told myself.

I picked the receiver up, lay it on the desk.

"Okay you," Myrtle's voice said.

I put the receiver to my ear.

"Okay, you lousy Irish bastard, put Tommy on this phone."

"He's not here. What do you need him for?"

"Never mind."

"You're calling for money," I said.

"Train fare, if it's any of your business. Blame me for burning up your crappy farm. It shows what you think of me."

"Myrtle, you were drinking heavy. You talked like you had set the fire."

"Yeah?"

"Yeah."

"I don't remember."

"I'm leaving town in about an hour. I'll pick you up before sunset."

"The hell you will."

"Where are you?"

"The Rogers. I'm a little behind in the rent."

"What's the Rogers?"

"A quaint little dump in Beaver Dam."

"I'll be in the lobby by sundown. If you're there, we're going away together, permanent. If you're not there, I'll keep going alone."

Silence.

"So what do you say? You going to be there?"

"Drive over and find out," she said.

And then she hung up.

Tommy showed in two hours with a belching, fuming Chevy coupe, just big enough for two passengers, or one man and two small dogs. He rummaged in his desk and handed me a driver's license made out in the name of Christopher Paul Bacon.

"Chris P. Bacon, get it?"

"So funny I forgot to laugh."

We ventured into the chill alley. Tom slapped me on the back.

"May the road rise to meet you," he said.

"Don't give me that Irish shit."

"May you be parked in Heaven before the Devil knows you need a tank of gas. I filled it up for you, by the way."

"Thanks, Tom, I appreciate all you've done."

I opened the door of the coupe.

"Dogs," I said.

They leaped in, panting and eager for a road trip.

I backed careful and slow out of the alley, and turned on Wabasha, headed south. On the bridge over the Mississippi, I stopped abrupt, yanked the handbrake, and rushed the bridge rail. Over the side went the sawed-off shotgun and the .45 automatic. Plunk, plunk, they disappeared into the river, to lay undiscovered, I hoped, until the Mississippi changed course.

I got back into the coupe and told the dogs: "We'll stop for breakfast, but it's got to be quick. We want to make Beaver Dam by sundown."

Dogs, God bless 'em, rarely talk back. They settled next to each other in the passenger seat, curled up into comma shapes. I zoomed away, the skyline of my hometown in the rearview. I was almost out of the city when a police siren wailed behind me. A red light flashed. I pulled over to the side. I told myself to be calm: I had a clean car, legit plates, a convincing fake ID, money in my wallet to grease a palm.

But it was a Saint Paul cop.

Siren wailing, chasing the wrong man as usual, he sped right past me.

A PREVIEW

MICK POWERS BOOK #4

DEAD
MESSENGER

This preview has not undergone its final editing.

CHAPTER ONE

The week after New Years, the phone calls began. Afraid it might be the sheriff, I didn't pick up.

Being a wanted man preys on your mind, ceaseless. You never know when they'll come for you: just as you finish dinner, in the middle of your restless sleep, when you've just stepped into the bath. I was isolated, deep in the forest that winter, and anyone who motored down the driveway would only be trouble: Burglars, the sheriff, or, worst case, the friends of Swede Fanlund.

So for days, I let the phone ring. It wasn't out of the question, here in rube country, that the sheriff would phone and ask me to turn myself in. The would save him the trouble of driving through snow drifts.

One cloudy, cold afternoon I could stand the ringing no more. "Hello?"

Silence. It was not a hang-up, but I could get no response. After several impatient shouts I slammed the earpiece into its cradle.

I thought of cialing O and asking questions, but the telephone exchange was downtown, next to the jail. Deputies were in the exchange flirting with the operators day and night.

Every day I took the dogs for a long walk in the snow-packed woods. They were enjoying Eagle River, I was not. Snowflake was fluffy, white, and loved to roll in the snowdrifts. Hula Girl, a black miniature Border Collie, amused herself by sniffing mouse trails underneath the snow.

We climbed the hill behind the cottage, me on snowshoes, and stomped into a pine forest. A path followed the single strand of overhead power line, and led to the burned ruins of my aunt Doris's farm. Those ruined acres belonged to my sisters and I now, but weren't worth much, having been torched by Swede Fanlund. Our charred potato farm was almost surrounded by Cousin Cindy's 120 acres of forest, lakefront and swamp.

One mild day, when we returned to the cabin after a walk, I made coffee in a French press and sat with the dogs near the big roaring brick fireplace. I had become quite the reader in my isolation. I'd just finished *The Thin Man* and was beginning Dorothy Sayers' *Murder Must Advertise*. I was imagining London when the phone rang.

I picked it up. I listened without saying anything. Someone was breathing into the other end.

"Hello?"

No answer.

"Who are you? Why are you calling here?"

Nothing. No hang-up, no voice, no more breathing.

I put down the phone, unnerved.

Last summer, in a surge of guilt, I had thrown my weapons into the Mississippi, a decision I now regretted.

On the lake side of the cottage was a porch that doubled as a spare bedroom. I walked into it and stared out the windows and up the snowy driveway. Nobody could drive down it without me hearing the crunching of tires. There were times this winter when nobody could drive down it all, without a snowplow. Still my guilty mind whispered that they would come for me on foot, on snowshoes, on skis through the woods. Swede's men or the sheriff, it didn't matter much anymore. I had lost the means, or even the will, to resist.

This kind of isolation gets to you. Although it was prison I feared, up here I was living in jail of my own, with a view of an ice-bound lake. The radio, the books, the dogs were my only friends. And the radio station, beamed from Rhinelander, came in garbled. I dared not go into town except on grocery and hardware dashes, and only when the stores were busy. I had the urge, somehow, to attend Mass, but didn't want to risk being seen, a stranger in a small congregation. So I visited Saint Peter The Fisherman at off times, lighting a candle for the good departed souls: Mom, Dad, nutty Uncle Joe, cranky Aunt Doris. Since Swede Fanlund's specialty had been arson, I lit one for him too.

The phone woke me the next morning, and the calls came, two or three a day, all week. I answered every time now, sometimes raging into the phone, sometimes silent with contempt, but the caller's routine never varied. Was it a child playing a prank? A lunatic in an asylum? I considered cutting the wire, but that phone, and a trusty Essex Terraplane, were my only connections to the warmer world.

On Tuesday, January 16th, the phone rang all day it seemed, and I let it ring except for that last call, deep into the night.

"Nice of you to think of me," I said. "Call back when you have something to say."

On Wednesday the phone didn't ring at all. That afternoon, I heard a car in the forest, slipping and grinding down the long driveway.

The dogs were howling for blood and my hair stood on end when I saw Swede's blue Pontiac slaloming down the hill. For a spooky moment I believed in ghosts but then realized it must be Swede's friends coming to kill me. I had the instinct to run for the kitchen door, open it, and at least let the dogs escape. But they were both herding dogs, bred to stick with the shepherd, and I rehearsed a plea: Let the dogs live, they've done nothing wrong. I saw in a flash that a gangland death wouldn't be so bad. Clean, efficient, painless. There were rules to our game, and torture was out of bounds.

As the car rolled to a stop in a snowdrift between cottage and lake, I experienced a moment of pure madness. Swede was dead, right? The Gates of Hell had not opened. The laws of physics had not been suspended. My heart was pounding as if that big pale bully, resurrected, might actually step out of the car. The dogs by now were insane with fury.

The Pontiac's passenger door opened and around the long blue hood strode Alvin Karpis.

He wore a brown fedora and a long tweed coat, and his oxfords, polished, disappeared in the snow. I saw no weapon, but that did not ease my panic. Karpis and Swede were connected, although I did not know how deep their fellowship had been.

Karpis mounted the stone stairway.

I had no feelings now. I was watching myself from Heaven, a place of peace and indifference to these ridiculous, puny Earthlings.

I opened the door.

"Well," Karpis said, "aren't you going to invite me in?"

I stepped back. That Pontiac behind him was idling, all doors closed, huffing smoke into the pure piney air. Men were inside that car, but looking over Karpis' shoulder at frosty windows, I could not tell how many.

I stepped back. Uninvited, Karpis unbuttoned his coat. He threw it on the couch, and topped it with his fedora. His outerwear gave the impression of a bank president, but underneath he wore a hunting outfit: plaid shirt and rough wool trousers. He did not seem to be carrying a pistol. He had lost weight since I'd last seen him, in summer. Even then he'd barely weighed 120 pounds.

"Nice," Karpis said, looking around like he was considering buying the place. "Stylish."

Cindy's place was elegant, for a lake cabin. It had hardwood floors in the living room, a big picture window framing Snipe Lake, an impressive brick fireplace, plush furniture, brass floor lamps, and a grand piano.

"They said we'd find you here," said Karpis.

"Who said?"

"Can you put a couple of old friends up until the weekend?"

With Karpis in the house, the dogs had calmed down, circling and sniffing him with reluctant acceptance. I too began to recover my nerve and said:

"Who are these old friends?"

But I knew he meant Fred and Doc Barker.

"You know them all right," Karpis said. "And more important, they know you."

I stammered. "There's only one bedroom," I lied.

"We're hardy," said Karpis. "We'll sleep on the floor."

He peered into the kitchen, then stepped over to the parlor's windows for a view of the snowy backyard. "Powers, I hate to intrude on an old friendship, but we're in a situation."

He unbuttoned his padded shirt, stood in front of the fireplace.

"Nice and warm," he said.

"Well, I came out here to get away," I said. "You know, from things. Peace and quiet. I like that."

"Maybe you were a little quick on the draw," he said. "But I had no use for the Swede."

"I have no idea what you're talking about."

Karpis clapped me on the shoulder. "That's the spirit."

"How many are you and how long do you want to stay?"

Karpis, removing his leather driving gloves, held up four fingers.

"Four. Four of us. Just until the weekend, at most. We'll probably be gone by Friday. We'll take care of the groceries and the booze, and we'll leave money for the house."

He lit a Chesterfield, stepped over to the ashtray, an amber glass dish held up by a brass stand. It was next to Cindy's piano. Upon that piano was a framed photo of a young girl.

"Cute," said Karpis.

"The owner," I said. "Long time ago." Cindy had played a haunting piano before the disease struck her. She's bitter now, and living in a sanitarium in Milwaukee. Angry and proud, she tolerates no visitors. Nobody was to see her in her ruined, crippled state, but remember her always as a beautiful, promising child.

"Powers, don't give me that blank look," Karpis said. "You're a hunted man. We know what it's like. Guys like us stick together or they pick us off one by one."

I began to realize I had nothing to lose by letting them stay. If the state of Minnesota had its way, I'd be locked up for a lifetime at Stillwater. Harboring gangsters wouldn't be the worst of my crimes. Like most people who knew him, I had come to loathe Karpis. He was a greedy opportunist with no conscience or feeling. He was cavalier about destroying whoever and whatever stood in his way. I feared what he might do if I shut him out. I certainly couldn't call the sheriff. If I refused to host this gang, they might move in here anyway. They'd shoot me and the dogs, and let our corpses freeze in the woods, to be devoured by raccoons and wolves. If I was busted for harboring gangsters, so what? Those charges would be dropped as I stood trial for two murders I did commit, both in front of witnesses.

Karpis blew smoke.

"Until the weekend," I said. "That's it, though. No longer. This place is really too small for houseguests."

"You won't even know we're here," said Karpis.

Karpis opened the front door, waved, and shut it quick against the cold. I stepped over to the windows that framed a view of the lake. Three bundled men struggled out of Swede's Pontiac. Two wore hats and one had a bloody white rag tied around his head. The bloody man's eyes were covered with dark goggles. He was a easily a foot taller than his escorts. They hustled him up the stairway and I recognized him the moment they pushed him blind through the door.

This was Ricky Alt, millionaire son of the Saint Paul brewer.

I had never said more than hello to him, but had seen him often around Saint Paul. He stood a rugged six-foot-three. About seven years ago, he had been on the Notre Dame football squad. He'd been a second-stringer and played only a few downs under Coach Rockne. But those fleeting moments of Fighting Irish glory made him a minor celebrity. He'd come back from college to learn the brewing trade. But he had a princely arrogance, and had alienated Altwasser's brew-master. Papa Alt, who couldn't brew a cup of tea himself, bowed to the brew-master and banished his only son from the works. Ricky'd been sent downtown to be president of the family bank.

And here he stood, a giant among these jockey-sized guys who made up the Barker Gang. Karpis was the tallest, at five-five. The brothers Doc and Fred barely hit five-and-a-couple inches tall.

The Barker brothers steered Ricky to the couch. Karpis lifted the dark-glass goggles from Ricky's eyes, ripped the bloody t-shirt from his head, dropped it to my polished floor. Ricky's head was a mess of dried blood. He seemed doped or dazed, his eyes registering nothing.

"What do you have in the way of bandages?" Karpis asked me.

I backed toward the bathroom.

"What do you want?" Fred asked the dazed man. Unbuttoning his own cashmere coat, Fred asked: "Can we get you tea?"

"And crumpets," said Doc.

Ricky sat on the couch, blinking, his eyes adjusting to the light.

"What do you got to eat?" Fred asked me.

"Uh ah," I stammered from the bathroom doorway.

"The man's famished," said Fred.

"I ah roasted a turkey a couple of days ago."

"Well carve it up, man," barked Doc.

"And tea," said Fred. "He's a tea man. Aren't you, Ricky?"

I detoured into the kitchen. If I could have joined my dogs cowering under the table, I would have. It was electricity that made it bearable to live here year-round. A refrigerator and toaster were plugged, in their turn, into the kitchen's single electric outlet. The main occupier of that fridge was a small roast turkey, which had been feeding me and the dogs for breakfast, lunch and dinner. I pulled it, draped in aluminum foil, out of the fridge and set it on the pink Formica-topped kitchen table. That brought the dogs out from their hiding places and got them standing on hind legs.

Fred appeared at the kitchen door.

"Pardon us for barging in," he said.

He stepped into the kitchen.

"We was raised with manners but…" he shrugged. "Business is business. It took us a couple of weeks to find you."

"That's good, I guess."

I carved turkey breast with a long, sharp knife. Through the doorway I had a framed view of Doc, hustling in two rifles, and a shotgun and tommygun. This knife was the weapon I'd mentally reserved in case of intruders. As a weapon, it was now about as useful as a ping-pong paddle.

With the wood cookstove always burning, it was a hot kitchen, but I got the shivers when I realized these gangsters would make a stand in this cottage, if they had to. I pictured it. The woods full of deputies and G-men, ferocious firefight, bullets ripping through windows and walls. These guys did not fear police but seemed to relish the chance to fight them. Every copper could be outwitted, bribed, or shot down, that was the Barker view of the world.

Fred stepped into the kitchen, picked off a slice of turkey, popped it into his mouth. He had a severe hairdo, thick and greasy red on top, shaved on the sides. It was a haircut for hard times, as the buzz-shaved styled would minimize trips to the barber. And barber shops were not only expensive. With all those detective magazines lying around, they were dangerous places for a wanted man.

Fred salted a turkey slice using Mr. and Mrs. Happy Pig, the salt and pepper shakers Cindy had won at the Vilas County Fair.

Fred tossed turkey bits to the dogs.

"How did he get hurt?" I asked.

"Aw it's nothing," said Fred. "Head wound."

"Lot of blood," I said.

"Couldn't be helped. He's a fighter."

In the parlor, Nurse Karpis was ripping one of my t-shirts into a bandage.

"We couldn't figure you was living alone or not," said Fred. "Looks like you are. No signs of a woman."

He stared through the kitchen windows. "How's the deer hunting?"

"Season's over."

"Hell, season's don't matter. Where's your nearest neighbor?"

Snipe Lake lay between us an anyone to the West, and those cottages across the lake were half a mile away. To the east, you'd have to trudge past Aunt Doris' burned acres, down Sunset Road and around the bend just to come upon two abandoned homesteads. To the north lay a swamp. And to the south, a bunch of snow-bound cottages without heat or occupants this time of year. But the less Fred knew about Snipe Lake geography, the better, so I shrugged and said:

"Down the road apiece."

"Then there's nobody to know if we're hunting, is there? Doc," Fred shouted into the living room. "Deer a plenty."

"No hunting, no shots, no noise," warned Karpis from the living room.

Karpis seemed to know the layout of the house, and led Ricky stumbling through the kitchen toward the little back bedroom, a child's room. Ricky hadn't uttered a sound, and walked like a drunk.

"Rough on the kid," I said after they passed.

"Nah," said Fred. "Don't worry, he can take it. He's a football player, right? It's nothing worse than a tackle."

On the tabletop I set five fluted white dinner plates and silverware. I ladled onto them cold, cooked-down cranberries. On the stove I set a cast iron frying pan, filled it with gravy and sliced turkey. Into the oven went a steel platter mounded with cold mashed potatoes. I opened the fire door, glowing logs in there.

"Where's a liquor store in these here woods?" asked Doc, picking meat off the turkey carcass.

I told him how he could get there. But I warned him: "You noticed my car at the head of the driveway."

"Yeah, almost on the road," said Doc.

"I don't park down here," I said, "because you can get snowed in. If it snows heavy tonight, your car could be stuck down here for days. Hard to get up that hill if it ices over."

"Bah," said Doc.

"I park up there and snowshoe down."

"Carrying groceries?" Doc asked.

"There's a sled out back."

"Well ain't you rustic." He turned to Fred. "Freddy, he's a son-of-a-bitching Eskimo."

"Mind your manners," said Fred. "He's our host. You're a houseguest."

Doc smirked. He teased the dogs, holding a turkey leg above their snapping jaws.

"Go asshole," said Fred.

"Who you calling asshole?" said Doc.

But Doc worked into a fisherman's jacket and left, slamming the front door so hard it rattled the dishes in the china cabinet. He sped up the driveway, tires spinning, and I could hear that Pontiac's engine whine even after it reached Sunset Road.

With our meal warming up, I followed Fred into the living room. I looked around for those weapons, but they had been stowed, maybe in a closet or under a bed. Karpis was sitting on the couch, smoking a cigarette, leafing through a copy of Startling Detective Adventures.

"I should ask," I said. "Just out of curiosity."

Karpis looked up, blank.

"Can I ask?" I said.

Karpis shrugged.

"How much?" I asked.

Fred looked at Karpis and they both laughed.

"Double," said Karpis.

"Twice as nice," said Fred.

WEDNESDAY NIGHT

Rick's soft moaning wafted like a musical wail from Cindy's childhood bedroom. We, his captors, played poker in front of the flaming fireplace. The dogs snoozed, turkey-stuffed and content under the card table. I played a losing game, distracted, imagining myself on trial for kidnapping. No juror would believe I was innocent of the original conspiracy. My fear came in waves. In between I was calmed somewhat by recalling the result of the William Hamm kidnapping trial. A disastrous federal prosecution had targeted the wrong gang, even as the Barker-Karpis boys celebrated in Reno, blowing the ransom in high gangster style. There was no reason to believe the G-men had gotten smarter in the two months since the Hamm trial went sour.

It was Doc's turn to sit with Rick in the little bedroom. At the poker table, Karpis, bored with a nickel-ante game, yawned and pushed back his chair. Fred, on a lucky streak, stacked coins. I walked to the picture window and looked out, pure darkness. Not a light in the cabins across the lake, all stars obscured by a cloudy sky.

Fred stood beside me, swirling bourbon in a squat glass.

"Ever been ice fishing?" he asked.

"Nope," I said.

"I'd like to go ice fishing."

"Now? I mean, tomorrow?"

"No, you know," he said and drank. "Someday. What's to catch?"

"Don't know. Not much of a fisherman."

"What? You live on a lake and you don't…" He turned toward Karpis. "Hey, Ray he…"

"I heard," said Karpis. "The man doesn't fish. So what?"

"A man don't fish, he's wasting his life," said Fred.

Karpis wandered over to join us, put a hand on my shoulder. "George likes this man."

"Fuck George," said Fred, "and fuck his college education and fuck his hundred-dollar suits."

"Now now," said Karpis, "we're all in this together, George too."

"I don't mean no offense to you, personally, Powers," said Fred. "It's George is a little high-falutin for us simple hill folk."

"You're not simple and I'm not a hillbilly," said Karpis.

Maybe there's some strange psychic connection between all human beings, something beyond understanding, I don't know, but we'd hardly finished talking about George when the phone rang.

"Get it, Powers," said Karpis.

It was a female voice: "Person to person, long distance for Mister Ray."

"Just a moment, operator."

I held the black candlestick phone toward Karpis. He snatched the base in one hand and the earpiece in the other and snarled: "This is Mister Ray, I accept."

Then he listened. With every moment his face grew darker, angrier.

"I've heard enough," he barked. "Don't call again. We'll send someone to see you."

He slammed the earpiece onto the table so hard the phone's bells rang.

"Well?" said Fred.

"They're giving us the stall," said Ray.

"What kind of stall?"

"Blood in the cab," Karpis said.

"So?"

"Papa Alt thinks his kid is dead. I told Doc and I told Weaver: Don't get rough."

"So what's the old bastard saying?"

"He wants proof," Karpis said, "that Lord Fauntelroy's alive."

"Who was on the phone?" Doc asked from the kitchen doorway.

"Shotgun," said Karpis.

"They got the dough ready?" asked Doc.

"Not even close," said Karpis. He swept into the kitchen, returned with a carving knife and severed the phone line.

"What the hell!" I said.

"Precautions," said Karpis.

"The sneaky pricks got wiretaps," said Fred.

"Federal sons of bitches," said Doc.

Karpis said: "We end up making five, ten calls a day between here and Saint Paul, how long before the operators notice?"

"Nosy bitches," said Doc.

"I imagined he was calling with good news," said Karpis.

"Good news? George?" said Fred. "He lectures you to death."

"What are we going to do?" said Doc. He approached the poker table, swigged from the bourbon bottle.

"Use a glass, pig," said Fred.

"Afraid of my cooties?" said Doc. "Too late. You had the Barker cooties since you was a kid. I say we kill the son-of-a-bitch and snatch another one. You'll see how fast they pay up after that."

"My genius brother," said Fred.

"Enough bickering," said Karpis. "We've got to think our way out of this one."

"Now that you boys cut the phone line," I said, "how the hell are you going to know the money's delivered?"

Karpis looked at the ceiling, impatient.

"Look, it's already arranged," he said. "Doc goes to a certain tavern down in the town. What is it, Doc?"

"White Buck."

"He's there every day at five," Karpis said. "Like he's just got off of work, wanting a quick beer. When the ransom dough comes in, the tavern gets a call at five exactly. Asking for Mister Red if something's gone wrong, asking for Mister Green if the money's okay."

"They pour a good beer in this state," said Doc.

"Never mind that," said Fred. "Papa Alt wants... what does he want?"

"He thinks his kid is dead," said Karpis.

"So what?" said Fred. "We're supposed to take a photo of his kid holding today's newspaper?"

"With what camera?" said Doc, "the one we aint' got?"

"Buy a cheap one," said Fred.

"No no no," said Karpis. "A town this small, a stranger buys a camera, these people have nothing to do but gossip about small events. Somebody will put two and two together."

"Mick's known in town," suggested Doc. "He could buy it."

"No I'm not," I said. "I keep a low profile, deliberate."

"Well ain't that the shits," said Doc.

"What time do the Chicago papers get here?" asked Karpis.

THURSDAY MORNING

That night was the coldest of my life. There weren't enough
blankets and quilts for five people. The cottage was steam-heated
from a basement coal furnace, but the porch/guest-bedroom had
no radiator. It was about ten degrees outside that night, the cold
leaking in around the windows. It got into my bones. I slept only in
snatches. I dreamed of Swede Fanlund. He was falling off the roof
of my apartment building, endlessly falling, screaming in agony.
Although in the actual horrible event, he went silent to his death
over the wall.

I dreamed of being arrested for his murder. I saw delight in the
sadistic faces of Inspector Crumley and his partner The Bulldog. I
dreamed they beat me, bruised me, and worse they mocked me as I
was tied to a chair in the basement of the police station.

Somewhere in the middle of that long night I begged my patron
saint, the Archangel Michael, for relief, for warmth and sleep. Just
before dawn, he delivered.

By 11 a.m. I was in town, at Bonson's Cash and Carry, buying
potatoes, eggs, sausage and onions. Fred and Karpis knew I would
return. Although nobody said it out loud, the Barker-Karpis gang
was holding my dogs hostage.

With the clarity of morning thought, I realized why they had
chosen me. I had worked well with Shotgun George during the
Hamm snatch. I lived on an isolated property. I could not go to the
police under any circumstances. Once the gang had decided on

using me, they only needed to know that I was out here, and alone, which explained all those phone calls.

Bagged groceries in the car, I sat with its engine and heater running. I watched through frosty windows as the Eagle River flowed out of the lake. Here it ran fast and open, despite the bitter cold. Bald eagles circled, master predators, swooping over the water. One of them snatched up a big catch. Too big. With that fish its talons it could hardly fly, and had to drop it writhing and bloody into the bay.

The train from Chicago delivered the newspapers at 11:35, only one bundle. It was lugged away on a sled by the son of Beatrice, the widow who owned Eagle River World of News. Unfortunately, she did know me. There was no choice here. Eagle River was a town of 1,200 hardy souls, and two blocks of downtown shops. If you wanted reading material of any kind, you had to patronize Beatrice's narrow dark store. She trapped patrons at the cash register, regaling them with stories of every malady she'd suffered.

And she'd suffered plenty.

I bought the Chicago Tribune, along with a few local papers for camouflage. Beatrice took my quarter, complaining that her hands were so arthritic now she had to trust the customers to pick out their own change. She was a sweet-natured, but tormented plump old lady with blue eyes and a curly cloud of platinum hair.

She asked after my cousin Cindy.

"It's the polio, ain't it?" said Beatrice.

"Multiple sclerosis," I said.

"That's not so bad," said Beatrice.

"She's in a wheelchair now. Carton of Chesterfields, please."

"Lord," said Beatrice. "That's where I'm heading. A wheelchair."

"Oh, I hope not."

"You smoke Chesterfields now?"

"Switching from my pipe," I said. "They say Chesterfields are easier on the throat."

"My knees got no car-ludge left," Beatrice said. "So the doctors tell me. They're a pack of bald-faced liars. I keep telling them I'm going to die any day now. I can't stand on these weak knees. My head throbs day and night, and my blood pressure could drive a locomotive. If I'm dead before sundown, I won't be surprised. Jimmy," she said, nodding toward her son, who was browsing the girlie magazines, "he'll be off before I'm cold in the ground. Off for Chicago."

The Alt Kidnapping did not make the front page of the Chicago papers, and the Saint Paul papers arrived, at best, a day late. There was a story on Page Three of the Chicago Tribune, though, four-paragraphs jammed in, bottom of the page. Sketchy in the extreme, the story said Richard Alt, president of the River State Bank, was last seen getting into a taxi outside his office in Downtown Saint Paul. The taxi was discovered at the edge of the Highland Golf Course, its driver half-frozen in the trunk. The rear seat of the taxi was spattered in blood. Police and the Alt family had gotten a telephone message from the abductors, but would not publicly disclose its contents.

I drove back to the woodsy intersection of Sunset Road and Cindy's driveway. I parked in a snow rut, hauled groceries, cigarettes and newspapers to the cottage on a Flexible Flyer, its red runners gliding beautiful over the sparkling snow. Hula Girl and Snowflake trotted up the hill to greet me, tails wagging. Hula Girl stuck her snout into the grocery bag. Snowflake ran ahead. If dogs know anything, they know breakfast.

Bags in my gloved hands, I struggled through the kitchen door. Karpis and Fred were leaning over the kitchen table, reading from a yellow legal pad. I set the groceries on the table.

"Ask Powers," said Fred.

"Read it," said Karpis, and handed me the pad.

It was block-printed in a nervous hand:

Pa:

I am quite alive thank you for your concern and they are treating me well. Please do as they ask for these are serious men of business. I am comfortable but it won't be long before they loose patience. Give a hug to Minnie and my love to Marie, and I hope to soon be back in the embrace of our family.

Richard

"Well?" Karpis demanded.

"Comma after ask," I said.

"The hell with commas," Karpis said. "Is it spelled okay?"

"To hell with spelling," Fred said and snatched the pad from me. "I'm looking for secret messages."

Karpis rolled his eyes.

"We make the Chicago papers?" Doc called from the bedroom.

"Page three," I called back.

"Son of a bitch," said Doc.

"You see any secret messages in what he wrote?" Fred asked me.

"Like…"

"Code. Trying to give away where we're at."

"I… don't see it."

Karpis grabbed the carton of Chesterfields. He set it on the dusty shelf above the stove, alongside tin pots and a ceramic cookie jar that looked like a gigantic apple.

"I'll take that newspaper," Karpis said.

"Make it big and bold," said Fred.

"Big as his bankroll," said Karpis, and walked into Cindy's little bedroom.

He returned a minute later with the top of the newspaper ripped off. The signature RICHARD WILHELM ALT was scrawled underneath the printed words: CHICAGO TRIBUNE. Karpis had torn that newspaper header off just below the date, Thursday, January 18, 1934. He wrapped that signed newspaper header and the letter into a thick envelope, which he licked and sealed.

"Well," Karpis set the letter atop the flour bin. "Who's cooking breakfast." He clapped his hands.

I had mentally prepared for this battle on the drive back. These guys were prison-hardened. They were always probing for soft spots in the people around them. If you showed too much weakness, they were ruthless enough to conclude that, ultimately, you didn't deserve to live. Maybe once you had served your purpose, they'd do the world a favor and bump you off.

"Not me," I said, "I went for the groceries."

"Well, I can't fry an egg," said Fred.

"Don't look at me," said Doc in the doorway.

"Well somebody's got to cook," said Karpis.

"Let the college boy cook his own breakfast," said Fred.

"Low card draw," said Doc, shuffling cards.

Doc lost. Standing at the cook-stove, wearing a sleeveless t-shirt that exposed his ugly prison tattoos, Doc dumped sausage into a cast-iron pan. He refused to cook potatoes, claiming they had no part in a good Southern breakfast.

In self defense, I made coffee in the French press. Cup of fresh coffee in hand, with Doc cursing, clattering and cooking behind me, I stared out the kitchen window. I saw forest, but my mind envisioned my Saint Paul penthouse. I remembered another winter night, when I awoke with a headache after a hellish nightmare, looked out to see a fire on the river docks. Those flames turned out to be the funeral pyre of Sadie and Rose. They were bad girls, but not evil, and no justice would ever avenge their deaths now. I could not forget that their fatal mistake had been to snitch on the Barker gang.

"Chow's ready," called Doc, and banged the cast iron pan with an egg-turner. By the time we sat for breakfast, the kitchen was sweating hot. I cracked a window to let in some winter air.

"Who's going to take pretty boy his breakfast?" asked Fred.

"Your turn," said Doc.

We piled our own plates greasy with fat sausages and scorched eggs. Karpis, not a coffee man, drank milk. Doc bitched that I forgot to buy oranges. Fred ate in the bedroom with the prisoner. When we had wolfed down the breakfast, Doc swigged whiskey from his pocket flask and said: "I ain't cleaning up. I ain't your mother."

Doc glared at me. In those eyes I saw it was Doc against the world, and he hated all of us.

"Powers will be leaving us," Karpis said.

"We need a son-of-a-bitching maid, then" Doc said.

"Mick," Karpis said, "George is waiting for you at the Hotel Saint Paul, room 914. It's seven knocks exactly or he won't open the door. Give him this envelope, and await instructions."

"How long we going to be in this son-of-a-bitching forest?" Doc groused.

Karpis handed me the sealed envelope, ransom note inside.

"You should leave now," he said. "What's time's sunset?"

THURSDAY EVENING

Weeks back, I had arrived at my Eagle River hideout in a Chevy coupe. It was a get-away car stolen by one of Tom Filben's minions in Saint Paul. I soon traded that Chevy in at a Rhinelander dealer for a 1933 Essex Terraplane K. This was a two-door sedan which itself had been traded in after skidding sideways into a tree. The passenger-side running board was crushed, and the dented door was stuck shut, but that damage made it affordable. Just as important, it was a fast car, capable of 80 mph. It could outrun the four-cylinder jalopies used by most coppers.

So cruising behind six powerful cylinders, I made Saint Paul an hour after dark. The city was winter-quiet, snow-frosted, weeknight dull. I parked on the dark side of the Library, sneaked across Rice Park, and slipped into the service entrance of the Hotel Saint Paul. It was chilly in the stairwell. I was desperate for warmth after hours in a car that leaked air through its wounded passenger door. In my inside overcoat pocket was a letter that would send me to Alcatraz for life if the G-men across the street got their mitts on me.

I huffed and puffed up the stairwell to the fourth floor, and took the elevator from there to the 9th. I slipped into the warm, plush carpeted hallway, and knocked seven times exactly at room 914.

The door opened a cautious crack, then was flung wide by Shotgun George Ziegler.

He wore underwear and a loosely-tied bathrobe. His boxer shorts depicted red-faced, cheerful Santas. The bathrobe was hotel-issued, a deep blue emblazoned with gold royal crest.

He shut the door, discreet, behind me. He latched the security chain. The room was lit only by a single lamp near the windows.

"What have you got?" he whispered, hoarse.

His hair was combed straight back and wet, as if he'd just showered. His big blue eyes searched mine for signs of betrayal. My leather-gloved hand trembled as I handed him the ransom envelope.

He sniffed it.

"What am I to do with this?" he said.

"I thought you'd know," I said.

"I don't deliver messages, Powers, I author them."

He tapped the envelope twice to the side of his head, then slipped it into a desk drawer.

"I have made my one and only call to the Bavarian mansion," he said. "They are aware of the price we demand. The also know that we require them to name three potential emissaries, from which list we will make our choice."

He retrieved the envelope. "On second thought," he said, "I have lost all trust in that simpleton from Missouri."

Who he meant, I had no idea.

"So congratulations, Powers."

He handed the envelope toward me.

"You performed so splendidly in our last adventure," he said.

I stared at the envelope.

"Go on, take it," he said.

He dropped it into my overcoat pocket.

"Powers, God gave you an imagination, use it."

"Hey, that's not my role, George, I…"

"Well it is now. Would you like a quick drink?"

He stepped toward the bar. "I had a veritable lifetime's worth of liquor delivered yesterday." He raised a bottle from the bar.

"Martell Cognac," he said. "Just off the boat from Hong Kong. It's going to be a while before the very best liquor makes it here from the civilized world. Prohibition. What on earth were we thinking?"

He poured generously into two gleaming snifters.

"Legal at last. I like to imagine all the world's ships, loaded with booze, headed for our fair Republic."

He handed me a glass. "You do know that we're a Republic and not a Democracy."

"Hadn't thought much about it," I said.

He offered a toast: "To the Alt tribe, and their ill-gotten fortune."

I clinked. I sipped. I felt myself slipping into a cold, dark nowhere. I threw myself a lifeline.

"I'm not your delivery boy," I said.

"Well you see, Powers," he said, sipping, "there simply is no one else. The simpleton from Missouri is a psychological basket case. I have no idea why our friends dragged him up here, but it was a dreadful mistake. And Handsome Curly is in charge of herding the women." He shrugged. "So you see, it's just you and me, and I, according to the master plan, am not to budge from this over-priced dungeon. Strict orders from the hillbilly hierarchy, you see."

He held his glass toward me and said: "We don't want to disappoint the boys, do we?"

I had never met either Curly or this simpleton from Missouri. I worried about the Barker-Karpis gang kept getting bigger. This was a danger, since more gangsters meant more potential snitches.

George said: "We've got to send them back an answer, they're deaf, dumb and blind without us, Powers. We're their eyes and ears in Saint Paul. So I recommend you secure accommodations, although definitely not…" he waved the snifter … "within sight of this hotel."

He dug into his bathrobe pocket, brought out a pack of Camels, offered me one. I declined. He slipped his cigarette into an ivory holder, and held it bobbing in his lips.

"How was the drive?"

"Cold," I said.

"We'll all be enjoying a warmer climate soon," he said.

Yes, Hell, I thought. I removed my gloves, unbuttoned my overcoat, as if I already could feel the heat of Satan's realm.

"Powers, were you a paper boy in your youth?"

"Who wasn't?" I said.

"Oh, I wasn't," he said. "Mother would not permit it. She never allowed me to get my hands dirty. I was college-bound from birth, you see. My admission to the University of Illinois was a grave disappointment to the old woman. She had her heart set on Harvard or Yale or at the very worst Northwestern. The family traces its noble lineage back to the Holy Roman Empire. *Reichsritter*, you see. The heritage of *junker*. But for the unfortunate events of 1848 …" he waved that cigarette-and-holder. "As a lad, you threw the newspapers, did you?"

I wasn't quite following that, having just been taken back to the Holy Roman Empire.

"Pardon?"

"You threw newspapers on people's porches. From a filthy sack, carried around your shoulders."

"Something like that."

"Well, you already know how to make the delivery."

"Look here, George," I said. "I never used those tickets."

"Tickets?"

"To the Barber of Seville."

"I'm not quite following you."

"The last time you and I had a working agreement," I said, "you paid me with two tickets to the opera."

"Oh, that," George said, and slapped his head. "Strictly an oversight, I assure you."

"Even half a share would have been a couple of thousand dollars."

"Well I doubt we were talking quite half a share, in any event. That would have been extravagant."

"Some amount of cash was expected, can we agree on that?"

"You see my man," said George, and put his arm around me like he was my uncle, "the hillbillies had an extraordinarily difficult time cleaning up the money. They are, after all, sixth grade dropouts. They hopped the train to Reno, you see, but their friends out there thought the money was too hot. They finally found an agent in San Francisco who used it to purchase a shipload of bootleg booze. So you see, it was absolutely months after the event in question that clean money was available. And by then, unfortunately, you and I had simply lost touch."

He reached for his wallet.

"Keep it George. I'm out of this."

"I'm afraid you're very much in."

He held out a $100 bill.

"Expense money," he said. "To be followed by many more of its brethren."

"No thanks," I said. "I'm known here. If I spend a bill that big, tongues will wag."

That was my excuse, but actually, I was already preparing for the inevitable trial. The Barker-Karpis Gang, whether they knew it or not, had snatched the son of a man whose father had a friend in the White House. During the Presidential campaign, when Franklin Roosevelt stepped off the train at Saint Paul's Union Depot, it was Papa Alt first in line to greet him. They were natural allies, and had become personal friends. FDR campaigned to bring back beer, and that rang the money bell in Papa Alt's mansion. The Barker gang might have been blind to it, but I knew the federal heat in this case was going to make Hell seem like the North Pole. Sure, the Feds blew the Hamm prosecution, but I had the feeling this kidnapping case was going to be different.

I wanted to be able to say: Your Honor, I did it under threat, and did not take a dime.

"I'm a patient man," I told George, "I'll wait for my share."

"Then let us create," he said, "a masterpiece of the genre."

At a rolltop desk sat a Corona portable typewriter and a stack of heavy bond paper. It was letterhead paper featuring the big bold word Blackstone and the silhouette of a hotel. I sat before the typewriter. I rolled in a sheet of this letterhead as George hovered over my shoulder.

"Powers, there will be a thousand hoaxers, lunatics and charlatans calling the family and the police over the next few days. I have advised the Alts that genuine communications will be delivered on this letterhead. Also, any telephonic messages will include the key word Blackstone."

"Blackstone," I said.

"Ready for dictation?" he said. "We have enclosed proof that your son is alive and well. You are to place in the window of your son's office the blue eagle sticker of the National Recovery Administration. By this sign we will be apprised that the money is ready for delivery. Once that sign is appropriately posted, you will be notified of the necessary steps to deliver the money to us and thereby procure your son's release."

I finished typing and said: "That's all?"

"My man," he clapped me on the shoulder, "I believe that brevity is the very soul of communication."

As I slunk down the hotel's back stairway, I knew George was right about one thing: I was in. I would never get the Barker Gang out of my cottage unless I delivered their message.

George's plan, however, was flawed. He imagined I would steal a newsboy's sack of newspapers, walk down the boulevard delivering them, and casually throw a paper on the Alt's porch. But it was nearing 7 p.m. and the Evening Dispatch and Daily News had long since been delivered. Any paperboy out now would raise questions in the minds of whoever saw him. I modified George's idea and bought just one copy of the Dispatch in a downtown drugstore. Its screaming half-page block of headlines said:

RICHARD ALT KIDNAPPED
$200,000 RANSOM ASKED

It was a spooky feeling, to hold both that newspaper and the ransom note. In my idling Terraplane, I read in the news columns that the family had named three go-betweensm as the kidnappers had demanded via telephone. They were: R.L Pearson, a real estate consultant; Father McCarthy O'Sullivan, family priest; and Andrew Stockwell, an executive at Altwasser Brewery.

I knew them all. The Dispatch had committed its usual sins of omission. R.L. Pearson was known around Saint Paul as Serious Bobby. For years he'd been the city's top underworld diplomat. He had been the chosen go-between in last summer's kidnapping of William Hamm, and was now a "consultant" to the Hamm Brewery. His "consulting," had nothing to do with real estate.

Father McCarthy O'Sullivan, an honest man as far as I knew, was Cathedral Provost. He was the Archbishop's tough guy and emissary to the underworld.

Andrew Stockwell had, for the last years of Prohibition, been manager of Alt-backed speakeasies all over town, which also meant he was in charge of bribery.

When I finished reading between the lines, I gave the Dispatch a newsboy fold and slipped the ransom envelope in tight.

The Alt Mansion stood on a side street just across from the Altwasser Brewery. A more grandiose beer baron would have lived up on Summit Hill, but Papa Alt, apparently, liked to keep an eye on the shop. His mansion, on the banks of the Mississippi, overlooked both river and brewery. I parked a block away, behind the concrete loading dock of a machine shop.

I watched.

The brewery's iron gates were locked against the night, the great works vibrating, throwing off the stench of rotten vegetables. The hum of its machinery echoed all over the neighborhood. With beer legal now, bricklayers were half-finished a building that would double down on Papa Alt's plan to inebriate the Northwest. I studied the Alt's white stone mansion for a while. There were many cars parked on either side of the street, and the home glowed with lights intense from every room.

Some of those cars belonged to G-men, since kidnapping was now against the federal law. It was only a couple of months ago that J. Edgar Hoover had slammed Machine Gun Kelly into Alcatraz on a kidnapping rap. This new island prison was escape-proof, the feds boasted. Kidnappers especially were warned of harsh discipline, shark-infested waters, and damp, cold cells.

A car circled the block. It revealed itself underneath each streetlamp, first as a luxury car with a hood five feet long. Then as a dark red sedan with white sidewalls. Then as a brand new Cadillac-LaSalle. On its second time around it settled for far-off parking. It was such a flashy, extravagant car I figured it belonged to a very important man, perhaps a representative of the governor or state's attorney general. As it sat idling, lights ablaze, I memorized the license number.

Then its engine shut off and out got two men. One was a giant, the other a mere mortal carrying a doctor's black bag. Underdressed in only a dark suit, the doctor hustled toward the Alt Mansion, climbed the steps and into the porch's light. Behind him, that giant was revealed to be Father McCarthy O'Sullivan.

A doctor and a priest. Desperate medical measures and Extreme Unction? Maybe old Otto Alt was having a heart attack. Great. Worries galloped like a panicked horse through my mind. Add a second-degree murder charge to the kidnapping.

What if I walked into Roland Heater's office and told all I knew? Well, the feds were as bloodthirsty as the gangsters. J. Edgar was eager to prove his college boys could slug it out with tommygunners. A few hours after I turned rat, G-men, the Wisconsin State Patrol, and sheriff's deputies would assemble in the forest outside Cindy's cottage. A horseshoe-shaped ambush would trap the gangsters against the lakeshore. A gun battle would leave several cops dead and wounded. And hell, half of them would be deputies, just farmers picking up part time dough by carrying a badge. The firefight would kill Snowflake, Hula Girl and Ricky Alt, as well as the three gangsters. Karpis might surrender if he were the last one left alive. But the Barker brothers would rather burn in Hell than rot in Alcatraz.

On the other hand, if I delivered this message, Papa Alt would pay $200,000, which he could well afford. Hell, he had donated more than that to the Roosevelt campaign. Ricky would be let go unharmed, as William Hamm was. Hamm was let go because the ransom was beside the point. The kidnappings were a dramatic warning to these brewers, that they should bring their gangster friends along into the profitable future.

So I had a big decision to make, me, a lowly gangland messenger, sitting in a banged-up car on a frosty night in an industrial parking lot. Death and destruction on a terrible scale, or clipping off a piece of a fat-cat's fortune.

A woman in hooded parka walked a sweater-wrapped dog down a lamplit street. She glanced at me, suspicious, a dark figure in an idling car. I shut the engine and wondered if just freezing to death would be my best option. But my dogs! I imagined Doc Barker shooting them because they barked too much. That vision got me going. I started the car again, rolled down the window. When the dog-walking-lady was out of sight, I sped past the Alt Mansion, heaved the newspaper over the iron fence, and it bounced off the bottom step. I made a vicious right turn at the river road, slid sideways, banged against the curb. The car tilted as if it might roll into the Mississippi, then righted. It stalled. With frantic looks in the mirror I started it and zoomed toward the better part of town.

Up on Grand Avenue I parked, thrilled by my escape, shuddering with relief. I popped out of the car behind the Barking Dog Tavern. I sneaked around to the back entrance, where a long dark hallway led to the restrooms and a bank of three public telephones. I grabbed a receiver, dropped a nickel, dialed the number George had given me. A female answered, maybe one of Ricky's sisters, maybe a maid. After a glance over my shoulder for eavesdroppers I choked out: "Newspaper. Porch. Message."

As I was about to hang up I remembered to blurt out: "Blackstone."

I hustled out the door and down the back alley.

It was a couple of icy blocks to Myrtle's luxury apartment. The lights were blazing, but they shades were down, her alley windows. Those lights about broke my heart, something warm flooding me after all this cold and frantic fear. Myrtle! In my winter's isolation I realized I missed the woman, I probably loved her, bad girl that she was.

I mounted the stairs, breathless. From inside her apartment I heard chirping parakeets. I rapped lightly on the door.

"Go away you bum," said Myrtle. "I'm not home."

"Myrtle," I said, trying to whisper through the door. "It's Powers."

The door cracked open as far as the security chain would allow.

The door closed and then swung wide. Myrtle grabbed the lapel of my overcoat and dragged me in.

"Get in here, are you crazy?"

"Somebody looking for me?"

"Everybody's looking for you."

"Well, it's nice to be wanted," I said and shrugged off my coat. I embraced her, kissed her, held her away. She wore a Chinese bathrobe, black, red and gold. Her breath smelled heavy of booze.

"Hey," I said.

"It's nothing," I said.

I held her chin in my hands. She looked like she'd gone a couple of rounds with a heavyweight palooka. Her cheek was bruised, her eye socket swollen, black and blue, her eyelid half shut over the damage.

"Who the hell did that to you?"

She pushed my hand away. "Nobody, Mick, it's nothing. What do you want to drink?"

The room, now that I got a look at it, might have been the scene left by wild animals. A rose-painted glass lamp was shattered, lying on the hardwood floor near the radiator. Unruffled, though, were Charles and Amelia, chirping merry in their tall golden cage.

"I ain't got around to cleaning up yet," she said. "It's the maid's year off."

A framed drawing of Japanese lovers in erotic positions hung crooked on the wall. The telephone had been torn away from its moorings and lay at the leg of an easy chair. A coffee table stood legs up on a Persian rug.

"I just got home myself," she said.

"Where from?"

"Loretta's."

I threw my overcoat on the telephone table, took a long look around and said: "Who's the mug?"

"Forget it, Mick, I got drunk and fell down the stairs."

"Right," I said.

"You know how it is."

"I certainly do. Now give me his name."

"What are you going to do, tough guy? You spit on the sidewalk, they'll send you to Stillwater."

"I know some guys."

"Mick, butt out. I can handle it."

"Apparently not."

Her face darkened with anger. "You too? You're going to humiliate me too? I thought we were old friends. Let's have a drink like we were old friends. Old friends don't tell each other what to do. Old friends are kind to each other. Because they're old and because they're friends, and because this life is killing them little by little. Don't judge me, Mick, I been in a courtroom, and if there's anything I hate it's a rotten, smug-face judge."

"Okay, but if you need a tough guy to square this up…"

"I know, thanks, Mick, now I'm dying for a drink."

We walked into the kitchen, where the booze was. The Myrtle I once knew had an antiseptic kitchen, because she never cooked. But this kitchen was piled with greasy pots. The sink was a monument to unwashed plates. Every burner on the stove hosted a crusty pan. Silverware, stolen from the best hotels, lay scattered and soiled on the drain board.

Myrtle opened a cupboard to reveal a selection of booze that could stock a tavern. She had never been much of a home drinker, doing her boozing in public, preferably with an orchestra in the background and a squire paying the tab.

"Canadian Club, Four Roses, Crab Orchard?"

"Crab," I said.

"Soda, ginger, straight?"

"Soda," I said.

She nudged aside a pile of dishes and fixed me a drink, knocking ice out of an aluminum tray she fetched from the tiny frost-crusted freezer.

"I'm looking for a place to stay," I said.

"Don't look here."

"I've been spending a lot of time alone," I said.

"I'm not in the mood for company. Ever again if I can help it. I'm through with your kind, Mick. I hate you all. Except you. And a couple of others. A million men in this city and only six of them got any heart."

We clinked glasses.

"So what are you doing in town?" she asked.

I sighed. "That, I can't tell you."

"Huh," said Myrtle. "I'll bet."

"I missed you, kid."

"Oh cut the baloney." She turned away and set her glass on the stained white porcelain sink. "I'm used up Mick." She lifted the shade and stared into the dark alley. "Victor died you know. Christmas Day."

The glass in her hand shook, ice cubes rattled. I lay both hands, gentle on her shoulders.

"I heard."

To spare Myrtle's feelings, I wasn't going to say that I knew how. "Professor Banks," as he was known all over gangland, was found hanged in his cell. He'd played prison Santa on Christmas Eve, then hanged himself with the big black belt.

"No funeral," she muttered. "He didn't want one."

And now she began to cry, huge tears running down her cheeks, I could see her reflection in the dark window.

"My Professor," she sniffled. "He taught me everything."

She wiped tears.

"And he never laid a hand on me. A gentleman. Where am I going to find a gentleman, Mick, I'm so old and fat."

"And enticing," I said.

"You always were Mister Flattery."

"I'm sorry about the Professor," I said.

"Thanks, I guess," she said, and picked up soiled napkin and wiped her tears, snuffling. "I shouldn't cry, what's to cry about, bad news, it oughta make you happy, it just proves what a rotten world we live in."

"There's a big mess going on, all right."

"Mick, I'm not asking, because look, I know the answer. The Alt kid gets snatched and all of a sudden you show up like a ghost. I hope junior's all right but even if he is, I'm afraid, Mick. I'm afraid they're going to drag you down into darkness."

"Aw, Myrtle, what are you talking about?"

"I heard them Mick. They were right here. Right in that living room. I was in here, penned up with their women, and the boys were out there talking, and you know Gladys' little daughter had to go to the bathroom and I walked her out to it and I heard them. Fred and Doc and Ray, sitting with Harry, and they got a pop-in visit from Big Ryan too."

"Harry's the finger-man?" I asked.

"It's Harry's job, so now you know what you're mixed up in."

"I'm mixed up in nothing," I said.

"I can see right through you, Mick, you always was a terrible liar, you got the mug of a disappointed altar boy."

"Harry," I said.

"The mastermind," she said, "with the usual assistance of the Saint Paul Police."

She drained her drink.

"Is the junior banker okay?" she asked.

"How would I know?"

"Just wink if he's okay."

"Got something in my eye," I said.

"Thanks, you're quite the blabbermouth."

"Myrtle, you could be an accessory if you knew too much."

"Are you listening to me, or do my words pass right through you? They planned it," and these last two words she shouted: "*right here.*"

"Okay, but that doesn't have to come out in the Saturday Evening Post."

"If them federals crack one acorn, Mick, the whole tree comes down. Come on, drink up, sugar, I can't afford to have you here."

I checked in at my favorite hideout, the Commodore. On the front desk were stacked the evening papers, Dispatch and Daily News. I bought a copy of each to bring upstairs.

BLOODY ALT TAXI

FEDERAL AGENTS GRILL CABBIE

According to the stories, Bank President Richard Alt had gotten into a cab outside the bank just before noon yesterday. Passersby had noted that the cab contained a second man up front, assumed to be a driver in training. Police had discovered that taxi an hour later at the Highland Golf Course, the shivering cabbie trapped in the trunk. The back seat of the cab was bloody. Otto "Papa" Alt had a brief phone conversation with someone claiming to represent the kidnappers. They had demanded that the family name three go-betweens and prepare a $200,000 ransom. Other than empty boasts and idle threats from various authorities, that was pretty much all the story said.

But I was electrified by the sidebar. That story itself was a tepid rundown of the shady history of Saint Paul kidnappings. It was the byline that shocked me.

By Janie Vetter
United Press

Only when she and her baby left Saint Paul for her parents' farm could I admit I was half in love with Janie, although she was far too young for me. Maybe it wasn't Janie herself, maybe it was youth and innocence I pined for. There is a point in your youth when you still have options. That was long since past for me, but Janie had a future, and my feelings for her were a mixture of admiration and envy.

I stared out into the dark courtyard. The radio blared so many bulletins that there was scarcely time for music. J. Edgar Hoover was thumping his chest like a Washington gorilla. Squads of G-men were headed to Saint Paul by car, by train, by airplane. Reporters and newsreel men were pouring in from all over the nation. Something crazy was eating at me, everything was eating at me, I worked into my overcoat and gloves and ran down the Commodore's back stairs.

I caught a taxi to downtown, grateful that the doorman was off shift for the evening. It was approaching ten at night but the morning papers had a midnight deadline and Janie might be working right up to it. I counted on my fingers: Her baby Dane was now seven months old. Was the baby okay? Why had Janie returned to Saint Paul?

A sick feeling settled into me, like it would never leave. The Hamm Kidnapping had been over quick, and had never become a world-wide story. The Alt Kidnapping, maybe because of the family's White House connections, was news in Washington, was news in Paris, for all I knew it was on the radio in Peking. At the Daily News building I found a bundled-up kid running a broom over the loading dock. I asked him where the United Press office was. Usually, he said, the UP reporter worked out of a cubbyhole behind then press room, but there were so many reporters in town now, they'd rented a room at the Hotel Saint Paul.

I hustled up there, through dark icy streets lit only by tavern signs, four dark blocks over the streetcar tracks up a gentle rise to the Hotel Saint Paul. I slipped in the back way. The office suites were on the third floor: R.G. Tietz, Dentist. Graf and Graf accountants. The Saint Paul Protective Association. All those offices were dark. On the other side of the gilded elevators, the clattering of a teletype machine, along with cigarette smoke, drifted out of an open transom.

I backed into a dark alcove and listened: Muffled voices. Soft curses coming over the transom. A young harried man opened the door and I glimpsed Janie, working like she was chained to the teletype, bent over it, intent, sweaty, typing. She looked older, she looked awful in that harsh light.

The harried man closed the door and rang for the elevator. I, ghost in the darkness, waited him out. I slipped out the back door of the hotel and walked, leaning into the brutal wind. It was below-zero cold but I could not risk hailing a cab in the gangster part of town. At the Commodore I slunk into my room. The arctic wind rattled the windows. The radio played the National Anthem and faded to static. I went to bed, rolled up in itchy wool covers. I expected a miserable night and that's what I got. No warmth, no refuge, no love, no sleep.

BOOKS IN THE GANGSTER ERA SERIES:.

No. 1 IF THE DEAD COULD SPEAK
Actual crime: the murder and incineration of Sadie Carmacher and Rose Perry, March 1932.

No. 2 DEAD A LONG TIME
Actual crime: The December, 1932 robbing of a Minneapolis bank and the murder of two cops and one civilian.

No. 3 DEAD LIKE LAZARUS
Actual crime: The kidnapping of millionaire brewer William Hamm, June, 1933.

No. 4 DEAD MESSENGER
Actual crimes: focuses on the last major crimes of the Barker-Karpis gang.

No.5 THE RESURRECTION OF SAINT JOHNNY is not a Mick Powers book but features many of the characters that inhabit the previous four novels. It is based on the spring, 1934 appearance of John Dillinger in the Twin Cities.